The crush

PENELOPE WARD

First Edition

ISBN-10 : 1951045467
ISBN-13 : 978-1951045463

Edited by: Jessica Royer Ocken
Proofreading and Formatting by: Elaine York
www.allusionpublishing.com
Proofreading by: Julia Griffis
Cover Photographer: Harol Baez
Cover Model: Jeremy Santucci, Instagram:
@jeremysantucci
Cover Design: Letitia Hasser, RBA Designs
www.rbadesigns.com

The crush

For Brandon

Thanks for brainstorming with me on this one, son.

(P.S. You need a haircut.)

Prologue

Life can change in a flash—even in what, at first, seem like the most routine of circumstances.

It was one of those busy days at work where the time seemed to go by faster than usual. The Japanese restaurant where I waitressed was packed—the side with hibachi tables and the regular dining section. I bounced back and forth between the two.

"I'm gonna need you to take over table six as well," my manager told me.

"Sure, no problem," I answered, taking an order of sukiyaki off the counter.

I'd been waitressing at Mayaka to help make ends meet while paying for school. At twenty-four, I'd gotten a late start on my college education after a few rough years, but I was finally getting my shit together.

Today I'd picked up an earlier shift. That turned out to be a very bad idea, because taking over table six forever changed my day—and perhaps my life.

"Can I start you off with some..." I lost my words. My heart nearly stopped as I looked into a familiar but long-lost face—a face I wasn't sure I'd ever see again.

His eyes widened.

My notepad fell to the floor.

Jace.

Oh my God.

A woman sat across from him.

Who is that?

My throat closed.

The only thing that felt right was running—so I did.

"Excuse me." I shook my head and turned around swiftly, making my way to the other side of the restaurant, past the shooting flames of the hibachi tables.

Bursting through the swinging doors, I entered the kitchen. "I have an emergency, Mae. I need to get home. I'm sorry to leave during a busy time, but I really need to go."

"Is everything alright?" she asked.

My words were rushed. "I hope so. Can't get into it now. I have to head out. I'm so sorry."

I bolted out of the kitchen. The sun blinded me as I opened the front door of the restaurant and raced through the parking lot to the sidewalk by the main road. Was leaving work a cowardly thing to do? Absolutely. Had I risked my job? Possibly. But no way was I ready to face him. The last time I'd seen Jace was three years ago, and he'd broken my heart into smithereens. Up until that moment, my heart had only ever belonged to him—since the time I was practically a child.

What was he even doing back in Florida? I'd thought he was gone for good. From the look on his face, he hadn't been expecting to see me working at Mayaka. Who was that woman with him? Why did he have to look even better than I remembered?

My heart felt heavy as I continued to pound the pavement. Of course I'd decided to *walk* to work today for exercise. A car would've been much better when it came to fleeing my past.

I was just about to cross the busy street when I felt a hand on my shoulder.

"Jesus, Farrah. Slow the fuck down."

I flinched, my heart nearly pounding out of my chest.

When I turned around, his steely blue eyes pierced through me, and I wondered how I'd ever thought I could escape having to face him.

Jace forced a sad smile. "If I didn't know better, I'd think you were running away from me."

We both panted. I flashed a nervous grin, not sure whether to laugh or cry.

His question was ironic.

Jace had been gone for three years, and he had the nerve to say I'd run from him? He was the one who'd run away.

Chapter 1

Farrah

Three-and-a-Half Years Earlier

"Whoa. Where are you going dressed like that?" Jace's deep voice stopped me in my tracks.

Bingo.

He noticed.

A chill traveled down my spine as I answered, "The Iguana."

"A bar. Interesting. I thought people wore clothes there." Jace smirked, opening a pistachio. He popped the nut into his mouth before throwing the shell aside.

I looked down at the crop top that showcased my stomach. I'd worn it specifically to flaunt my new belly ring. My jean shorts barely covered my butt.

Pretending to be peeved, I said, "Last I checked, what I wear isn't any of your business, Jace."

"It *is* my business if I have to go beat some guy's ass because he gets too drunk and puts his hands where they don't belong."

Jace was protective of me, which I both loved and hated. It would've been better if he didn't look at me like a little sister, though. His attitude came from an innocent place. That's the opposite of what I wanted. None of *my* feelings for this man were brotherly. But that was my little secret, I supposed.

"I'll be fine." I shrugged, opening the refrigerator and taking out a jug. I poured some water into a glass, feeling tingly because I could still feel his eyes on me, even if he was only concerned.

"I can't tell you what to do...but speaking from a guy's point of view, if I see a girl dressed the way you are now, it sends me a certain message about her. You know what I'm saying?"

Jace was clueless. Totally clueless. Little did he know *he* was the only guy whose attention I wanted lately. Anytime I dressed provocatively, it was an attempt to rile him up.

Ever since he'd moved in two months ago, getting Jace's attention was one of my pastimes. But unlike the pistachios he was chomping on, he was a hard nut to crack. Sure, I'd caught him looking at me from time to time, but I never knew what he was actually thinking. And truly, I didn't know what *I* was thinking trying to get him to notice me. Jace wouldn't touch me with a ten-foot pole—not just because he was living with us now, but because I was his best friend's sister. Thus, he looked at me like a sister, too—which I hated. As much as he'd been like family over the years, I'd never looked at him like a brother. My attraction was too strong. I'd had a crush on him from the moment I'd met him, when I was probably around six.

"Last I checked," I said, "the girls you hang out with don't dress any more conservatively than this."

He licked some of the salt off his lips. "Well, that's... different."

I cocked a brow. "How so?"

Jace's jaw tightened. He didn't have an answer.

Exactly.

I took the liberty of answering for him. "I know why you think it's different. You seem to forget that I'm twenty-one now. Some of the girls you date are practically my age, but you don't see me as mature, because when you left for college, I was twelve. That's the person you remember." I sighed. "I'm not twelve anymore. Reverse the numbers."

My brother, Nathan, walked in at that moment. "I don't care how old you are. You're dressed like a whore."

I rolled my eyes.

Jace glared at him. "Don't say shit like that to her."

"It's my job to tell her the truth."

"But you don't have to use those words, jackass."

I chuckled. "Yeah. Jace basically told me the same thing, except he was a lot nicer about it." I gulped the last of my water and placed the glass on the counter. "Anyway, it's hot as balls at The Iguana. Their air conditioning is sucky. Everyone dresses like this," I lied.

They looked at me in unison, both with skeptical expressions.

Jace and Nathan had been best friends since childhood. He and my brother were six years older than me. I'd spent the majority of my preteen years lusting after Jace in secret. In those days, he'd come over to the house all sweaty after football practice, and my hormones would mimic Mexican jumping beans. Whenever he'd so much as talk to me, I'd get weak in the knees. If you looked at my diary entries from back then, there was something about Jace on every other page. Wanting someone and knowing I couldn't have him had been pure torture. Especially during those last couple of years before Jace went away to college, I was hopelessly lovesick.

And then? He was gone. My twelve-year-old heart had been devastated when Jace moved away to attend school in North Carolina. And he only came home in the summer for the first few years.

He'd stayed away for nine years in total and had only recently moved back home to Florida. I certainly never imagined he'd end up living with us. At twenty-seven, Jace was the boy I remembered lusting after, but even bigger and better. He was a full-fledged man now. And I wasn't a child anymore. So you can imagine where my head had been lately.

Nathan snapped me out of my thoughts. "You'd better bring the pepper spray with you if your stubborn ass won't change into something decent."

"You know I always carry it."

Sometimes my brother didn't hold back, but I couldn't blame him for being protective. I was an adult now, but old habits died hard. Nathan had become my caretaker after our parents were killed during a robbery seven years ago. I was fourteen, and Nathan was twenty when we lost them. Jace had been home from college that summer, working for my dad's landscaping company. Sadly, he was with my parents when they died. That was still so hard to fathom. To this day, Jace couldn't talk about it. I knew he suffered from survivor's guilt. He'd been shot at as well, but he'd gotten lucky. Still, the trauma of having witnessed my parents' murder had inflicted a different kind of damage—not physical, but it had scarred his soul for life. None of us really talked about what had happened. Our painful past was a ghost that followed us around, one we never acknowledged.

I knew from the police report that my father and Jace had been driving back from a landscaping job. They'd stopped to pick up my mother at the convenience store where she worked. My father had felt like someone was following them from the moment he and Jace left the job site. The man eventually tried to run them off the road before pulling out a gun. My dad had a ton of cash on him, since his landscaping clients typically paid him that way. The investigators believe the man had somehow known about that money, which was why he'd been following their truck. Perhaps he'd been tipped off by someone working for my dad.

According to the report, the victims, Ronald and Elizabeth Spade, had cooperated, handing over the cash, but the man, who was high on drugs, fatally shot my parents anyway. A bullet grazed Jace, but he was unharmed. Based on the description of his vehicle, police later found the man holed up in his apartment. He was shot and killed following a standoff. And that was the end of it. Our lives changed forever, and the innocent, idyllic childhood I'd enjoyed became a memory.

After that summer, Jace never came home again. That was understandable.

Though it had now been seven years since my parents died, I knew I hadn't properly dealt with that loss. Some mornings, I still woke up expecting my mother and father to be here. If it weren't for Nathan, I wouldn't have made it. He did his best to fill the void they left. As miserable as we both were in the beginning, he'd tried to make life as normal as possible—like continuing our tradition of family movie night, even though it was just the two of us now. To this day, we picked one night a month to watch a movie together.

Nathan and I still lived in the neighborhood where we'd grown up in Palm Creek, Florida. After Mom and Dad died, staying in our childhood home had been too painful, so Nathan used the money we'd inherited for a down payment on a house a couple of streets over. Unfortunately, my brother had been recently laid off from his car-sales job and needed some help paying the bills. Around the same time, Jace moved home to temporarily manage his dad's business. Nathan asked Jace if he would rent out our spare bedroom to help with our mortgage payment. Since Jace was in limbo, waiting to buy property until he knew whether or not he'd be staying in Florida permanently, moving in with us was a good, temporary solution. It benefited everyone. So that's how we became a party of three.

I turned to my brother. "Can I have a ride to the bar?"

"What's wrong with your car now?"

"It might be the alternator this time. It's in the shop again."

"That piece of shit."

The old, rust-colored Toyota Corolla I drove constantly gave me trouble. Thankfully, our local mechanic—ironically named "Rusty"—always offered me a good deal. Nathan was convinced Rusty had ulterior motives when it came to me, but I gladly accepted the price break without questioning the reason for it.

"I'm saving up for something else," I assured him. "Until then, I have to deal with it. Not like I could get any money for that piece of junk if I tried to sell it."

"Next time, don't take it to Rusty," Jace said. "I can try to fix it."

The idea of Jace shirtless and sweaty under my car wasn't exactly unpleasant.

"Thanks. I hadn't thought to ask you. I appreciate the offer."

"When do you need to be at The Iguana?" Nathan asked.

"I have to leave now. I just need a ride there. Kellianne says she can drive me home."

He looked over at the clock. "I can't take you now. Someone's coming in ten minutes to look at the lawn mower I'm selling. I can take you after, though."

I frowned. "I'll miss the beginning if I don't leave now."

"Why is that such a big deal?" Nathan asked. "It's just a bunch of drunk people spewing dumb shit."

"It's not dumb. It's captivating."

Once a week, The Iguana held their open mic "Pour Your Heart Out" night, and I'd been obsessed with going as of late. Patrons—mostly somewhat drunk ones—were encouraged to get on stage and reveal anything they wanted to a room full of strangers. It could be something they needed to get off their chest, or their deepest, darkest secret. You never knew what you were going to get. Some of the confessions were sad, things I could relate to after years of harboring the pain of my parents' murder. Other times, it was a sexy secret. Some people held nothing back. It was definitely eighteen-plus. Even though I loved listening to it all, I hadn't had the guts to get up on stage yet. *Someday*.

"I can take her," Jace interrupted.

I inwardly celebrated.

"Thanks, man. I appreciate it," Nathan said.

Jace stood up from the table and tossed the pistachio shells he'd accumulated on a paper napkin into the trash.

He grabbed his keys from the counter and threw them up in the air. "Let's go."

A surge of adrenaline coursed through me as I followed Jace outside to his shiny black pickup truck, parked in our driveway. It was almost 8PM, and the hot Florida air had started to cool down. A warm breeze blew around the palm trees in front of our house. We lived on a quiet street of similar-looking stucco homes. Our house was only one level, but it was pretty big in comparison to the other properties. We had three bedrooms and a large, screened-in pool in the back. Because the homeowners' association was very strict, all of the houses were kept in good condition. Otherwise, you'd have to pay a fine. Members of the association drove by periodically and would send nastygrams if they so much as noticed the paint chipping. Fortunately, Nathan could fix pretty much anything himself.

The black leather seat felt hot against my skin. The truck was huge, too big for our small garage, which was where Nathan parked his little Hyundai. Jace always had to park outside in the heat.

He started the ignition but didn't back out, instead looking down at my navel. For a split second, I thought he might have been checking me out. "Put your seatbelt on."

Well, now I feel dumb. "Oh." I grabbed it and placed it over my chest before locking it in. "Sorry."

I flinched when he wrapped his hand around my seat as he backed out of the driveway.

Did you think he was going to touch you, Farrah?

I had to giggle.

"What are you laughing at?" he asked as he drove down the road.

Wracking my brain, I made something up. "You know what they say about men with big trucks, right?"

He rolled his eyes. "That their vehicles are proportional to the size of their manhood? Yup. Live that every day."

"That's not exactly what I heard. But whatever you say." I winked.

"Wiseass." He laughed.

The smell of his cologne, mixed with the smallest hint of cigar, filled the air. He'd never smoked in front of me, but I knew he enjoyed the occasional cigar while he drove. I loved the smell of his truck, because it was basically the smell of *him* condensed into a small space. It was heaven.

If I'm coming across as a bit desperate for this man—well, I guess that's right. But consider the fact that he was my very first crush. *The* crush. My only crush. Many years of unrequited longing had led me here. Also consider that he's ten times more attractive now, having morphed into a full-on man. The additional fact that I was now actually old enough to entertain my fantasies didn't help. I didn't *want* to want him. I just did. He was the last person I should've been setting my sights on, because this was futile. But you can't choose who you're attracted to.

We drove in silence for a couple of minutes until I said, "Thank you for driving me. I appreciate it."

He glanced over. "No problem."

I braced myself. "What are you doing tonight?"

He hesitated. "Probably heading to Linnea's."

Linnea was a girl I knew he'd been seeing. I'd heard him talking to Nathan about her and spotted her in his truck once.

"Are things getting serious with her?"

He shrugged. "I don't really get serious with anyone. I just spend more time with certain people than others."

I nodded slowly. "I see."

While that made me feel a tad better, it also meant there was likely more than one girl he'd been "spending time" with.

"Do you regret moving back to Palm Creek?" I asked.

"Why would you think that?" he asked after a moment.

"Isn't it obvious? In North Carolina, you owned your own place. You had a great job, from what I understand. Now you're living with Nathan and me and working for your father. That's a big change." I paused to think. "Besides...I know not all of the memories here are good ones. I just thought—"

"It's fine," he interrupted. "My father needed me to run his business for a while. I had little choice in the matter, but being home has actually made me realize how much I missed it here. It's not all bad."

Jace's dad, Phil, owned Muldoon Construction. Phil Muldoon had been undergoing treatment for throat cancer and needed help running the business side of things for a while. Since he had a business degree, Jace was the most equipped of his siblings to handle the task. Actually, Jace's older half-brothers weren't capable of anything at all, considering they were both unemployed drug addicts. So Jace had quit his property manager job in Charlotte before moving back here.

"Do you think you'll stay permanently?"

"That depends on a lot of things. I'm just taking it one day at a time."

"I know Nathan really appreciates the fact that you moved in with us. He's not always the best with words and expressing his thanks. His pride gets in the way. But he sleeps better at night knowing we can pay the mortgage. I'm glad he wasn't afraid to ask you to move in."

"I kind of feel like I owe him, to be honest."

"Why is that?"

He paused. "When things...happened...I disappeared. Went straight back to school. You know..."

This was the first time Jace had even vaguely alluded to what had "happened." I'd never realized he felt guilty for going back to North Carolina after my parents were killed. That made sense, I supposed. But I certainly never faulted him for that decision. What was he supposed to do? Drop out of school, stay in Palm Creek, and suffer along with the rest of us? At the time, I'd envied the fact that he had somewhere else to go. Heck, I would've gone with him if I could've.

"You had to get back to school, had to continue your life. You had no choice—"

"There's always a choice. And I do regret not being there for him...and for you. Now's my opportunity to make up for that." He glanced over at me. "You guys are like family."

While a part of me liked hearing that, the other part didn't care for the incestuous undertone of his statement.

He cleared his throat. "What is it about this confession thing at the bar you like so much?"

I shrugged. "I guess when you bottle up your feelings a lot, you envy those who have the courage to let them out."

"You've never actually gone up there, then."

"No...not yet anyway. Maybe at some point."

He raised his eyebrows. "What are you waiting for?"

I chuckled. "Guts."

"What are you scared of specifically?"

"Losing my ability to speak mostly, or worse, speaking in gibberish if I do manage to get the words out... Fainting, collapsing, being carted away to a mental hospital with padded walls. Stuff like that."

"Catastrophic much?" He laughed. "But I get it. It's not easy doing anything in front of an audience. I can't blame you."

"Yeah. I prefer to just listen for now. I find it very inspiring, even though I wish I had the balls to do it."

"There's no rush. When you're ready, you will. Public speaking does take balls, but I would imagine it's even harder when you're sharing something personal."

I nodded. "That's exactly it. And I'd also need something interesting to confess. Sometimes people talk about painful things that have happened to them, but I'd prefer not to go there. I'd rather confess something juicy or funny rather than start bawling in front of strangers."

"Don't go doing anything stupid just so you have something to talk about. You'll give your brother a heart attack."

"It doesn't take much to upset Nathan."

He turned to me. "You don't talk to him much, do you? He told me he never knows what you're thinking."

My brother has talked to Jace about me? "He did?"

"Yeah. I think he wishes you'd open up to him more."

"I'm not very good at talking about certain things with anyone. I write down my thoughts to express myself, or sometimes I write fiction where the characters have gone through what I have. But I keep everything private. Even listening to certain songs that resonate helps me get stuff out. I meditate and do yoga sometimes, too. Talking has never been my thing, though."

"As long as you have an outlet."

"What's *your* outlet?"

"Nothing as respectable as writing and yoga."

"Sex and cigars?" I suggested.

"I haven't had a cigar in a week." He winked.

Jesus. So I guess it's sex then.

"Maybe I should learn to meditate instead," he added. "When do you do it?"

"Whenever I can find the time. I use an app on my phone for guided meditation. It helps calm me down when I'm stressed. I also feel like it helps me connect to my subconscious."

Glancing over at me, he smiled. "You're way deeper than the little girl who used to chew on her hair."

I felt my cheeks heat. "I can't believe you remember that."

"Some things are kind of hard to forget."

I sighed. "Life was certainly simpler back then. Glad I got out of that habit, though. If I chewed on my hair when I got stressed now, I wouldn't have any left."

"You do a good job of not seeming like you're stressed all the time. I guess you can hide a lot behind a smile, huh?"

I shrugged. "Fake it 'til you make it."

He turned to me briefly before his eyes returned to the road. "What's got you stressed?"

"It's nothing I can pinpoint. Just the overall uncertainty of the future. I want to make something of myself but have no idea what it is I want to do. I feel like I'm stuck in limbo. I stay in the same mundane secretarial job—getting up every day and doing the same thing—but I feel time ticking away."

"You're so young. You've got a lot of time."

"I'm not *that* young," I felt compelled to say.

"I know you're not a kid anymore, but you're young."

"I should've almost graduated college by now, and I haven't even started. My mother was married with a baby at my age."

He grimaced. "You wouldn't want to be married with a kid right now."

"No, but I want a purpose, deeper meaning in my life. It's frustrating that I haven't found it."

"There's no timetable, Farrah. You've been through a lot—more than most people your age. And honestly, I'm proud of the way you and Nathan have handled everything. You've got a roof over your head, and you look out for each other. You're doing amazing, even if you don't always feel like you have your shit together. In the end, we're all just trying to get through the day, you know? Don't be so hard on yourself."

Admiring his gorgeous cheekbones and the way the streetlights reflected on his jet-black hair, I smiled. "I'll try to look at it that way."

We finally approached the strip of businesses where The Iguana was located.

Jace slowed the truck. "Is this it?"

"Yup."

He pulled up in front. The last of the daylight had diminished during the course of our ride, and the blue neon sign atop the bar lit up the night.

"You said you have a ride back?" He placed his hand on my headrest.

Once again, my body was all too aware of his proximity.

"Yeah. Kellianne is meeting me here and driving me home."

Jace gave me a look. "Does she drink?"

"Don't worry. She'll only have one drink if she's driving."

"Okay. If anything changes and you need a ride, text me."

It was tempting to create a situation later that might warrant that scenario.

"I will."

"Be careful," he warned.

Not eager to leave his truck, I lingered for a moment. I wanted to stay with him all night, talk more about life, learn more about what made him tick and what types of things he longed for. I wanted to know everything about him, pick him apart layer by layer.

Instead, I forced myself to open the door. Before exiting, I paused and leaned in to give him a quick hug. "Thanks again."

His body stiffened, yet he wrapped his arm around my back. I savored those few seconds before pulling away. From all appearances, it was an innocent gesture. But on the inside, I was burning up. I didn't have many opportunities to "thank" him in that way.

Jace waited for me to go in before he drove off.

Once the door closed behind me, I made a beeline for the bar. I hated being the first to arrive. Kellianne was coming straight from work.

After finding a seat at a table that faced the stage, I sat alone and sipped my mojito.

About ten minutes later, I spotted my friend rushing toward me.

I'd met Kellianne at the law firm where I worked as an administrative assistant. She'd since moved on to another job, but we'd stayed in contact. Physically, we were opposites. Kellianne was short with curly blond hair. I was five-foot-seven with long, straight, brown locks.

"Sorry, I'm late. Traffic sucked," she said.

"No worries." I lifted my drink. "As you can see, I got a head start."

"Anyone go up there yet?"

"No. They haven't started."

The confessionals usually started at nine and would last for about an hour, maybe more, depending on how many people were willing to spill their guts.

"Your brother drove you here?"

"No. Jace gave me a ride."

"Ah...Jace." She sighed. "He's so freaking hot. I ran into him pumping gas the other day. Well, he didn't see me. He had a girl in the truck with him."

I rolled my eyes. "Did she have red hair?"

"Yeah, actually."

"That's Linnea. He's been seeing her for a couple of weeks. He's with her tonight."

Her brow lifted. "Does that bother you?"

I shrugged. "A little. Yeah."

I'd never spoken to Kellianne about my recent feelings for Jace. She only knew about my crush on him when I was younger. A hopeless crush was excusable, even cute, at twelve. At twenty-one? Not so much.

But she didn't seem surprised by my response. "I thought so..."

"I don't want to get into it."

"But *I* want to hear about this."

"There's not much to say. You already know I had a crush on him when I was a little girl. Being around him again has brought out some of those old feelings."

She held out her index finger. "Hold that thought. I need a drink for this."

She ran to the bar. When she returned to her seat with a rum and Coke, she took up where she'd left off.

"Okay, so...some of the old feelings for him came back...or rather, they just never went away?"

I slurped the last of my drink and shook around the ice. "When he was living in North Carolina, it was easier not to think about him, but now that he's here again, I can't help how I feel. It's like my emotions just picked up where they left off. And, now that he's living with us, I'm getting to know him on a different level. We never talked much when I was a kid. Back then it was just me admiring him from afar. We're both more mature now, so it's different."

Her eyes brimmed with excitement. "Do you think there's a chance something could happen?"

"No. I really don't. He treats me the same way Nathan does–like a sister. Which sucks."

"Well, you never know. Keep dressing like you did tonight, and that might change."

"I don't know. He cares about me. I do know that. I think that's exactly why he'd never try anything." I tipped some of the ice into my mouth. "Honestly, I don't know what I'd do if he returned the attraction. Nathan would kill us both."

"Okay, so hypothetically, if an opportunity arose... you wouldn't go there?"

"I don't know." I sighed. "Anyway, that's a fantasy, not reality."

"It's weird to know the person you're obsessed with cares about you, just not in the way you want. Sort of a unique situation."

Her use of the word *obsessed* weirded me out. I thought I'd downplayed my feelings toward Jace, but apparently she could see through me.

Fiddling with my straw, I looked down into my empty glass. "He does care about me. I care about him, too. It's not just lust. For so many years, he was a big part of my life. He spent a lot of time with our family. When his team lost a football game, he'd lament to us at the dinner table.

I had a front-row seat to a lot of important times in his life, like when he and Nathan went to prom and graduated from high school. I watched him grow up." I closed my eyes. "And of course, as I've told you before, he was there when my parents died. He was *with* them, because he was working for my dad that summer."

Kellianne shook her head. "That's so crazy."

"Yeah. He won't talk about it. And I don't blame him." I blew out a long breath. "I can't imagine how traumatic that was. It hurts me to even think about it." Wiping a tear, I said, "Okay, we need to move on to another subject, stat."

Kellianne clapped her hands. "Okay then. I know what we can talk about. What do I have to do to get you to go up there tonight and confess your secret crush on your brother's best friend?"

That wasn't the change of subject I was hoping for.

"Figure out how to make pigs fly?"

Chapter 2

Farrah

In our house, everyone did their own laundry. We kept our washer and dryer in a corner of the garage, since we didn't have a separate laundry room. About once a week, I'd wash my clothes after I got back from work, which was before Nathan or Jace got home.

One such afternoon, I carried my items in a basket to the garage and noticed a pile of Jace's clothes sitting in a canvas bag next to the washing machine. I recognized the red shirt on top as the one he'd worn yesterday. He'd smelled amazing in it while sitting across from me at the table. It had to smell just as good today.

On impulse, I picked up the shirt and lifted it to my nose, keeping it over my face as I breathed in deeply for several seconds. Inhaling the earthy cologne mixed with a delicious scent that was all Jace was sweet torture. This made it easy to imagine what it would be like to have him up against me. Closing my eyes, I rubbed my face against the soft material, pretending he was inside of it. This was as close as I was going to get, so I let myself enjoy it.

"What the hell are you doing?" a gruff voice demanded.

My heart nearly stopped. The shirt fell to the ground as I lifted my chin to meet Jace's incendiary stare. He'd apparently entered the garage through the side door while I was immersed in my olfactory fantasy.

Feigning calm, I said, "Oh...hi. You're home."

"Yeah. I had to take my dad to an appointment, so I left work early. Is...*this* what you do when we're not here? Sniff the dirty laundry?"

His confused expression held a mix of anger and amusement.

I pulled the most insane excuse out of my butt. "I have this...strange habit of smelling things that aren't mine. Sort of like...a compulsion."

My heart thumped out the word *liar...liar...liar* repeatedly.

"So you decided to smell my shirt out of everything in here?"

I gulped. "Yeah, I guess. It was bright red—caught my attention. Not to mention, your cologne is...nice."

He chuckled. "You're weird, Farrah."

"Never claimed not to be."

His brow lifted. "How did it smell otherwise?"

Letting out a shaky breath, I nodded. "Good. No strange odors or anything—unlike Nathan's shirts. His smell like tacos."

Jace chuckled. "I guess if I'm on the fence about throwing something in the wash, I should consult you from now on?"

"Could've been worse, right? I could have been, like, smelling your underwear or something. I'm not *that* weird." I snorted and closed my eyes in shame.

"Well, thank fuck for that." After an awkward pause, he said, "I'll...let you get back to what you were doing—whatever it was."

Saluting him, I smiled. "Thanks."

After he left, I turned around and let out a silent scream of horror.

Once I put my load in the washer, I decided to take a walk around the block to burn off some nervous energy and avoid having to face him inside so soon. The more time that passed the better.

After I circled the block, I headed toward my yard, planning to pick an avocado off our tree. As I passed the side of the house, I spotted Jace through his bedroom window. Sweat glistened on his back as he pumped iron. Since he wasn't facing me, I took a few moments to admire his physique. Gorgeous ripples of carved muscle. Round, hard ass. Perfectly tanned skin. Jace had always had a nice body, but at twenty-seven, he was in the best shape of his life.

A rush of water suddenly emerged from under my feet. If only the shock hadn't caused me to scream. *If only.* If only Jace hadn't turned around to find me standing there, looking like an idiot—a drenched idiot who didn't even realize Nathan had installed a new sprinkler on this side of our grass.

Jace rushed to the window and opened it. "What the hell are you doing? Are you wet?"

Um... Not even going to go there with that.

Covering my soaked chest, I said, "It's so...hot today. I thought I'd let the water run over me for a bit."

"I thought I heard you scream."

"Wasn't expecting it to be so cold."

He squinted. "Are you okay, Farrah? You seem off today."

"Yes, of course I'm okay." I laughed nervously when he continued to look at me. "I'm fine. I swear."

"You know you can tell me if something is up, right?"

"Yup." I nodded vigorously.

"Okay." His eyes lingered for a moment. Then he shut the window and went back to his weights.

Is 4PM too early for vodka?

• • •

The following evening, Nathan and I had scheduled a family movie night. He'd somehow guilted Jace into staying in and joining us. Our one must-have on movie night was ice cream, and since my car was still at Rusty's, and Nathan was still at work, Jace drove me to the market to buy some.

The ride to the grocery store was a bit tense. I assumed maybe Jace was quiet because he might've still been thinking about me sniffing his shirt, or the sprinkler incident outside his window yesterday. Maybe I assumed that because getting caught *twice* in the act of stupidity was all I could think about.

When we got to the supermarket's freezer aisle, I grabbed a container of Rocky Road and sniffed it. You know...to throw him off.

A look of horror crossed Jace's face. "You're doing it again."

"You caught me. See? Told you I like to sniff things," I lied. "If you breathe in hard enough, you can get a feel for the taste."

He shook his head and laughed. "It's you, isn't it?"

"What's me?"

"That person captured on store camera footage, opening up the ice cream containers, tasting what's inside, and putting them back. They're looking for you, you know."

"Guilty," I joked. "Actually, I think that's super gross. I would never do that."

I continued to pick through the containers, sniffing the various flavors like an idiot. "I'm sorry if I'm taking a long time," I said. "This is always a big decision for me."

After several more minutes, Jace reached over me. "I'm gonna put you out of your misery." A waft of his scent dominated anything else I might have been pretending to smell. "There is no flavor better than cookie dough." He tossed a container into the cart. "Done."

"I beg to differ, but okay. If you feel that strongly, we'll go with that."

We went to the register, and the cashier's eyes danced over Jace. That was a typical reaction. Younger girls and older women alike constantly checked him out. It was funny, because people very likely assumed I was his girlfriend. That certainly didn't stop them from looking.

Before we left, I gave the cashier a sly grin that said, *yeah, look what's mine and not yours*. Even if that was the furthest thing from the truth, it gave me a sense of pleasure.

We hopped back inside Jace's truck, which once again smelled divine.

"Put your seatbelt on."

I'd been too busy staring at his big hands as they wrapped around the steering wheel.

"Thanks for the reminder."

"Why do I always have to remind you? It should be second nature."

Because you distract me. "Sorry, bossy. I'll try to remember next time." I clicked the belt in place and settled in. "Oh, I forgot to tell you someone came by for you today."

He headed out of the parking lot. "Who?"

"His name was James...Moore? He said he would text you, so I assume you spoke to him?"

He raised his tone. "James Moore?"

"Yeah. He didn't seem too friendly, either."

Jace banged on the steering wheel. "Fuck. He's looking for money the company owes him for a paving job he did for us. He has no patience. He had no business coming to the house."

"It was no big deal. I told him you weren't home, and he left right away."

"I don't like the idea of him coming in contact with you. The same goes for a lot of the guys who do work for us. What were you doing opening the door anyway?"

Jace was probably right to be a little alarmed, but this felt like an overreaction. "It's my house. Why wouldn't I open the door? It's not like I'm a child home alone after school."

"No, but you're an attractive woman who could set off the wrong kind of guy, someone who's looking for revenge. You wouldn't be able to fend him off. This has nothing to do with age. I don't care how old you are. You should never open the door to talk to anyone if you're alone."

Attractive woman.

He called me an attractive woman, and I basically heard nothing after that. This was the first indication he'd ever given that he felt I was attractive.

"I'll try to be more careful."

"You need to, Farrah. There are a lot of bad people in this world. If someone comes to the door and you don't recognize them, let them leave. There's nothing important enough to risk your safety." He let out an exasperated breath. "I don't even know how the fuck he got our address. I don't list it anywhere."

Jace continued swearing under his breath.

"You made your point. I won't answer the door when I'm alone unless it's a Girl Scout selling cookies or something."

"I would never forgive myself if something happened to you," he mumbled.

I felt those words deep in my heart.

• • •

"What did we finally settle on?" I asked.

Nathan was using my phone to peruse the movie options for tonight. "It's a toss-up between the Pete Davidson movie or that one with The Rock," he said before tossing the phone on the counter. "By the way, Farrah, why in God's name were you Googling 'vibrating vagina'?"

My face froze. *Shit.* I must not have closed out of that window.

Jace's eyes widened as he looked up from his laptop.

Any excuse I could have conjured up probably would have sounded weirder than the truth. So I decided to be honest. "I had a weird symptom this morning. It felt like I had a cell phone going off in my panties—like it was on vibrate. I think it was a muscle twitch. I was worried it was some kind of neurological issue. Apparently, I'm not the only person in the world who's gotten it. This girl in India posted the same thing."

Nathan bent his head back in laughter. "Did you guys agree to call each other sometime?"

I glared at him.

He continued to tease, laughing harder. "Seriously, though, when it rings, do you answer it?"

Jace shook his head. "Leave her alone, jackass. You shouldn't have been looking at her search history."

"I wasn't expecting to see that shit! It was on the screen when I grabbed the phone to search for a damn movie."

"Imagine if she searched *your* history, all the shit she'd find. And then called you out on it?"

"That would definitely not be a good thing." Nathan chuckled.

Thankfully, Nathan dropped the subject, and I went to busy myself by getting the dessert ready. These past few days had been *full* of embarrassing moments.

Opening the container of cookie dough ice cream, I decided to let it sit for a bit so it could soften. After grabbing three bowls, I sifted through the silverware drawer.

Then the doorbell rang.

I turned to Nathan. "Are you expecting someone?"

"It's Linnea. I invited her to join us," Jace called, heading to the door.

My heart sank. *Great.* Up until now, he hadn't brought her over to the house. I'd hoped it would stay that way.

"Did you know he invited her?" I asked.

"Yeah." Nathan took one of the spoons and dug into the ice cream. "What's the big deal? It's his house, too."

"This is a family thing. I don't like letting strangers join."

"Well, she's *hardly* a stranger to him." He wriggled his brows.

I couldn't roll my eyes back far enough.

A few seconds later, Jace and Linnea entered the kitchen.

"Linnea, you've met Nathan once before, but I don't think you know his little sister, Farrah."

Ouch.

Little sister.

Bite me.

She looked me up and down and flicked her red hair off her shoulder. "Nice to meet you. Farrah's such a pretty name. Your mother must have liked *Charlie's Angels.*"

"Why?"

"Farrah...Fawcett? The actress? She was one of Charlie's Angels. It was a TV show years back. She's iconic. She's dead now, unfortunately."

"Oh." I knew about the actress. I also knew my mother thought of her when naming me. But I'd forgotten the name of the show she was on.

Jace flashed a mischievous smile. "My dad used to have a vintage poster of Farrah Fawcett hanging in our garage. It was definitely one of my first pieces of… material."

Material? It took me a few seconds. *Oh.*

And now I was jealous of a dead actress because Jace had whacked off to her picture?

"I remember that poster!" Nathan laughed. "She was so hot."

"That time we met before, Nathan," Linnea said, "I don't think I realized you and Jace grew up together."

Nathan sighed exaggeratedly. "Yeah. I've been stuck with this guy my entire life."

"That's so great. It's rare to have long-lasting friendships." She turned to me. "You're a lot younger than they are, right? Are you in high school?"

No, she didn't.

Jace chuckled under his breath.

"High school? No. I'm twenty-one."

"Oh. Sorry. My bad. You look younger."

So much for dressing provocatively to appear older. But it seemed this chick was *looking* for ways to insult me.

"And are you thirty?" I asked, tilting my head to the side.

Her expression dampened. "Twenty-six."

"Ah."

Jace disappeared into the bathroom off the kitchen, leaving Nathan and me alone with Linnea.

She took a seat on one of the stools by the small center island. "Do you go to college around here?"

It really wasn't any of her business, but I explained anyway. "I took classes at Palm Creek Community College for a while, but I'm taking a break at the moment. Hoping to enroll somewhere next year. I don't want to waste time until I'm sure what I want to major in. Leaning toward education."

"You should teach English," Jace said from behind me as he emerged from the bathroom.

"Why do you say that?"

"Because you said you like to write. Might be a subject you'd enjoy teaching."

I nodded. "It's definitely on my short list. Although, if I'm going to teach someday, I guess I'd better get over my fear of public speaking."

Linnea nodded. "Oh...I hate to get up in front of a crowd."

No one asked you, but okay.

Seeing as though we now had another mouth to feed tonight, I guessed I'd try to be cordial, even if having her here irked me. I walked over to the cabinet. "We're having ice cream. You want some?"

"I'd love some," she answered.

I almost wished she'd refused "because she was on a diet" so I could hate her even more.

After distributing an equal amount of cookie dough ice cream into each bowl, I took mine and left the others on the counter.

I was first to venture into the living room, plopping down on the couch and selecting the video-on-demand options. Nathan sat on the chaise lounge, which meant the only spots for Jace and Linnea were on the couch next to me. I shifted over when they approached. To my delight, Jace sat on the side next to me. Silver lining? At least with three people on the couch, I was forced to sit closer to him than I would have if it were just the two of us.

We decided on the Pete Davidson movie, and everyone seemed to be into it. It was set in Staten Island, New York. I loved any movie set in or around New York City. One of my dreams had once been to live there, even if just for a couple of years to experience something that was the polar opposite of Florida.

At one point in the middle of the film, Jace stood up and grabbed Linnea's empty bowl, piling it atop his. He reached out to me, and I handed him my bowl as well. He was thoughtful like that sometimes. Jace didn't bother grabbing Nathan's bowl, though, which was on the floor next to my brother's feet.

Jace returned holding two bottles of beer and handed one to Linnea. This time when he sat down, he was much closer to my side than before. In fact, I could practically feel the warmth emanating from his body. The fine blond hairs on my legs stood at attention. If I shifted my thigh just a couple of inches in his direction, my leg would be up against his.

Then, about a half-hour later, Jace stretched his leg out. His knee now happened to be grazing my thigh. I didn't dare move. Instead, I enjoyed the feel of his hard knee through the denim of his jeans. This was okay, I told myself, as he was the one who'd shifted in my direction.

From where she sat on the other side, I wasn't sure if Linnea had noticed my leg was touching Jace's. Was it a coincidence when she repositioned her body to be closer to him? Maybe I was ballsier than I thought, because as soon as she did that, I did the same—moved just a hair closer so a bit more of my leg pressed against his. If he hadn't realized that our legs were touching before, there was no way he didn't know now. Yet he didn't shift away from me.

The fact that he stayed put likely didn't mean anything. But still. He stayed in the same position for ten whole minutes. Trying to figure out what it meant was likely going to consume me later, but for now, I pretended to watch the movie, pretended like my entire body wasn't on fire.

After the movie finished, Jace grabbed his keys. "Ready to leave?"

Linnea stretched and yawned. "Yup."

"You coming back tonight?" Nathan asked.

"Nah. Probably gonna sleep at her place."

I swallowed the lump in my throat.

Linnea said goodbye, but Jace never made eye contact with me before he left. My delusional mind proceeded to create a story in which he felt guilty for enjoying the contact of my leg.

I guess I should've been happy that he went to her place. The last thing I wanted was to hear anything happening in his room. But all night, the memory of Jace's leg pressed against mine continued to torment me. And I couldn't stop thinking about what he might have been doing with Linnea. She got to lie next to him, to be held. As attracted to Jace as I was, if given a choice between getting to have sex with him once or just being held all night, I wasn't sure which I would choose.

Okay. Sex would probably win.

I'd slept with two people in my life, but neither was someone I truly cared about. Maybe that's why I'd never fantasized about being held by either of them. My first time was with my prom date my junior year of high school. It was a miserable and painful experience, and we never even went out again after that. The second person I slept with was my one and only serious boyfriend, Jordan. We'd broken up a few years ago when he got a scholarship to an out-of-state school. I couldn't blame him for leaving, but it had hurt all the same.

My thoughts returned to Jace, and I tossed and turned all night—my body still on fire.

Chapter 3

Farrah

The next time I encountered Jace was a few days later. It was still the afternoon, so I was surprised to see him home from work already.

He had his head in his hands as he stared down at the kitchen table.

Something is wrong. "Hey," I said.

He looked up, his eyes tired. "Hey."

I couldn't remember the last time he'd seemed so down. My heart sank. "Are you okay?"

He shook his head. "No."

I pulled out a chair and sat across from him. "What's wrong?"

Jace let out a long, exasperated breath that I felt on my skin from across the table. "It's work-related."

"Well, sometimes talking it through helps."

He laughed angrily. "This isn't a problem that talking is gonna solve, unfortunately."

"Why not?"

"Because I need a hundred-thousand dollars. Can we talk our way to that kind of money?"

My jaw dropped, but I caught myself and closed it, trying not to freak him out even more. “Likely not,” I said.

He chuckled.

“But okay, Jace. Let’s think about this.” I paused. “First...try to be positive.”

His eyes widened. “Oh yeah? So if I’m positive enough it’s gonna make cash magically appear?”

“Crazier things have happened.” I sighed. “Seriously... what’s going on? Why do you need that kind of money?”

He bounced his legs nervously. “You remember when that guy James Moore came by looking for money we owed him?”

“Yeah.”

“Well, apparently that was part of a bigger problem I’ve only recently become aware of.”

“What problem?”

“I guess James has been owed that money for a much longer time than I was led to believe. My father has defaulted on payment to several of the people he contracted to work for Muldoon.”

“Why hasn’t he paid them? I thought the company was doing well.”

“Well, that’s the worst part. Business *is* good. But apparently, Dad has a gambling problem. He blew money at the tables that was supposed to be paid out to various vendors.”

I closed my eyes. “Shit.”

“This is not what I signed up for when I agreed to manage the company while my father got treatment. I have no idea how I’m supposed to rectify this. The old man never even fucking told me about it. A heads-up would’ve been nice. Now I have a bunch of shady guys on *my* ass because of what he did."

"Is there a way to explain the situation to those who are owed money? Maybe agree to pay them back with interest over time?"

"I haven't gotten that far." He shook his head. "But I do know there are far more people angry at my father and me than I realized. Not to mention, once word gets out that we're not paying people, no one is gonna want to work for us. We'll never be able to keep up with demand with no one to do the labor."

My imagination ran wild. Would someone try to harm Jace if he couldn't come up with the money?

I tried to get that out of my mind. "I'm sorry. I know it may seem hopeless, but things have a way of working themselves out. You have to have faith. Now that you know about this, you can figure out a solution." I frowned. "I know that advice isn't very specific. I just want to make you feel better."

His mouth spread into a reluctant smile, and my heart ached a little.

"No, you're good." He rubbed his temples. "Thank you for trying. It's not your job to make me feel better. You were right, though. Telling you did ease some of the load, even if it doesn't change anything. So, thank you for listening."

I nodded. "You've overcome obstacles before. Even though this one might seem unsolvable—you'll get through this, too." I smiled. "After all, we're talkin' about the same guy who managed to take his team to victory in that Pee Wee game after five consecutive losses, the guy who got the highest score on the Algebra Two final after a D on the previous test. The guy who taught himself Morse code on a dare..."

He shook his head. "How the hell do you remember all that?"

Uh-oh. This would be the part of our conversation where I admit my history as a secret Jace connoisseur. "I...always looked up to you and Nathan. I paid close attention, listened to all the conversations at the dinner table—watched and learned. You were too busy being popular and kicking ass in football to notice my brace face back then."

"Well..." He grinned. "I do recall a certain backyard cat rescue."

Wow. "I can't believe you remember *that.*"

"Nathan and I came home to find your ass hanging on for dear life while you tried to get it down." He chuckled. "You were sweet then, and you're still sweet now. I see how you go check on that kid next door. You're still the kind girl you always were." He stared into my eyes. "I also see you putting on a brave face every day, but I know your life hasn't been easy. You were forced to grow up way faster than you should have."

This was the most candid Jace had ever been.

I shrugged. "You're right. It *hasn't* been easy. But I'm lucky. At least I have Nathan."

"He's lucky to have *you.*"

I paused, but ultimately I went for it. "And I have you now, too. I'm glad you're here."

After several seconds of silence, he said, "I'm glad I'm here, too."

My heart fluttered. "Whatever you do, never believe that it's impossible to come up with that money, Jace. I've been reading this book. It talks about the power in positive thinking. Even if it seems crazy, you have to make yourself believe you can rectify this situation. That will help manifest it."

He chuckled. "Manifest it? You want me to believe some hocus pocus will solve this mess my dad caused?"

"I promise you, manifesting isn't witchcraft or anything. It's more like visualization. What's the alternative? Feeling hopeless? Negative energy will hamper things. You have to envision a positive outcome and actually believe it. That's what manifesting is."

"And what exactly have you manifested lately?" he asked.

I'm currently manifesting you. Hard. "I'm working on a few things."

"Oh yeah? How's that going?"

"It's going." I blushed.

He looked like he wanted to say something, but remained silent. "I have another memory of you, actually," he finally said. "Something I'll never forget. I don't know if you'll remember this one, though. You were really young."

I cocked my head. "What was it?"

He looked down at his hands. "You know I used to have a stuttering problem when I was a kid..."

"I do vaguely remember that, yeah."

"By the time I met you and Nathan, my parents had paid for speech therapy, but the stammering would still come out when I was nervous or stressed. Anyway...I think I was, like, fourteen. Nathan and I had gotten in trouble with your parents for breaking one of the windows. It was my fault. I threw the baseball that broke the glass." His mouth curved into a slight smile. "Your dad was so pissed. I was trying to explain myself, and I couldn't get the words out without stuttering. It freaked me out. I ran out to the yard mid-conversation, and you came after me. You must have been, like, eight years old, but you were so perceptive. You somehow knew why I'd escaped. You said the cutest freaking thing to me."

"What was it?"

"You said, 'Don't worry. Porky Pig is my favorite Looney Tunes character.'"

Oh my God. "Because he stutters?" I laughed. "I don't remember saying that, but I still stand by it. He was always my favorite. Honestly, that was probably *because* of his stutter. It gave him character."

"What you said calmed me down that day. I went back inside and explained myself to your parents. I was still stuttering, but I got through it. No one else seemed to realize why I'd even left." Jace flashed a gorgeous smile. "Anyway, when I look in your eyes, I still see that sweet little girl sometimes. Even though you're far from a little girl anymore."

I felt warm all over—not sure if it was because he'd called me sweet or had acknowledged I'd grown up.

He suddenly stood and walked over to the snack cabinet, opening it and perusing the selection. He ran his hand through his inky hair before closing the cabinet. Then he turned around and said, "Anyway, thank you for the talk."

"Anytime."

I was just about to head to my room when he stopped me. "Do you have plans for dinner?"

"No."

"What time is Nathan coming back tonight?"

"He said he won't be home until late. He had a job interview this afternoon, and then he was going to see some girl he met online. She lives about two hours away. That's a long-ass drive. Hope she's worth it." I snorted.

"Ah. Okay. That's good he's putting himself out there, though. I was getting worried." Jace scratched his chin before grabbing his keys. "I'm in the mood for Checkers. Would you want something if I go and bring it back?"

My stomach growled. "That sounds good." I walked over to my purse on the counter. "Let me get some money."

He held out his hand. "No, no, no. My treat."

"You need to come up with a hundred grand. I'm not letting you cover my dinner."

"I'll live. Put it away. What do you want?"

I pulled up their online menu on my phone. "I'll take a Mother Cruncher chicken sandwich and a Diet Coke."

"That's it? No fries?"

"No. I'll just steal a few of yours."

"I'll get you your own." He winked. "Be back."

I stood by the window, watching him pull away. I didn't know what to do with myself. Since he'd moved in, Jace and I hadn't eaten dinner together without Nathan. I warned myself not to get too excited. For all I knew, Jace would take his food to his room and eat by himself. It wasn't like he'd asked me out on a date. He'd merely asked if I wanted something from a fast-food joint since he was going there anyway.

It was a hot day, so while I waited, I ventured to my room and changed into a bikini. Regardless of whether Jace wanted to join me for dinner, I decided I'd eat at the table by our pool after my swim. I grabbed a towel and laid it on one of the loungers in our screened-in pool area. It was seriously the most beautiful part of our house. Surrounded by breezy palm trees, it was like being outside—minus the mosquitos or rain when it suddenly poured. It was the best of both worlds: being outside *inside.*

I dove into the pool and began swimming laps, one of my favorite ways to expend nervous energy. I must have lost track of time because when I finally emerged from the water, pushing the wet hair off my face, I looked up to find Jace standing by the edge of the pool. *How long has he been watching me swim?*

"Hey." I wrung some of the water out of my hair. "Didn't realize you were back."

"I just got here."

I stepped up the ladder. Oddly, I felt a bit self-conscious and immediately walked over to wrap my towel around me. I liked to try to look sexy around Jace, but this was my first time in a swimsuit. And being in a bikini was basically like wearing underwear and a bra. As daring as I'd been with my clothing choices lately, I was surprised to find I wasn't *that* daring.

Jace had set the food on the table where I'd planned to eat. I guess he'd decided to join me out here.

"Thanks again. I'm famished. Swimming always makes me hungry."

"Yeah. Looks like you worked up an appetite."

"I love to swim. That pool sold me on this house when Nathan and I were looking."

"It's hot as fuck today. I might just go in later myself."

I pulled out my chair. "You should. I haven't seen you swim once since you got here."

Jace and I opened our sandwiches and began to eat.

I went to the kitchen to grab extra ketchup, and when I returned, Jace's eyes went wide as he watched me pour the red stuff over my pile of fries until they were totally covered.

"Care for some fries with that ketchup?" he teased.

"I put it on everything. I love ketchup."

"I can see that."

I peeked over at his burger. "What did you get?"

"A jalapeño burger. Wanna bite?"

"Sure." I wasn't going to refuse putting my mouth where his had just been. Plus, it did look good.

I leaned in as he reached across the table and offered me a taste. One of the hot peppers fell onto my chest near where the towel was wrapped around my bikini top. Not wanting to seem gluttonous, I took only a small bite and chewed, licking the corner of my mouth. "Mmm... It's really good."

Jace watched as I picked the pepper off of myself and placed it into my mouth.

When my eyes met his, he quickly looked down at his sandwich before getting up from his seat.

What is that about?

"I'm gonna grab a beer," he said. "You want something?"

"I'll take a beer, too."

He chuckled. "Is it bad that I had to think for a second whether you're legal to drink? It feels wrong giving you alcohol, for some reason."

"You've dropped me off at the damn bar! How could you think that?"

"I know. It's fucked-up." He laughed as he walked backwards into the house. "Be right back."

A minute later, Jace returned with two chilled bottles of Miller Lite. He popped one open and handed it to me.

"Thanks." I took a long sip that felt great going down.

We polished off the rest of the food, and by the time I finished the beer, I felt pretty tipsy. Between the soft breeze blowing Jace's scent my way and the buzz, I was on cloud nine.

Jace took it upon himself to clear our wrappers and napkins, stuffing everything into the paper bag. As he went back into the kitchen, he asked, "Want another beer?"

"I'd love one."

When he returned, he set the bottle in front of me and sat back down. He put his feet up on an empty chair and leaned his head back, closing his eyes.

He sighed. "This is exactly what I needed...to chill at home."

That made me happy. "Give your head a break tonight. You can always worry about work tomorrow."

"Yeah. I think I'm gonna take your advice on that."

While his eyes were closed, I was able to enjoy staring at his profile—his strong, angular jaw and slightly cleft chin, his perfect nose and kissable lips, the way the sun brought out a reddish tone in his otherwise black hair. Jace was even more beautiful with the sun shining on him.

I eventually closed my eyes as well, enjoying the breeze that offset a little of the heat. My eyes opened suddenly when I heard his chair skid against the cement.

"Fuck it." He got up. "I'll be right back."

My heart raced a little. *What is he doing?*

A few minutes later, Jace returned in his swim trunks. They were blue with tiny anchors, a nautical pattern. Not that I was looking closely at his lower half or anything. I'd just started to make my way up to his chest when he dove into the pool, his gorgeous, hard body disappearing under the sky blue water.

He emerged and shook his head to clear the water from his hair. "You comin' in or what?"

I got goose bumps. I hadn't planned to, but I couldn't resist the invitation.

"Sure." I got up from my seat and unwrapped the towel.

Jace watched as I entered the pool. But what was he thinking?

I dove in and swam toward him, feeling more comfortable in my bathing suit now that I was submerged in the water.

He flashed a mischievous grin. "Wanna race?"

I splashed him. "Why? You think you can beat me just cuz your legs are longer?"

He cocked a brow. "There's only one way to find out, right?"

Over the next several minutes, Jace and I swam in tandem from one end of the pool to the other. Sometimes he'd beat me to the other side, and a few times, I beat him.

Eventually, we got into a water fight. The next thing I knew, he was chasing me, then lifting me up and tossing me in the water. He did that several times. It was the most fun I'd had in a long time. I hadn't a care in the world.

Then he lifted me up again, and I was certain he was going to toss me into the water, just like all of the other times. Instead, though, he just held me. Our eyes locked as my legs wrapped around his waist. He was going to have to drop me, because I sure as hell wasn't climbing off him willingly. As he continued to hold me, the world seemed to stop. I could see the reflection of the palm trees in his gorgeous eyes, made luminescent by the sun. Those eyes then dropped to my lips. I could see his chest rising and falling. He swallowed hard. *Holy shit.* Something was happening. My heart was going a mile a minute.

And then...

"What are you doing?"

Jace dropped me like a hot potato at the sound of Nathan's voice. My body hit the water with a loud splash.

What the hell is he doing here? My voice was shaky as I wiped the water from my eyes. "Wha...why are you home? I thought you were driving to meet that girl."

"She canceled on me, so I came back after the job interview." Nathan's eyes traveled between Jace and me. He seemed suspicious.

"Oh." I exhaled, moving a strand of hair out of my mouth. "How...how did the interview go?"

"It was okay. Too hard to tell if they're gonna call me back, though." He looked straight at Jace. "You guys seemed to be having fun. Didn't realize I was missing out on a...pool party."

Jace was silent.

I felt the need to chime in. "Jace decided to take his debut dip in the pool. We were just playing around."

Nathan looked between us again. "I see."

Jace finally spoke. "Well, it's hot as all hell today. So..."

"You guys down if I make some dinner?" Nathan finally asked.

"We actually already ate," I told him. "Jace went to Checkers."

Nathan turned to his friend. "Since when do you eat dinner this early?"

Jace cleared his throat. "I was starving."

"We didn't think you were going to be home," I said. "Otherwise, we would've waited."

"I guess I'll give you that."

Jace got out of the water and dried himself off. He then laid out on one of the loungers, displaying his gorgeous, tanned body in all of its glistening glory. His feet dangled off the end of the chair.

Nathan snapped his fingers in front of my face. "I asked if I got anything in the mail. Earth to Farrah."

Jesus. I hadn't even heard him the first time. "Oh. No. Nothing came for you today."

"Shit. I'm waiting for a part to come so I can fix the toilet in the master bath."

"Bummer," I said, still itching to look back over at Jace.

"Guess I'd better figure out something for dinner if you guys aren't eating with me."

When Nathan disappeared into the house, relief washed over me. Rather than put my towel back around me, I went over to where Jace was lounging and lay down on the chair next to him.

"How are you holding up?" I asked.

He opened his eyes and turned toward me. "Good. You?"

"Great." I smiled.

"When we were swimming..." he said. "It definitely got my mind off things. But as soon as Nathan came home, all the shit in my head started to hit me again."

"Nathan is a buzzkill?" I chuckled. "Is that what you're saying?"

He laughed. "Basically. It was a nice escape while it lasted."

"Are you going to tell Nathan about what's going on at work?"

"I will eventually. But I don't want him to worry. He's got a lot on his plate now with the job search and all. So, if you don't mind, don't mention what I told you about the money. Let me tell him myself, okay?"

I nodded. "Okay. No worries. I won't."

"Thanks."

"Are you...going to Linnea's tonight?"

He shook his head. "Nah. I need a break."

"Yeah. You've been spending a lot of time with her. Although, you shouldn't really need a break from someone so early in a relationship."

"It's not a relationship," he was quick to clarify.

"Something tells me she doesn't see it that way."

"Well, I never promised her anything. I don't lead people on. I can't help it if she draws the wrong conclusion."

"If you hang out with someone several nights in a row, they're going to draw certain conclusions, whether or not you define anything. I'm a girl. I know how we think."

"Thank you for the reminder that you're a girl."

I laughed. "Smartass."

"Anyway..." He sighed. "That's why I'm taking a night off. It got to be too much. And I'm...not ready for that."

I turned my body a little more toward him. "Can I ask you a personal question?"

"Depends on the question."

"Do you think you'll ever be ready for a serious relationship? Or do you just see yourself dating casually for the rest of your life, moving from one girl to the next?"

He sighed. "I can't answer that."

"Because you're not sure?"

"Because I've never only wanted to be with one woman, yet I do feel like there's probably someone out there who could make me not want anyone else. I just haven't found that person. So the answer depends on something I don't have control over."

And now I was incredibly jealous of some fictitious, perfect woman who would get to have Jace all to herself one day—someone who could make him never need anyone else. She probably looked like a young Farrah Fawcett.

"I guess that's a fair answer."

He turned the tables. "What about you? Why haven't I had to beat up any dudes trying to come around here lately?"

"Well, you missed one a few years back. I would've loved for you to beat his ass."

His forehead crinkled. "Who was that?"

I sighed. "Jordan Rhodes. My high-school boyfriend. He broke up with me when he got a basketball scholarship to an out-of-state school. It wasn't like I'd expected him to stay here for me. But he'd led me to believe we'd try to make it work, and then right before he left, he ended it."

"He strung you along with false promises until it was time to leave."

"Exactly."

Jace grimaced. "It's not too late, you know."

"For what?"

"For me to beat his ass. Does he come home in the summer?"

I smiled. "I'll let you know."

"Seriously, though, very few people end up with their high school girlfriend or boyfriend. You remember Grace?"

Grace.

Ugh.

How could I forget Jace's high school girlfriend? *Jace and Grace. Gag me.* She was enemy number one for a long time—the focus of much of my preteen angst. How I'd wanted to be Grace Wethers back then.

"Yeah. I do remember her."

"I bet she's relieved she didn't end up with my ass. Breaking up with her was the best thing I ever did. She's married to some plastic surgeon now. She just had a baby."

"All thanks to you for breaking up with her?"

"Basically. She was in love with me and wouldn't have been the first to end things. I did to her what that asshole did to you—broke up with her before I left for school, because I didn't want to be tied down. But she was probably the closest I've ever come to loving someone."

Jealousy coursed through me at the mention of him *almost* loving someone.

"And yet you let her go..."

"Yeah. I respected her. I knew I wasn't going to be faithful in college. It all worked out for her in the end, though."

I had to respect that, I guessed. "What about for you? No regrets there?" I braced for his answer.

"About not being with her? No. Not at all. It wasn't meant to be."

I, for one, was grateful Jace wasn't married to his high school sweetheart right about now—even if I didn't stand a chance in hell with him. At least he was still on the market.

Closing my eyes, I relished the last of the sun.

When I opened them a few minutes later, I was surprised to find that Jace's eyes weren't closed—they were on me.

Chapter 4

Jace

Nathan really needed to get out of the house and earn a little cash, so I hired him to help me out with some cleanup at one of our work sites on Saturday. When I went to check things out over there, he said he hadn't eaten yet, so I decided to fetch lunch and bring it back.

Halfway to the restaurant, I realized I'd left my wallet at home. So I had no choice but to swing by the house to get it.

When I opened the door, Farrah was sitting on the floor in the living room with her legs crossed. She wore fitted yoga pants and a purple sports bra. Her belly ring sparkled against her tight stomach. I'd tried to put that "thing" that had happened between us in the pool a few days ago out of my mind. Walking in on her like this, though? It wasn't helping.

She stood up from her exercise mat. "I thought you left to go check on Nathan."

"Yeah. I went to pick up lunch for him and realized I forgot my wallet. I'm just gonna get it and head back out." I pried my eyes upward. They wanted desperately to explore the soft mounds peeking out from her bra, even if that was wrong as hell.

She ran her hand along her hair. "Ah."

Soft music played from the television, where I could see the menu of her yoga DVD. Two lit candles sat on the mantel at each side of the TV.

"Is this what you do when we're not home? Turn this place into your own little Zen kingdom?"

"Sometimes." Her eyes twinkled. "You guys probably watch porn when you have the house to yourself. I do yoga for stress relief."

I'm not going to touch that comment. Clearing my throat, I said, "Does it really work? This yoga? To calm you down?"

"Yes. I mean, it's not just about stress reduction. This particular type is supposed to activate the spiritual energy at the base of your spine. It's designed to help you rid yourself of your ego. It's called cunnilingus yoga."

What did she just say? "Say what?"

"Cunnilingus yoga," she repeated.

What the fuck? "Pretty sure that's not what it's called, Farrah."

Her eyes widened. "What did I just say?"

"You said *cunnilingus* yoga."

She reached for the DVD cover on the couch and shook her head. "Kundalini!" Her face turned beet red. "Kundalini! I didn't mean to say *cunnilingus*. I don't know where that came from."

"It was a slip of the *tongue*."

"Shit." She laughed.

"Although, I have to say, cunnilingus yoga would be very interesting." Okay, I needed to stop. This was my best friend's little sister, and I was going to hell for that innuendo.

She wiped her forehead. "Oh man."

"Anyway, I'd better find my wallet."

"Do you...want to try it with me?"

Try it? Cunnilingus? "Uh...yoga?" I stupidly asked.

She smiled shyly. "Yeah."

"I would...but Nathan is waiting for me to pick up lunch."

"I bet it would help you with all the stress you're going through. Try it for five minutes. See if you like it."

I looked over at the candles and back at her.

Am I crazy for entertaining this? "What the hell. Five minutes won't kill me."

Farrah's face lit up. "Get down on the floor. Sit behind me so you can see what I do. Cross your legs. Take a deep breath in and just listen to the instructions."

I must have been sick, because when she demanded that I get down on the floor, I continued to think nothing but dirty things. A vision of pulling off her yoga pants and going down on her flashed through my mind. *Cunnilingus yoga.*

This is Farrah we're talking about. Cut the shit.

Sitting down, I crossed my legs as the guy in the DVD instructed. Farrah turned around to check on me, flashing her gorgeous smile. She was naturally beautiful. She didn't have a drop of makeup on, and she certainly didn't need it. And I was glad she didn't wear any, because I preferred being able to see how her smooth skin changed colors when she was embarrassed. That happened a lot. Especially around me. I definitely had an effect on her, and I'd be lying if I said I didn't get off on it a little. But I'd take that to the grave.

I watched the video, following Farrah's lead for what I knew had to be more than my five-minute allotment. She was right. As I bent my body forward into child's pose, I could tell this was calming me.

The short-lived peacefulness ended the moment the guy on the TV instructed us to get into a pose called *triangle*. That's when I got into trouble. Farrah bent over in front of me, providing a clear view of her butt sticking straight in my face. Her pants were so tight that it almost looked like she wasn't wearing anything, and I could easily make out the outline of her ass.

Christ.

Thank fuck I was behind her, because it turned out I had no control over my body's reaction. I was so damn relaxed right before this, I hadn't put my guard up, and my dick moved to fully erect before I had a chance to talk it down. I needed to get the fuck out of here before she turned around. It was bad enough that I'd just gotten hard over Nathan's sister, but I sure as hell wasn't going to let her notice.

I bolted toward the kitchen.

She called after me. "Are you okay?"

"Yeah. I guess yoga really makes you have to go," I hollered from the hallway.

Once in the bathroom, I locked the door behind me. Splashing some water on my face, I stared at myself in the mirror.

What is wrong with you?

I kept waiting for my stiffy to go down, but it wouldn't. There was no way I could go back out there like this.

My phone went off. It was a text from Nathan.

Nathan: Where the hell are you?

Feeling like absolute shit, I typed.

Jace: Stuck in some traffic. Sorry.

I looked down at myself and decided that unless I did something about this, I'd be stuck in the bathroom for the rest of the day. Unzipping my jeans, I took out my swollen cock. Positioning myself over the toilet, I thought back to the visual that had gotten me here—Farrah bent over in front of me—and it took all of ten seconds to shoot my load. My orgasm might have been quick, but it was intense. Apparently, I needed to get laid. Meanwhile, Farrah probably thought I had yoga-induced diarrhea in here.

I flushed the toilet and washed my hands, destroying all evidence of my transgression before heading back out. With my head still stuck up my ass, I nearly forgot the entire reason I came home in the first place. But I didn't. Stopping in my room, I picked up my wallet from the desk before returning to the living room.

Farrah lifted her foot behind her back as she stretched.

When she spotted me, she set her leg down. "You good?"

"Yeah. I'd better get going."

"It was nice having company while it lasted." She smiled. "We should do it again sometime."

No fucking way unless you blindfold me and cut my dick off. I nodded. "See you later."

By the time I got back to the job site to drop off Nathan's lunch, it had been over an hour.

"What the hell? Did you go to Africa for lunch or something?"

I shrugged. "Sorry."

Wouldn't the truth have been interesting?

Well, Nathan, I went home to get my wallet and instead decided to partake in cunnilingus yoga with your sister. Then I locked myself in the bathroom and jerked off. Here's your sandwich. Enjoy.

• • •

The following day, my father was released from the hospital after his final round of chemo. I'd decided not to bother him with work stuff while he was hospitalized, but I needed to talk to him now that he was home.

When I arrived, my mother was out running errands, so I was happy to have the alone time with him. It was our first opportunity to really talk since the day I'd learned the real reason behind the company's financial problems.

Pacing in my dad's room, I took a deep breath and told him exactly what I thought about what he'd done. Then I went through it again, just to get it all off my chest. When I finally came up for air, he looked a little shell-shocked.

"I'm so sorry to have disappointed you, son. I'm sorry I wasn't a stronger person. And I'm sorry I put the company in jeopardy."

While I tried not to yell, I couldn't help the harshness of my tone. "It's not even the gambling so much as the fact that you kept this from me. You let me uproot my life to come here to help you. I didn't know I was walking into a clusterfuck." I pulled on my hair. "How the hell are we supposed to come up with that money?"

"We have options. We have the house."

The house? "Mom has to suffer for your misgivings? I'm not letting you sell our family home. That's not an option."

"When I explained to her what I'd done, she was upset, but she accepted my apology. She said she'd be willing to sell this place and downsize."

I sighed. "Well, let's keep that as a last resort. I have an appointment at the bank tomorrow to talk about a business loan. If we get approved, that's the answer. But my question to you is, how do I know this won't happen again when you're healthy enough to be out and about?"

"I promise you, I'll seek therapy. I won't even resume my position until I'm confident I won't do any further harm to the company. I know you've sacrificed a lot to come here. And I'm very sorry to have dragged you into this."

It was hard to be mad at him when he seemed so weak. "I just wish I'd known so I could've helped you."

"Me too, son." He examined my face. "How are *you* doing?"

"What do you mean 'How am I doing?' Isn't it obvious? I'm fucking pissed."

"I didn't mean in terms of this situation. I know you're upset. I mean in general."

"I don't know." I shrugged. "Fine. I guess."

"You still living with Nathan?"

"Yeah. I'm mainly doing it to help him out, but honestly, it's the best thing for now. I don't want to commit to any property until I know whether I'm staying. After this fiasco, I might just get myself a one-way ticket out of here and say *fuck it all.*"

"You know you can do that, right? No one is making you stay here."

My voice rose again. "Then what? Who's gonna run the company while you're sick? Who's gonna be here for Mom? It's not like Kenny or Thomas is gonna step up to the plate. It's just me."

My two older brothers, Kenny and Thomas, were my dad's children from his previous marriage. They were ten and eleven years older than me, and both had gotten into trouble with drugs over the years. Neither had finished school, and the only time I ever saw them was when they were trying to mooch money off of my parents. For the most part, I was an only child. I'd vowed not to be anything like them, so I'd always excelled at school and sports, and when I left home for college, I promised to make something of myself, not be a burden on my parents. Before leaving Charlotte, I'd been thriving in my property manager position. It was a job where I could have continued to grow. But my time there ended when I tried to do the right thing in coming home to help Dad. He'd certainly made me second-guess that decision.

"You shouldn't have to bear the sole responsibility of getting us out of the mess I made," my father said. "You could let it all burn."

He knew me better than that.

"I wouldn't be able to live with myself. You know you can count on me, and that's probably part of why you weren't more careful. Unlike some people in this family, I actually have a conscience."

He huffed. "Thanks a lot, Jace."

"You deserve it, old man." I shook my head. "I love you, but you deserve it."

My mother appeared in the doorway. "There's my handsome son!"

"Hey, Mom." I walked over and kissed her on the cheek.

She placed a paper bag on my father's bedside table. "I brought you your favorite soup from the bistro. I hope you're feeling well enough to eat it."

"Well, that depends on whether our son decides to forgive me for sabotaging my own business."

"Whether I forgive you or not doesn't change the fact that we need a way out of this, Dad. The last thing I want is a dozen angry vendors on my ass for their money."

"No one is gonna come after you."

Is he that naïve? "Are you kidding me? James Moore already came to my freaking house looking for his money. Farrah answered the door. If he'd done something to her, I would've never been able to forgive myself."

"Shit." My father closed his eyes briefly. "I didn't realize that."

"Is she okay?" my mother asked.

"Yeah. He didn't do anything, but he was pissed. I told her not to open the door like that ever again."

Mom tilted her head. "How *is* Farrah?"

"She's good...sweet as always."

"And quite the looker," my father chimed in.

I whipped my head toward him. "How the hell would you know, you dirty old man?"

"Saw her at the mini-mart a couple of months back. Barely recognized her with those long legs. Beautiful woman."

I gritted my teeth. "Get your mind out of the gutter."

"I'm not dead yet. Noticing a woman's beauty isn't a crime."

"It is when she's practically a kid," I said.

That felt a little hypocritical coming from me. Even before the escalation of these last uncomfortable weeks, I'd inappropriately checked Farrah out many times—too many to count. More troubling, I found myself inexplicably drawn to her. The sweetness in her eyes. The way she looked at me like I could do no wrong. The way she made me feel. Maybe I was angry with myself, not my dad, where Farrah was concerned.

"Give her my best, will you? Such a tough situation she's in," Mom said. "Having to grow up without her parents."

I stiffened against the pain in my chest at the mention of Farrah's parents. "She's actually doing pretty well, all things considered," I said, clearing my throat. "She's independent, and she seems happy overall. It's Nathan I worry about. Not sure where he'd be if he didn't have his sister around. The kid's gotta find a new job. He hasn't been having any luck. I was planning to offer him full-time work with us, but that was before I realized we didn't have the money to pay him." I glared at my father. "The best I could do was hire him for cleanup over at the old mall site yesterday."

Mom gave me a sympathetic look. "Things have a way of working themselves out. I can ask around at church and see if anyone knows of anything opening up for Nathan."

"That would be great. I know he'd appreciate that."

"It's the least I can do. Nathan was always like a brother to you."

"Yeah, especially since the brothers I *do* have are always out of commission."

I lifted my keys off the table next to my father's bed. "Anyway, I gotta go. I'm supposed to grab some dinner with Nathan. I haven't told him about our financial situation, but I think I'm going to tonight. He needs to be alert in case someone tries to come to the house and pull shit again. I've put off telling him long enough." I turned to my father and shook my head.

Mom placed her hand on my arm. "Try to go easy on your dad. He's sick. Stress will make him worse."

"Maybe if *you* weren't so easy on him, we wouldn't be in this situation in the first place."

She hugged me. "I'm sorry. I know. I love you."

"I love you, too." I looked over at my dad. "I love you, old man. Take care of yourself. I'm gonna get us out of this mess. But if I ever hear of you pissing money away again, you're gonna be on your own. Understand?"

My father nodded, his voice frail. "I understand, son."

• • •

Nathan and I had planned to meet at the house for dinner. I stopped off at a Mexican place for takeout on the way back from my parents'. Farrah was apparently out with her friends, so it would be just the two of us.

Nathan was waiting for me in the kitchen when I got back.

I dropped the paper bag of tortilla chips on the counter.

"Sorry I took so long. The line was out the door."

"No problem, man." Nathan opened the other bag and began taking out the contents, examining the writing on the burritos to determine which was his. "How's your dad?"

"Health wise? He seems to be stable. It's everything else that's screwed up."

He stopped messing with the food. "Everything else? What's going on?"

"There's something I haven't told you," I admitted.

His eyes narrowed. "Everything okay?"

"Let's take our food to the table."

We did, and I spent the next several minutes telling him about the situation my father had gotten Muldoon Construction into.

He shook his head. "God, I always thought Phil had a better head on his shoulders than that. I guess addiction sometimes gets the best of them. I mean, look at your brothers."

"Yeah." I gritted my teeth. "All the men in my family have issues, apparently."

"So, what are you gonna do?"

"I'm heading to the bank tomorrow to see if we qualify for a loan. I just want to pay these guys back and deal with the rest later."

He nodded. "Well, I wish I could help, but as we know, I am one broke-ass motherfucker right now."

"There *is* a way you can help."

"How?"

"You can be vigilant." I braced myself. "One of the guys we owe money to came by the house the other day looking for me. Farrah answered the door."

His face turned red. "That's not good."

I exhaled. "I know. I told her never to answer the door if one of us isn't home."

I knew nothing meant more to Nathan than his sister. She was the only family he had.

"I need to tell Farrah what's going on with your dad," he said.

"I already did."

His eyes went wide. "You did? When?"

"The other day—when we had dinner together. She came into the kitchen and saw me at my lowest point. It was right after I found out about it. She asked me what was wrong, so I told her."

"Wait...you told Farrah that day, and I'm only now finding out about it?"

Shit. "It's not that I was keeping it from you. I just didn't want to upset you. You seemed to be in a rare mood that day. So I opted to wait."

He raised his voice. "Maybe I was in a rare mood because I came home to find you all up in my sister."

Whoa. What the fuck? I feigned shock. *I had to.* "What are you talking about?"

"Things looked a little compromising when I found you two in the pool. Your hands were all over her. She was practically naked."

My pulse raced. "I don't know what you thought that was, but we were just playing around."

Several moments of silence passed. It was awkward as fuck, and I hated every second.

Then Nathan backed off and shrugged. "Okay. If you say so."

I tried my best to make myself believe what I said next. "There's nothing going on there, Nathan. I love Farrah... like a sister. She helped take my mind off everything that day. We were having fun, like a couple of kids in the pool. That's it. You got me?"

He looked at me for a few seconds. "Yeah."

I recognized the look in his eyes as one of cautious trust, which meant I needed to be careful moving forward.

"Good," I said.

The silence that followed as we finished dinner told me Nathan was still thinking about it. That sucked. I felt like shit. And I was sweating. Because deep down, I knew what had been happening with Farrah lately wasn't innocent.

Chapter 5

Farrah

My shift at the law firm ran from seven to three. It was a cushy job, and what some people might say was a waste of my time. I wasn't going anywhere in life by filing things and typing up correspondence. But it paid decently, and they didn't care whether I had a college degree, which made it kind of hard to give up. I'd been working there for the better part of a year. The hours were great because there was never any traffic at three in the afternoon.

One of the first things I did when I got home from the office was check on the girl next door. Nora's mother left her alone after school. I always felt bad for her because I could relate; I knew all too well what it was like to come home to an empty house when you needed a hug or someone to talk to.

Her mother had given me a key to use so Nora never had to answer the door—to avoid inadvertently opening for the wrong person. (Like I did the other day.) Nora was doing her homework when I came in.

She put down her pencil when she saw me. "Hey, what's up?"

"Not much. Just checking in on you."

"I'm still alive."

"I know. Figured I'd see if you needed anything."

"Shawn Mendes tickets," she said.

That made me chuckle. "I meant like something to eat. But is he coming to town?"

"Yeah. I want to see him. I'm desperate."

I sat down at the table next to her. "Will your mom buy you tickets?"

"She says she doesn't have the money."

"Maybe I can ask around and see if I can find affordable tickets."

To my surprise, she started to cry. "Oh my God. That would be awesome."

I'd nearly forgotten what it was like to be a lovesick child. *Oh wait.*

She sniffled. "I forgot to tell you, I saw you in the pool the other day with Jace."

Speaking of lovesick...

"I heard splashing, and I looked out the window and could see you."

I nodded. "Yeah...Jace and I were swimming."

"Do you like him?"

I didn't know how to answer. "You know Jace is like an older brother to me, right? He's Nathan's best friend... But..." I hesitated. *Am I really considering telling an eleven-year-old my dirtiest secret?* "Between you and me, I have a crush on him."

Her eyes were like saucers. "He's handsome."

"Yeah. He is."

"Not as cute as Shawn, though. Do you think he likes you?"

"You know...before the other day, I would've told you no. But I kind of got this vibe from him when we were hanging out. So, let's put it this way... If he does like me, I don't think he *wants* to like me. It's kind of depressing because I don't think anything can ever happen between us."

Okay, that was definitely way too much to be divulging to a kid.

She sighed. "That's like me and Shawn. I love him, but nothing can ever happen because he's a huge star. At least Jace knows you exist."

"I guess that could be a consolation." I laughed before becoming paranoid. "Please don't ever mention to anyone what I just told you, okay? It's a secret."

"I won't say anything."

"Okay. I'm choosing to trust you." I smiled.

She returned to writing on her worksheet before turning to me again. "Why do you come over and check on me all the time?"

Shrugging, I sighed. "I guess I can relate to the feeling of being alone. I know I like it when people check in on me, so I figured I would do the same for you."

"I'm sorry your mom isn't here. I mean, I'm sorry she died. Your dad, too."

Momentary sadness washed over me. "Thank you."

"It was an accident, right? My mom told me."

"Yeah. Sort of. I don't really like to talk about it, though, okay?"

Her mouth twisted. "Okay. I wouldn't want to talk about it, either."

After some silence, I asked, "Are you sure you don't want anything? I could make you a sandwich."

"Nope. I have a Coke in the fridge and some Sour Patch Kids. I'm good."

"Well, *you* may be good, but your teeth might think otherwise."

"I do have a cavity."

I raised my forehead. "You don't say..."

I hung around for about fifteen minutes before getting ready to go back home. "Okay, well, if you need me, you have my number. Just ring me, and I can be over in thirty seconds."

"Literally thirty seconds. How cool is that?" She giggled.

"Yup. *Literally.*"

"Good luck with Jace!" she shouted as I headed out the door.

Turning around, I placed my index finger over my mouth. "Shh... Remember what I said. Forget I told you about that."

"Sorry," she whispered.

I must have needed my head examined for telling a child about my feelings for Jace.

When I returned home, ironically, Jace's truck was in the driveway. Just like the other day when we'd hung out in the pool, he'd come home from work early.

A rush of excitement hit me, until I entered the house and noticed a pair of women's shoes under the small table in the foyer. I heard muffled laughter coming from Jace's bedroom at the far end of the hall.

My cheeks burned.

He brought a girl home in the middle of the day?

He'd never done that before.

Not only was I extremely jealous, but I felt like a complete idiot. Ever since our jaunt in the pool and our brief yoga session, I'd been so excited for the next opportunity to be alone with him. I'd convinced myself that maybe he'd felt something when he held me in his arms for those few moments. *God, I'm such a fool.*

No way could I stay at the house this afternoon. And he knew I got home from work around this time, so he didn't even have the decency to sneak her over here when the house would be empty. Why the hell wasn't he working, anyway?

I found my keys and walked back out to my piece-of-shit car. This pissed me off because I was trying to save on gas, and now I'd have to drive somewhere just to get the hell out of here. I started the ignition—or tried to, at least. My crappy vehicle had other ideas. It wouldn't start. I kept trying, to no avail. To make matters worse, my car was right outside Jace's bedroom window. So I knew he could hear me trying to start it.

Now what?

Jace was inside, probably fucking some girl, and I was stuck at the house unless I wanted to walk somewhere. I supposed I could go back over to Nora's...

Just as I'd had that thought, Jace came out of the house. His hair was mussed, and he looked so gosh darn sexy in his fitted, white T-shirt, and ripped jeans. I wanted to scream. I was mortified to have caused him to come out here.

He ran his hand through his dark mane. "That thing crapped the bed again, huh? Didn't you just get it back from Rusty?"

I exited the car and slammed the door. "Yeah. I, uh, need to get going, but it doesn't look like that's going to happen."

"Don't take it back to that pervert anymore. I'll take a look at it tonight."

"Yeah. Well, I don't want to bother you. You're clearly busy today. I know you have a friend over. Saw her shoes." I huffed. "Big feet." *Jesus, Farrah. Can you be more obviously upset?*

He didn't acknowledge my comment. "Like I said, I'll take a look at it tonight."

The sun shone on his beautiful eyes, causing them to glow.

I stared down at my shoes. "Thanks."

"Where do you need to be right now?"

"I, uh, was gonna meet a friend at the plaza down the street for coffee," I lied.

"You need a ride?"

I looked up. "How are you gonna give me a ride when you have someone in your room?"

"I'll tell her I'll be right back."

I concluded that interrupting Jace's late-afternoon fuck wasn't the worst thing in the world. I shrugged. "Sure. A ride would be great."

"Okay." He walked back toward the door. "Hang on."

As I waited on the sidewalk, I realized this was a stupid idea. But that's what I got for pretending I had somewhere important to be. I didn't dare follow him back into the house. Seeing *her* would make me more upset.

Jace reappeared and clicked to disarm his truck. I hopped in.

"So, who are you meeting?" he asked as he put his seatbelt on.

I locked myself in too. "Some guy." *Where did that come from?*

His brow furrowed. "Who?"

"Just someone I met online."

His eyes narrowed. "He doesn't have a name?"

"It's...Sheridan." *Sheridan? You couldn't have come up with a more common name?*

"Whatever you do, do *not* get into his car. You don't know this guy."

"I'm a big girl. Don't worry."

"I won't be worried as long as you stay at the coffee shop. Don't be getting in any cars with strangers. You hear me?"

I felt guilty that his genuine concern was in vain. But I had no choice now except to continue this charade.

"Jace, don't worry. If I get a weird vibe, I won't."

He slammed on the brakes and stopped in the middle of the road. "Okay, I'm not sure how to make myself clearer. I don't care what kind of *vibe* he gives you. Do not get in his fucking car." His face turned red as he took off slowly again.

I hated that I loved angry Jace. I hated that he was angry for no reason—because there was no guy. But most of all, I hated that he was going to take his anger out on that girl back in his bedroom, and not on me. I could only imagine how amazing it would feel to be angry fucked by this man.

I couldn't help myself. "Who's the girl back at the house?"

After a few seconds of nothing, he decided to grace me with an answer.

"Her name is Alyssa."

"Ah. A newbie?" I stared out the window, wanting to scratch my eyes out.

"I guess."

"So, you got tired of Linnea and moved on to... Alyssa?"

His eyes darted over. "Sounds like you're being a little judgy."

"No. I almost feel bad for them, though. You know... I can easily put myself in their shoes. Linnea really liked you. I could tell. And I'm sure this girl does too. Yet you left her in your bedroom to give me a ride. She must be pissed. She'll be even more pissed when you stop calling her eventually because you met someone else."

"Wow. Okay. So it's like that." He shook his head. "Why don't you just say what you mean and call me an asshole?"

"Sorry. I'm...cranky...because of my car."

"Tell me, Farrah, what am I supposed to be doing at this point in my life? Not dating anyone? How do you even know if you click with someone unless you try? I'm doing what I'm supposed to be doing at my age. I don't make promises to anyone, and I don't need you to be judging me for shit that's none of your damn business."

Ugh. I went too far. "I didn't mean to sound like I think you're an asshole. I just think..."

"That I'm an asshole." He chuckled.

I sighed. I'd let my jealousy get out of hand. The worst part? My emotions were rising to the surface. I was on the verge of admitting something I'd regret.

"No. I don't think you're an asshole. You have every right to live your life. You've been an amazing friend to me and my brother. You're not doing anything wrong. It's me. I really wish I didn't care about any of this. If I'm acting weird, it's because..."

Oh no.

No, no, no.

What the hell was I about to admit? I needed to tape my mouth shut because I apparently had no control over it right now.

His jaw tightened. "What were you going to say?"

"Nothing." My heart pounded. "Never mind."

"Tell me," he prodded.

"Please drop it, okay?" I whispered.

He did. He said nothing else, and I was grateful.

Tension filled the air for the remainder of the ride. Jace eventually turned on some music as a buffer, but from my perspective at least, it didn't help. Not at all, because the song that played—"Drive" by Halsey—was about a girl who's in love with someone and doesn't know how to tell him. As they drive around together, she hides her feelings, which eat her up inside. *Great.* The universe sure knew how to play games.

Jace finally pulled into the strip mall where the café was located.

He put the truck in park and turned to me. "Be careful."

"Okay," I said, exiting as quickly as possible.

Jace waited for me to enter the café before he drove off.

Once inside, I ordered a coffee and sat alone at my table, stewing over the fact that I'd almost confessed how I felt about him.

I was pretty sure my feelings would have come as no surprise to him, because why else would I have lashed out like that? I'd treated him unfairly for doing something men do every day.

About an hour into my café rumination, my phone chimed.

Jace: You okay?

My heartbeat accelerated as I typed.

Farrah: Yup.

The dots danced as he responded.

Jace: How are you getting home?

Kellianne had texted me a few minutes before Jace did. So I did have a ride. I told the truth.

Farrah: Kellianne is picking me up here. We're going to dinner and then to The Iguana later for Pour Your Heart Out.

Jace: What happened with the guy you met?

Ugh. I hated lying.

Farrah: A dud.

After about a minute, he responded.

Jace: Stay safe tonight.

Farrah: You too.

My head spun. I needed to get a life, needed to move past these feelings for a man who couldn't return them. Feeling a bit out of control, I knew I needed to do something tonight to expend all of this energy—and fast. I needed a distraction.

Chapter 6

Jace

Nathan walked in early that evening and seemed surprised to see I had a guest.

"Oh, hey. I wasn't sure if you'd be home," he said.

"Yeah. We were just hanging out."

Nathan coming home and catching me with Alyssa was *exactly* what I'd aimed for—and the only reason I'd brought her back here this afternoon. After the other day when he'd accosted me about my time in the pool with Farrah, I needed to distract him. I'd wanted both Nathan and Farrah to see me with her. I knew Nathan had gotten a one-day gig helping a friend paint a rental property, so I'd made sure Alyssa and I would still be at the house when he returned.

The mood with Alyssa was definitely ruined after I'd left to take Farrah to the coffee shop. She gave me an attitude after I returned. Apparently, she'd looked out the window of my bedroom and gotten a glimpse of Farrah. She'd grilled me about whether there was something going on with my "roommate." I did my best to explain that Farrah was like a sister to me, but apparently I was no better at convincing Alyssa of that than I was at convincing myself.

I hadn't been able to get Farrah off my mind all afternoon. My response to her meeting some dude was a bit of an overreaction. But I refused to let myself analyze why I'd blown it way out of proportion. Whatever strange feelings I'd been experiencing toward her lately needed to go. I mean, what the fuck? Why was I suddenly thinking about Nathan's little sister all the time? It made no sense. And it needed to stop.

After I introduced Nathan to Alyssa, the three of us sat outside by the pool and popped open a few beers. I lit up a stogie for the first time in ages and tried to relax. I probably needed something a fuck of a lot stronger than a cigar.

"Where's Farrah?" Nathan asked.

Alyssa gave me side eye as I answered.

"She apparently had a date. Her car shit the bed again, so I gave her a ride to the café over by the shopping plaza." I puffed and blew out some smoke.

His eyes narrowed. "A date with who?"

"Some guy. Name's Sheridan. She said she met him online. I texted her after to make sure she was okay, and she said he was a dud."

"How's she getting home?"

"Kellianne was picking her up. I told her not to get into that guy's car. Hopefully she's telling the truth."

Nathan stared out at the pool. "She'd better be."

"I think she's smart enough not to do anything dumb." I blew out more smoke, feeling relieved that Nathan seemed concerned about this *other* guy.

Alyssa suddenly hopped out of her chair. "Mind if I go for a swim?"

"Do you have a bathing suit?" I asked.

"No. But I can just go in my bra and underwear, if you don't mind."

Blowing smoke rings, I said, "Whatever floats your boat."

Alyssa pulled her dress over her head, and her tits bounced in her bra. Nathan's eyes practically bugged out of their sockets as he gawked at her. Before he could stare too long, she dove into the pool and began to swim laps. We watched her until Nathan interrupted the silence.

"So, I didn't want to ask you in front of Alyssa, but how did it go at the bank?"

One thing I'd managed to do today was take my mind off the problems at work. "Looks promising that we're gonna get approved for a loan. They just had to run some reports and look a little closer at our numbers. The guy I spoke to said I should know something within a week."

"Good. I'll be crossing my fingers for you."

"Thanks."

He looked over again at Alyssa, who was still swimming from one end of the pool to the other.

"What's the deal with this hot blonde? She's smokin'."

I shrugged. "Swiped right. It's new. Too early to tell."

He chuckled. "Linnea's totally out of the picture?"

"Yeah. It didn't work out."

"Why not?"

"She...wanted more than I could give her right now."

"Well, feel free to pass them my way when you're done, especially this one." He smiled from behind his beer bottle. "Just kidding. I know our rule still stands."

He was referring to our agreement never to touch each other's "leftovers." Only once had Nathan and I truly gotten into it over a girl, and that was Kaylee Little in middle school. We nearly lost our friendship over that one. I guess the hormones at that age made things crazier than they should have been.

Nathan definitely didn't have the luck I did in the female department. He would always comment on how I could get any woman I wanted. I suppose he had a point, but honestly, sometimes I enjoyed more of a chase. There was something arousing about wanting someone you couldn't have.

And now I'm thinking about Farrah again. I shook my head. Forcing myself to think of something else, I remembered something I needed to tell Nathan.

"Oh, I meant to let you know, my mother might have gotten you a job lead. She spoke to this woman at her church. Her husband owns the dealership on Route One."

"Really?"

"The Ford one."

"Yeah. Billings Ford. That's one of the bigger ones." His expression brightened. "Man, that would be awesome."

"She's getting me the details. I'll pass them along as soon as I have them."

"Wow. Thanks. For that and...for everything."

Guilt set in again. "You don't have to thank me again for staying here. It's benefitting me just as much as it's benefitting you because I'm not ready to buy anything. Besides, I sure as hell don't want to be living with my parents."

"Do you think you're staying in Palm Creek? I mean, if Phil gets better and doesn't need you anymore, you'll go back to North Carolina, right?"

I took another drag of my cigar and slowly exhaled. "I don't know. There are definitely things I missed about Florida. I'm just trying to be happy day to day, trying not to worry too much about the future."

"I wish I could be like you," he said.

"What do you mean?"

"I wish I could not worry about the future. I worry about everything. Maybe it's just the instability of not having a job that's freaking me out. I worry about that, and I also worry about Farrah way too much."

I swallowed. "Why are you worried about Farrah? She seems to have her shit together better than both of us."

"I don't know. I sometimes feel...like I'm holding her back. Like she wouldn't be here in Florida if it weren't for me. When she was younger, she always used to say she was going to college out of state. But she hasn't completed more than a couple of classes at the community college. She's stuck in limbo, and I can't help wondering what she'd be doing if things were different. At the same time, I don't know what I'd do without her here."

"She does care about you. I agree that she'd be very hesitant to leave you and move, but no one is really stopping her, either. It's still her choice in the end. There's nothing holding her back from enrolling in college when she's ready. She'll come around."

He gazed out at the pool. "She hides a lot of her pain, you know? I see her writing shit down a lot at night. I'll walk by her room, and she'll close her notebook real fast, like she doesn't want me to see. What is she hiding from me? She doesn't *talk* to me about how she's feeling. She just puts on a brave face and bottles everything up. I know that's partly my fault because I can hardly handle talking about stuff myself. It just sucks that she doesn't have any family to open up to but me—because I suck at it."

"Don't be so hard on yourself. I'm no better when it comes to opening up about difficult shit."

"Yeah." He grinned. "We both suck."

Alyssa emerged from the pool, her nipples fully visible through her wet bra. Nathan's mouth once again hung open. It was a little embarrassing.

"That was amazing. I feel so refreshed." She wrapped herself in a towel, and just like that, Nathan's little show was over.

The three of us ended up grilling some hotdogs for dinner, and Alyssa threw together a salad with the vegetables we had left in the crisper. We ate by the pool as the sun went down.

I could tell Alyssa was still annoyed that our time together earlier in my room had never amounted to anything. She kept hinting that she had nowhere to be tonight, but I wasn't feeling it. So I made up an excuse.

I stood and announced, "I actually told my parents I'd come by their place tonight. I can drive you home on the way."

Her lashes fluttered. "Oh...I assumed we were going to be hanging out tonight."

"Yeah, I'm sorry. Another time."

Alyssa grabbed her stuff and seemed silently annoyed as we got into my truck. She didn't have much to say when I dropped her off either.

After I left her house, I happened to pass the block where The Iguana was located. Farrah had told me she was headed there tonight. I wondered if maybe she'd lied about it so I wouldn't get on her case about getting in that dude Sheridan's car.

Curiosity got the best of me. I knew I'd regret it, but I impulsively pulled into a parking spot outside the bar. If she wasn't here, I'd know she was lying. I convinced myself this had nothing to do with being a stalker, that my checking up on her was for her own good. There would be no harm in peeking inside to see if I could spot her. Then I'd leave. I wasn't sure what I'd be doing with this information—it wasn't like I could text her if she wasn't here and say, *I know you're not really at The Iguana.* I'd have to keep this to myself either way. Yet I still felt compelled to do it.

When I walked into the bar, however, nothing could've prepared me for what I saw. Rather than being noisy, the place was almost completely quiet. In the center of the spotlight, up on stage, was Farrah.

My heart beat faster as I realized she was about to say something. You would've thought I was the one up there with how nervous I got. It felt like I stopped breathing for a moment until her voice finally rang out over the room.

"I'm Farrah."

"Hi, Farrah," the audience said in unison.

"This isn't going to be one of the sexy or embarrassing stories. So I apologize for that. Believe me, I've had many of the embarrassing ones lately. Maybe I'll confess one of those another day." She cleared her throat. "The reason I'm pouring my heart out today..." She paused for several seconds. "...is because my parents were murdered."

A few people gasped, followed by muffled whispering. My chest tightened with shock.

Farrah took a deep breath in and continued. "I don't think I've ever said those words aloud. I mean, how many people have lost both their parents to murder? I'm sure people like me exist—like, on *Dateline*. But we're few and far between. Most days I feel like the only person on Earth in this situation, even though I know that can't be true."

She ran her hand along her hair. "People typically don't know what to say to me when they find out what happened to my parents. It's hard for me to see shocked reactions like yours. Talking about it is an unwanted reality check, one that takes me out of the denial that's necessary for everyday survival. I know I'm probably supposed to give you more specifics about what happened, all of the salacious details... Because that's what we do here, right? Pour our hearts out? But sometimes, there are just no words. So I won't be able to go there tonight."

Farrah let out a breath, amplified by the mic. "I mainly come here every week to listen to you all, not only for the occasional juicy confessions, but for the sad ones. It's the sad ones that keep me coming. Those make me feel less alone. Listening to some of you has taught me that it's okay to not be okay, that human suffering is a collective experience. We all have *something*. No one gets out of this world unscathed. Maybe we're not put here to have it easy. Maybe life is about learning to survive pain and grief, two things that hit every person at some point. My turn just came at fourteen, when my life changed forever.

"If you didn't know me, you'd never know I'd been through something horrible. Because I'm really good at hiding behind my smile. So the next time you see someone you assume has it better than you do, remember that you can't know what someone is going through by looking at them. They might have been through something agonizing, yet still found a way to smile. And I hope whatever you're going through, you know you're not alone—and that you find a way to smile, too." She nodded once. "Thank you."

Farrah stepped down to a round of applause.

Wow. I was so proud of her for putting aside her fears.

I should've left sooner though. Should've turned right around and gotten the hell out of there. Instead, I froze. I'd been so into what she was saying, I hadn't realized I'd walked close enough to the stage that I was now in front of her. When she spotted me, I knew I was fucked.

How the hell am I supposed to explain this?

Chapter 7

Farrah

At first, I thought I might have been hallucinating. *What the hell is Jace doing here?* I had to blink several times to confirm I wasn't seeing things. *Oh my God.* He saw my entire speech? He heard every last, raw word? How could this have happened on the one night I'd decided to go for it?

Jace shifted on his feet. "Farrah...that was—"

"What are you doing here?"

He fumbled in search of words and finally said, "I don't have a good answer for that."

I turned to look over at Kellianne, who was beaming. She gave me a thumbs-up, clearly enjoying this a little too much.

"How could you possibly have known I was going to be speaking tonight?"

"That's the fucked-up thing. I had no clue. Getting to see you up there was pure luck."

"Why are you here?"

Jace bit his bottom lip. "Honestly? I was driving that girl back to her house, and I passed by here on my way home. Figured I'd check things out...see why you like it so much."

That seemed weird to me. "I'm still confused. You knew I was here. So...you were gonna say hello?"

"Possibly. But when I came in, you'd just gotten on stage. I was going to turn around and leave after you finished, but then you spotted me."

"Why would you have left?"

"Because I wasn't sure you'd be comfortable knowing I'd heard everything."

"Okay..." I shook my head. "Are you gonna stay?"

His eyes seared into mine. "Do you want me to?"

I swallowed. "Yeah."

"Okay," he said, looking around.

"I need a drink. What can I get you?"

He held his palm out. "Nothing for me. I'm driving."

My legs felt wobbly as I made my way to the bar—and I hadn't had anything to drink yet.

Jace was chatting with Kellianne when I returned to the table with a mojito for me and an ice water for him. I was still confused, but also thrilled that Jace had shown up here tonight. He'd been on my mind all day, and this meant that on some level, he was thinking about me, too. I couldn't be sure if I was reading into this too much, but how could I not? After all, I'd been trying to *manifest* this kind of attention from Jace for weeks now. Was it finally working?

"So..." Kellianne said. "Jace was telling me how he *happened* to be driving by and decided to check things out." She gave me a look that made me want to tell her to cut the shit.

I knew what she was thinking. But I also knew this could've had more to do with Jace acting as a spy on Nathan's behalf than anything else.

Jace looked anxiously around the room, like he was expecting the morality police to show up any minute and cart him away.

I'd been so emotional earlier today as I sat alone in that café, angry at my inability to control my feelings, my inability to move on from the impossible situation of wanting someone I couldn't have. My emotions had made me a little crazy, I guess. (Well, crazier than usual.) Over dinner with Kellianne, I'd decided I was going to get up on stage tonight come hell or high water, and I'd stuck to that promise. But because I'd kept waffling, I'd been the last person to speak. Jace had somehow made it just in time.

Eventually, Kellianne stood up from her chair. "I'm gonna get going. You coming with me or—"

"I'm taking her home," Jace said.

"I figured. Just didn't want to be presumptuous." She wriggled her brows at me.

I wished she wasn't so damn obvious.

After Kellianne left, Jace turned to me. "Ready to get out of here?"

"Yeah."

I sipped the last of my drink until the straw made a slurping sound. Then Jace led the way out the door.

The weather had cooled down a lot, and a swift breeze blew my hair around. Jace disarmed the truck and opened the passenger door for me. I settled into my seat and pulled the seatbelt over myself.

He started the truck and backed out of the space. He seemed to be driving slower than normal when he turned to me.

"I don't want Nathan to know I was with you tonight, okay? I'm gonna drop you off at the corner of our street so he doesn't see my truck."

"Where are you gonna go?"

"I'll just drive around for a while."

"Why do you not want Nathan to see us together?"

Jace sighed. "He told me he didn't like seeing us together that day in the pool. Deep down, he doesn't trust me with you. While I managed to calm his fears, I don't think he'll give me another pass if he finds us hanging out alone again."

Wow. "So, wait. He confronted you?"

"Not specifically about that. It came out in the midst of another conversation."

"What did you say to him?"

"That he doesn't have anything to worry about."

That stung. "Is that the truth? Does he *really* not have anything to worry about?"

Jace gritted his teeth. "He does *not* fucking have anything to worry about. He just thinks he does. Because of my track record with women, he assumes *all* women are the same in my mind." He ran his hand through his hair. "It's different with you."

I crossed my arms as we stopped at a red light. "Really...what makes me so different? You haven't been around me for the past nine years. Now you don't know whether to treat me like the girl you left behind or the woman I *am*. That doesn't change the fact that I am a woman now and not that girl."

He blew out a long breath as he stepped on the gas again. "It's not an age thing... It's a respect thing. I wouldn't make a move on you for the sheer fact that you're Nathan's sister and it would upset him. End of story."

"Would you want to, if things were different?"

He chewed on his bottom lip. "Want to what?"

"Make a move on me—if I wasn't Nathan's sister."

"That's irrelevant. It doesn't matter whether I would want to or not."

"It matters to me. I want to know."

He was right. What did it matter if he would never act on it? But I wanted to know if he wanted me, perhaps so I could marinate in that knowledge, fantasize about the what-ifs, and just have the general satisfaction of knowing my desire was reciprocated.

In search of the answer I needed, I rephrased my question. "Why did you come to The Iguana tonight?"

He briefly shut his eyes and exhaled. "I don't know, Farrah. I wish I could give you an answer that makes sense. It was an impulsive decision. I wasn't planning on staying. I guess I was curious as to whether you were telling me the truth about not getting into some guy's car."

"There was no guy," I blurted.

He narrowed his eyes. "What do you mean, there was no guy?"

My face felt hot. "I lied."

He raised his voice. "Why the fuck would you do that?"

There was no choice but to be honest. Any other explanation would have made me sound like a pathological liar. I'd already put everything on the line tonight by getting up on that stage...

Here goes.

"I felt really awkward, coming home and finding you with that girl. I was leaving so I didn't have to be there while you were doing God knows what with her in the next room. I tried to leave with little fanfare, but then my stupid car wouldn't start. When you asked me who I was meeting, I just said the first thing that came to mind."

Jace didn't respond. My heart beat faster with every second that passed.

Say something.

His eyes softened. "You didn't have to lie. You could've just told me you were uncomfortable. I would've left the house and gone somewhere else."

"Why should you have to do that? It's your house, too."

"Well, now that I know it makes you uncomfortable, I'll try to be more considerate."

"I wasn't mad because you brought a girl over to the house per se. It wasn't *only* that." I braced myself. "It was the timing. I was mad because I felt something between us when we were hanging out at the pool. And you bringing a girl over so soon after made me incredibly jealous." Every muscle in my body tightened.

The truck jerked as Jace turned from the main road and took off down a side street.

Where is he going?

He eventually pulled into an empty playground parking lot.

Looking a bit tormented, he shut off the truck and leaned his head back against his seat. Then he turned to me. "You need to get that moment that happened between us out of your head, okay?"

"Are you saying there *was* a moment? You felt it, too? It wasn't my imagination?"

"Whether or not I felt anything is irrelevant." He looked me in the eyes. "Nathan would kill me if I ever laid a hand on you."

"Does that moment we shared have anything to do with why you came to The Iguana tonight?" My breathing quickened. "Was it more than just checking to make sure I wasn't lying?"

You could have heard a pin drop in the truck as Jace stared out at the empty jungle gym.

Then he turned his whole body toward me. "Okay, look. Full disclosure...you're a beautiful girl. There's no denying it. And yes, there *was* a moment. But it was *just* a moment, okay? A slip in judgment on my part—just like showing up tonight was. That day in the pool... I was having a really good time with you. I felt more at peace and carefree than I had in a while—a long while. I don't know if it's that you remind me of a happy time in my life—my youth—or if it's more than that. But I can't investigate it. That's the point." He paused. "If things were different, it would feel very natural to be attracted to you."

My heart wanted to burst. "It's pretty surreal to hear you say that. For so long, it's seemed like you saw me as that twelve-year-old girl you left behind when you moved away to college."

He laughed as he looked up. "Let's put it this way: I *wish* I could still see you like that."

"I had the biggest crush on you back then," I admitted.

He nodded. "I know."

"What? What do you mean, *you know*?"

"I knew about that—your little crush on me." He smiled hesitantly.

I straightened in my seat. "How is that possible? I never told anyone. I only wrote about it in my diary."

A guilty look crossed his face.

"Jace...what are you not telling me?"

He placed his head on the steering wheel for a moment and muttered, "Shit."

"Did you look in my diary?"

Looking up, he laughed. "No. I didn't. I swear."

"Then how did you know? Because I thought I played it pretty cool."

"Your mother told me."

"My mother?" I blinked. "What?" That made no sense. My mother would never have betrayed my trust.

"Okay, before you get upset, try to understand that she had your best interests in mind when she let it slip."

"How could ratting me out possibly mean she had my best interests in mind?"

"I guess there was a period of time when I started bringing Grace around a lot. I invited her over to dinner at your parents' house more than once. I had no clue that you felt a certain way about me. One night, your mom had a little too much wine after dinner, I think. You'd disappeared to your room, and Grace had just left. I was sitting at the table with Nathan and your parents getting ready to play cards." He stared off. "I'll never forget it. She said, 'Do you mind putting my daughter out of her misery and not inviting Grace to dinner so much?' I had no idea what she was talking about. Then she explained."

"Ugh."

"Your mom was looking out for you." He smiled. "Your dad just sat there rolling his eyes."

I stared up at the night sky. "I don't know how to feel about this news. On one hand, it's kind of a sweet story, and on the other, I want to kill my mother posthumously." I shook my head. Then it hit me. "It's rare that you mention them."

Jace nodded. "Yeah, well, I guess listening to you speak tonight brought out the courage."

Crickets chirped as I thought about what to say next. I had to be careful not to open any old wounds. "I always just assume it hurts you too much, so I never talk about them in front of you or ask you anything...about...you know."

"It sucks because I feel like I should be able to talk about it...for you and Nathan...but I can't. I'm sorry for that."

I rested my hand on his knee. "No one expects you to open up if it's too painful. It's okay if you don't ever want to."

He exhaled. "It was definitely easier to be in Charlotte all these years. If you're trying not to have to deal with something, distance helps."

"You don't *need* to talk about it, but if you ever *want* to, you can talk about it with me. You know that, right? It's not easy for me either, but I'd be willing to go there with you."

His mouth curved. "How did you get to be so strong?"

"I try to be strong for Nathan, but that doesn't mean my mind doesn't travel to dark places."

"That's why tonight was so amazing. Whatever brought me to that damn bar...I never expected to see you up on stage. I'm proud of you for putting your fears aside."

I felt myself smiling. "Thank you."

"Your message—that it's okay to *not* be okay—undoubtedly helped someone in the audience tonight, myself included." Jace's eyes lingered on mine.

"What are you thinking about right now?" I asked.

He looked over at the time on the dashboard. "I'm thinking I'd better get you home. Nathan will worry if you're late. He thinks Kellianne is driving, and she would've had you back by now."

"He would've texted me if he was that worried." I paused, looking out at the playground in the darkness. "I like talking to you, Jace."

"I like talking to you, too," he whispered.

Despite what he'd just said, he looked conflicted.

I arched my brow. "But..."

"*But* this can't be anything more than talking."

No way was I going to make myself seem desperate and argue about that. But I refused to give up hope. *I wasn't imagining things that day in the pool.* It was real.

Without saying anything further, he started the truck and began driving down the palm-tree-lined streets toward our house.

As promised, Jace stopped around the corner. "I'll see you in a bit."

"Thank you for the ride, *Kellianne*," I teased as I opened the door.

"Wiseass," he muttered.

Jace stayed in the same spot until I turned the corner. In the distance, I could hear him take off. I hoped he wasn't going to some girl's house.

His instincts were apparently correct, though, because the second I walked in the door, Nathan was there, looking concerned. I couldn't imagine what he would have thought if Jace and I had walked in together.

"You had me worried," he said. "The bar closed a half hour ago. I thought you got into an accident."

"How come you didn't text me if you were worried?" I asked.

"I was just about to."

"You shouldn't have been worrying."

"Jace mentioned you'd gone out with some guy you met on the Internet earlier today. I wasn't sure if you were really with him and not Kellianne."

I felt terrible lying to my brother. So I attempted to avoid it. "I *was* with Kellianne at The Iguana. And you'll never believe what happened."

"What?"

"I finally got up and spoke."

"You did?"

"Yeah."

"What made you do that tonight?"

"My emotions were kind of going haywire all day, and I needed to get it out somehow. I spoke about what happened to Mom and Dad—without going into detail. I honestly surprised myself."

"Wow." He pulled me in for a hug. "Really proud of you. Wish I could've been there."

He and I talked for about fifteen minutes before the front door opened.

Our heads turned in unison as Jace walked in.

Nathan seemed surprised. "Hey. Didn't expect you to come back. Figured you went back to that girl's place after your parents' house. What a freaking hottie."

I felt my face go hot. I hadn't gotten a look at her, and now I was glad for that.

"No. She's not my girl. Staying here tonight."

Jace's eyes locked with mine for a moment, guilt written all over his face. Strangely, that gave me hope that whatever was happening between us was far from over.

• • •

In the middle of the night, I couldn't stop thinking about Jace. I reached for my phone and clicked on his name.

Farrah: Are you awake?

I stared at the screen, awaiting his response.

Jace: Why are you texting me?

Farrah: What do you mean?

Jace: You know your brother is always grabbing your fucking phone. You shouldn't be texting me.

His rationale made perfect sense, but his abrupt response still pissed me off.

Farrah: You can stalk me, but I can't text you?

He didn't respond, so after a few minutes, I typed again.

Farrah: I'm sorry for calling you a stalker. The fact that you showed up tonight made me really happy. But I went from feeling happy to bummed out after our conversation, and now I can't sleep.

The three dots moved around for a while. His response finally came through.

Jace: Try to get some sleep. And delete this message chain off your phone, okay?

Rolling my eyes, I resisted the urge to scream in frustration.

Farrah: Done.

I swiped over his name to delete our history.

Chapter 8

Jace

I vowed to stay away from the house as much as possible the following week. I'd worked on Farrah's car and got it running again, but I did my best to avoid her. Having crossed so many lines with her the other night, I wasn't going to risk doing or saying anything reckless again. It was bad enough that I'd gone to The Iguana to check on her, but I'd also pretty much told her I would want to fuck her if she weren't Nathan's sister. I cringed. I should've never admitted my attraction to her.

Despite the fact that Farrah could rival a freaking Victoria's Secret model in the looks department, it was more than a physical attraction that drew me to her. I felt very connected to Farrah—not only because we shared some of the same pain, but because whenever I looked in her eyes, I was reminded of innocence and passion and all that was good in the world. I always felt like she could see the good in *me*, even if I couldn't see it myself. For years, I'd known about her little crush, and I'd never felt deserving of it, or of the way she looked at me—then or now. But *especially* now.

No way was I going to fuck up again. I needed to keep my feelings tucked inside where they belonged—and my dick tucked away, too, while I was at it.

Today after work, I forced myself to pay a visit to my parents to avoid running into Farrah. I knew I couldn't stay away from the house forever, but I would until the tension between us blew over a little. It might have been dumb to assume it would just go away, but I was hopeful.

My father was sitting up in bed when I arrived.

I knocked lightly on his door. "What's up, old man? How are you feeling?"

"I'll be better if you tell me we were approved for the loan."

Sitting down on the chair next to his bed, I rubbed my temples. "The bank is taking its sweet time to get back to me. They asked for a couple more pieces of info, and I had Kristy pull what they needed. Hopefully we can get that straightened out."

"I can't thank you enough for everything you've done."

I nodded. "Let me ask again... How are you feeling?"

"I've been feeling sicker at night, but overall, I can't complain. Your mother takes good care of me."

"Her cooking would cure any ailment."

"It's not just her cooking." He winked.

"Excuse me while I go throw up."

"You know your father's a horn dog," my mother said from behind me. She had apparently been standing at the door.

Like father, like son. Wasn't it my dick that ultimately led me to The Iguana the other night? Infatuation is like an addiction.

Granted, I wouldn't characterize my feelings for Farrah as an addiction at Dad's level. But so far, I hadn't been able to shake her from my thoughts. I wished it were easier to forget about her.

"Hey, Dad. Let me ask you something."

"What is it, son?"

"I know you have the best of intentions when it comes to stopping the gambling, but *how* exactly do you plan to do it? I mean, you say you're gonna get help and you won't do it again, but if something is that difficult to resist, how do you really *know* you can stop?"

Asking for a friend.

He sighed. "I don't have any guarantees that I won't slip. I just pray to God that I can do it. The main thing is keeping myself out of the atmosphere that would trigger me. That means never stepping foot into a casino again. There's still online gambling, of course, but that was never my thing. There's nothing like the rush of being at the tables. Undoubtedly, it's not going to be easy, but I suppose you have to get to a point where you're willing to experience suffering in order to do what's best for your family."

Nodding silently, I soaked up my dad's words. They reminded me of a show I used to watch, *Intervention*, where drug addicts were confronted by family members about going to treatment. At least half the time the person featured in the show relapsed. Addictions were hard to break, even if everything was on the line. And I worried whether my need to protect Nathan would be enough to keep me away from Farrah. I could relate to being tempted into self-destructive behavior, even if it hurt people. Dad had a point, though, about keeping yourself out of the environment. Maybe I needed to consider moving out of Nathan's as soon as he found a job.

My mother interrupted my thoughts. "Did Nathan ever call Jack McGrath about the Ford dealership position?"

Speak of the devil. "I gave him the information. He told me he would. I hope it works out. He's been really down about not having a job."

"Well, tell him to think positively and it will happen."

I chuckled. "You sound like Farrah."

"Why is that?"

"When I told her about Muldoon's financial situation, that's exactly what she told me—to imagine that coming up with the money would be easy and somehow I could *manifest* it."

"Smart girl," my mother said. "Sounds like she's learned to turn lemons into lemonade over the years. That's the difference between someone who says 'woe is me' when they're dealt something unfair versus a person who perseveres. A great attitude is everything."

"Well, I know she's hiding a lot of pain," I said. "But she does the best she can. She tries to be strong for Nathan."

"You said she's not in college, right?"

"No. She's not."

"You should encourage her to enroll."

That's right, Jace. You should be mentoring her, trying to get her in school...not stalking her and fantasizing about sleeping with her.

"Maybe I will. I know she took some classes at the community college, but that's not the same. She has this law firm secretarial job that pays decently, considering she doesn't have a degree. It's enough to get by, but I think she knows she's limiting her potential by not continuing her education."

Mom nodded. "I would imagine with Nathan out of a job, she'll be even more reluctant to think about quitting for the time being."

"Yeah, even though he shouldn't be her responsibility, I think he impacts a lot of her decisions. She likely would've moved away to go to school were it not for wanting to be here for him."

"Maybe now *you* can be there for him, so she doesn't have to be so much." She smiled. "I'm biased in saying that, though. I was always happy that you had a chance to get out of Florida for a while, but I hope you'll consider staying here this time. I can't imagine living away from my only child forever."

Cue the guilt trip.

"I can't make any promises, Ma."

"I understand. I know you loved your life in Charlotte."

"Well, don't underestimate the need to be around family. As much as I did love Charlotte, I was alone out there." I laughed. "But if your family is a pain in the ass, that can be a good thing." I looked over at my dad and raised an eyebrow.

"I hope we can somehow convince you to stay," she said.

"I think a lot of that is going to be contingent upon whether or not I behave," my father chimed in.

"Damn straight, old man."

I was more concerned about whether or not he would survive the cancer. But I didn't want him to know how worried I was. No matter how things with the company played out, I wouldn't be leaving Palm Creek until I knew he was okay.

• • •

Road construction meant I had to take another route home from my parents' house that evening. That wouldn't have been a problem, except it forced me to take a path I typically avoided with all my might—the road where the robbery had happened seven years ago. I'd managed to bypass that stretch of road all this time, and now a detour had cruelly led me there.

My hands began to shake as I passed the spot where Farrah's parents were murdered. I stepped on the accelerator to get through as quickly as possible. Sweat beaded on my forehead as I gripped the wheel.

When I finally made it past, my pulse slowed.

So much of everything in life was out of sight, out of mind. I'd somehow managed to compartmentalize things, even while living with Nathan and Farrah. Maybe it was easier because they didn't live in the same house as they used to. But driving on that road had brought that terrible memory to the forefront. All the things I never wanted to remember flashed through my head: Elizabeth's screams as her husband was shot dead. The smell of the gunfire as she was killed shortly after. The horrible aftermath as I called 911. I wouldn't wish that experience on my worst enemy.

By the time I got back to the house, my nerves were shot. It felt like I'd run a marathon with a load of bricks on my back.

I made it inside but stayed in the kitchen, staring at the wall for a while. My mood brightened a bit when I caught the smile on Nathan's face as he entered the house. He was wearing a dress shirt and tie, which was odd.

"What's up?" I asked.

He spun around. "You're looking at the newest sales associate at Billings Ford."

I beamed. "You got it?"

"I did."

Smacking him on the shoulder, I said, "Congratulations, man. My mother was just asking me about it, and I told her I didn't even know if you'd called."

"Called this morning, and they told me to come in this afternoon for an interview. Hired me on the spot."

"Well, that's the best damn news I've heard all day."

He examined my face. "You okay?"

"Yeah. Why?"

"You seemed like you were down when I first walked in."

"Just work-related stress," I lied. "That's all."

Imagine if I'd admitted everything that was bothering me today—not only the fact that I'd driven by the site where his parents were murdered, but also that I felt guilty because I came hard last night while imagining his little sister's ass. Yeah. That probably wouldn't go over too well.

"Let's go grab a bite, get your mind off things," he said. "To celebrate my new job, too. I don't know where Farrah is, but no need to wait around."

As much as I wanted to flee, because being around Nathan put me on edge, I forced myself to do the opposite. Nathan deserved better than a friend who wouldn't celebrate his new job with him. Plus, it would be more time away from the house and a way to avoid a run-in with Farrah tonight.

I smiled. "You know what, man? That sounds really good. Let's go."

Nathan and I went to Applebee's and enjoyed burgers and beers. We reminisced about our childhood. I even made a point to flirt back with the waitress to further deflect from what was going on in my head about Farrah. At least on the surface, it seemed like everything was normal. But inside, I still felt like I was on the brink of messing up.

• • •

When we returned to the house, Farrah was sprawled out on the couch watching television, wearing nothing but a bikini top and short shorts.

Fuck me.

Really? I manage to avoid her for days, and this is how she's dressed the first time I see her again?

"It'd be nice if you put some freaking clothes on," Nathan said.

I swallowed hard.

"I thought I was alone." She sat up. "Where were you guys?"

"Applebee's. Celebrating," he added with a smile.

"Celebrating what?"

"I got the dealership job!"

Her tits bounced as she got up from the couch. *Jesus.* I forced my eyes away.

She pulled Nathan into a hug. "I'm so proud of you. That's the best news ever. I wish I had known you were going out to celebrate. I would've joined."

"Well, you weren't home, and it was an impromptu decision," he said.

"I'm so happy!" She patted him on the back.

"Thanks. I gotta take a piss," Nathan said, brushing past her to walk through the kitchen to the bathroom.

It took a few seconds for me to realize I hadn't moved, and that I was gawking again. Farrah smiled as she stood in front of me, seeming to appreciate my admiration of her body. Had I always been this obvious? In the past, I'd thought I'd only snuck looks at her, but maybe I hadn't been so slick. Maybe she'd noticed all along.

Clearing my throat, I said, "You should put some clothes on."

Her chest heaved. "Because you like looking at me?"

Yes. "It doesn't matter what I like."

"I can't stop thinking about you," she whispered.

The sound of Nathan's footsteps approaching caused my body to jerk into motion. Walking past Farrah, I headed straight to the main bathroom. I tore my clothes off and turned on the cold water. Getting in, I let the shower rain down over me, praying it would wash away my guilt.

Chapter 9

Farrah

I'd just gotten home from work when the doorbell rang.

Peeking through the peephole, I saw Nora holding a stack of pita bread.

I opened. "Is that for me?"

"I need something to spread on it. We don't have anything at my house. My mom needs to go shopping."

"Come on in."

Nora's uncle owned a Middle Eastern bakery nearby. She told me he got up at, like, two in the morning to bake bread and often had so much of it, he'd drop a pile off on their doorstep a few times a week. She shared it with me frequently because she and her mother had a surplus in their freezer. Although, she never seemed to have anything to eat it with.

I walked over to the fridge. "What did you have in mind? Cream cheese...peanut butter?"

"What about butter?"

"That sounds good. We can warm the bread first, make it nice and toasty."

She rubbed her belly as she took a seat at the counter. "Yum."

"I thought your mom told you not to leave the house," I said as I opened the package of bread.

"She did. But I don't think she would mind me being here."

"Okay, but can you text her that you're here so she knows?"

Nora nodded and pulled out her phone.

I took out some of the pita and popped it into the toaster oven. "How was school today?"

Nora shrugged. "It was okay."

"Learn anything interesting?"

"Not really," she muttered.

I chuckled. I used to give my mother the same kind of answer when she'd ask me. She used to pressure me to think of one thing I'd learned, and never accepted my original answer of "nothing much."

"Why do you look sad?" Nora asked.

"I do? I didn't realize that. I just remembered something that made me a little nostalgic." I shook the thought from my head. "Anyway, what else is new with you?"

"Not much. How's Jace?"

I still regretted telling her about my crush, so I skirted her question. "How's Shawn?"

"He still doesn't know I'm alive."

"Yeah, well, sometimes that can be better than the reality. He can never hurt you if he doesn't know you exist."

She looked over at the toaster oven. "The bread is gonna burn."

Shit! I jumped. "You're right. Thank you."

Having retrieved the bread just in the nick of time, I buttered it. The comfort I took in devouring that warm bread dripping with butter was just what the doctor ordered.

"This is really delicious," I said with my mouth full. "Thanks for bringing it."

"Thanks for being home so I didn't have to eat it alone." Nora grinned. "And for the butter."

"You're always welcome over here. I just like it when you ask permission first."

"Can we go swimming?"

I stopped chewing for a moment. "I suppose, but you'd have to ask your mom if it's okay."

She texted her mother again. After a moment, her phone dinged with a response and she frowned.

"Mom wants me to go home and do my homework instead. She says she doesn't want to be worrying about me swimming while she's at work."

I felt bad for Nora but could understand her mother's concern. "I'll tell you what, maybe we can ask your mom to come over one of these weekends with you. I bet she'd be more comfortable with you swimming in the pool if she was here to watch."

"Yeah, maybe." Still looking sad, she hopped down from her seat. "Well, I'd better go."

"Cheer up. Get your homework done so you can relax."

She waved. "Bye, Farrah."

After the door closed behind her, I let out a long sigh. Nora didn't have it easy being left alone so much; she deserved some fun.

A few seconds later, there was a knock at the door. I looked at the rest of the pita on the counter and figured Nora had come back for it. But my heart dropped the second I opened the door because it wasn't Nora—it was that angry man, James, the guy who'd come to the house before, looking for the money Muldoon Construction owed him.

My heart pounded as I shut the door halfway, with only my head peeking out. "How can I help you?"

"You can help me by telling me where the fuck Jace is. I just went to his office, but he's not there. I want my fucking money, and I'm not waiting another day for it."

My voice was shaky. "Listen...I totally understand how you feel. The company is in a bit of a predicament, and I know he's doing everything in his power to—"

"I said, I want my fucking money!" he shouted. "And I'm not leaving until I get it."

"Okay, well, I can't let you inside, so..."

"That's fine. I'll wait right fucking here until he gets back."

Fear consumed me. What exactly was he going to do if Jace couldn't come up with the money?

Just then Jace's truck appeared, screeching to a halt in front of the house. He didn't even bother to pull into the driveway properly before he slammed the door and ran toward us.

His anger was initially directed toward me as he panted. "I told you not to open the fucking door!"

"I thought it was Nora. She was just here a second ago. It's the only reason I didn't check."

He turned to James. "You have no right coming here."

"I'm not leaving until I get my money."

Jace scrubbed a hand over his face and blew out a long breath. "Get in your car and follow me to the bank on Wheeler Street."

James huffed and reluctantly got back into his vehicle. Adrenaline coursed through me as they both took off because I still wasn't sure what was happening. Was Jace going to take money out of his own account? Would James pull something if Jace couldn't come up with the full amount?

I spent the next half hour worrying my head off about what was happening down at the bank.

When Jace's truck finally pulled into the driveway and I could see he was safe, I let out a huge sigh of relief. I opened the front door and waited for him at the threshold.

"Is everything okay?" I asked as he approached.

He ignored my question and glared at me as he entered the house. "What did I tell you about opening the door when you're home alone, Farrah?"

"I told you, the only reason I answered was because Nora had just left. I assumed it was her—that she forgot something. It was bad luck. If I'd known it was him, I wouldn't have opened."

"He didn't touch you, did he?"

"No. He didn't lay a hand on me." I sighed. "I'm sorry I opened the door."

Jace expelled a long, slow breath and seemed to calm down. "It's okay. I'm sorry for yelling at you."

"What happened at the bank?"

"It's taken care of."

"How?"

"I gave him his twenty grand."

"From your own account?"

"Yeah. It sucks, but I want him to leave us alone."

It didn't surprise me that Jace had enough money in his account to pay James back. I knew his job in Charlotte had paid well, and he didn't seem to blow away money.

"I was so worried about you." I reached out and placed my hand on his cheek. I rubbed my thumb along his stubble.

He closed his eyes as his breathing quickened.

When he opened his eyes, he stared at me intensely. The heat of his body was palpable. I inched closer and could feel his breath on my lips.

"Please tell me I'm not the only one feeling this," I said.

To my surprise, he whispered, "You're not, Farrah."

I threaded my fingers through his gorgeous black hair as he muttered something under his breath and closed his eyes again. I leaned in, and before I could blink, he'd taken my mouth in his.

Relishing the deliciously warm feel of his lips, I melted into him. Jace groaned. I couldn't believe this was happening. Pressing my body into his, I immediately noticed his erection and could feel the heat through his jeans. My panties were already wet. His mouth moved down my face to my neck, where he sucked on the skin at my collarbone. Bending my head back, I let out a desperate sound, unable to contain my arousal. Jace pulled my hair as he bent my head back farther, sucking even harder on my neck.

"Fuck, Farrah...what are you doing to me? This is so wrong, but I can't stop."

"You don't have to stop."

He spoke over my skin. "Yes, I fucking do."

Jace pulled me harder against him as he moved his mouth back up to meet mine. His kiss was rough and hungry. He tasted better than I could have imagined, like sugar and spice. I could feel myself getting wetter by the second. My body had never come alive like this. I prayed he didn't stop.

When I felt him pulling away, I gripped his shirt and brought him back into me. He devoured my mouth, harder and faster. I lifted my leg to wrap it around his waist in the hopes that he'd scoop me up and take me to his room. That was apparently the straw that broke the camel's back.

Jace ripped himself away, coming out of the trance he'd been in. "I can't fucking do this."

I breathed heavily as I took in the sight of him: the hair I'd mussed up, the lips I'd made red and swollen, the erection I'd caused. Frenzied, my body continued to buzz with excitement.

He rubbed his lips with his fingertips. My mouth watered. I wanted him to kiss me again.

"We can't let that happen ever again, Farrah. I was way out of line just now. I don't even know what the fuck came over me."

"We're both adults."

Panting, he looked me in the eyes. "Do you really think Nathan could handle this? Be honest."

I didn't think Nathan *should* react negatively to the idea of Jace and me, but I knew better. I absolutely knew Nathan would never accept it. I'd have to defy him. If he found out, it would ruin his relationship with Jace; one of the only two people Nathan trusted would be gone from his life. Jace was right. I just didn't know *how* to erase my feelings, especially now that I knew they were returned... at least on a physical level.

"Okay. I admit he would take it really badly."

"You saw how he reacted when we were in the pool. We weren't even doing anything then, and he freaked out on me about it."

This felt hopeless. I just kept nodding, because there wasn't anything to argue. This would wreck Nathan. It was still a conundrum for me, though, because I wanted Jace more than I'd ever wanted anything in my life—and that was no exaggeration.

"I understand it would be a nightmare if he found out. But I don't know how to turn my feelings off. I was crazy about you before I knew you had any interest in me. But now that I know you have feelings, too, I—"

"Just get what you think you know out of your head, okay? Yes, I care about you, and that goes way back. And yes, I'm inappropriately attracted to you now. You've grown into a beautiful woman, and I'm a man—I can't help being drawn to you. But I *can* help my actions. I need to do what's best for all of us."

"So, what does that mean exactly?"

"It means...pretend the mistake I just made under an incredible amount of stress didn't happen. I got worked up. I was worried about you and stressed, and I came back here so freaking happy to see you, so relieved that you were okay. All you had to do was look at me, and I lost all sense of reality. I had no right to give in to my urges." His mouth fell to my lips. "The fucked-up thing is... I know how damn wrong it is, but I'm still standing here wanting to fucking do it again, and that scares the shit out of me. Because it has to stop."

His weakness gave me hope. "You don't trust yourself..."

"I don't. You shouldn't trust me, either."

"Why shouldn't I trust you? From what I can see, you're a hardworking, decent man and one of the few people in this world I actually *do* trust."

He pulled on his hair and stared up at the ceiling in frustration. "Even if Nathan weren't in the equation, Farrah, I'm not right for you. You deserve a guy who's good at relationships. I'm not. Never have been. And you deserve someone who's definitely staying in Palm Creek. I don't see myself here long term."

"That would change if you felt the right way about someone. I think you're just trying to make a case, when we both know if it weren't for Nathan, you'd probably be inside of me right now."

His eyes widened.

Heck, my words shocked me too. But it was the truth. Jace gritted his teeth and looked down at the ground. I took that to mean he agreed with me.

My gaze wandered down. "You're still hard. You want me."

His tone grew harsh. "It doesn't matter what my dick wants, Farrah. Nothing can happen. Okay? You know it. And I know it. We got a taste of it. Now we just have to forget."

I didn't want a taste of it. I wanted to bury myself in it, experience all of it—and not just sex, either. I wanted Jace in every way, and it felt so unfair to have to suppress these feelings forever. That felt like a daunting task.

I felt tears in my eyes, but I wouldn't let them fall. *Shit.* I didn't want to cry, but it was all too much. I knew he was right, but I felt desperate.

"Can't we just sneak around for a while?"

He let out a shaky breath and shook his head. "We can't do that."

"Says who? If Nathan doesn't find out, what's the harm?"

His eyes darted up to meet mine. "He *would* find out eventually. Not to mention, you're forgetting that we all live together. If anything goes wrong between us, even if Nathan didn't know about it, it would be impossible to deal with it while living under the same roof."

It was crazy that I'd be willing to be with him in secret, just to be able to experience it. But I was. If he'd agreed, I would have gone with it in a heartbeat.

I rubbed my arms. "Okay...so...I guess there's nothing more to talk about here." I felt a tear finally fall as I looked down at my feet, so frustrated and hopeless.

"Please don't cry, Farrah. Fuck. I'm not worth your tears."

"Things are supposed to just go back to normal now? I'm supposed to deal with you bringing girls around again...after you kissed me?"

"I won't bring anyone here. You have my word." His eyes softened, filled with regret, as he cupped my cheek. "The last thing I want is to hurt you."

The automatic garage door sounded, and Jace flinched. Nathan was home early.

I wiped my eyes. "Shit." I hurried out of the room so Jace would be alone when Nathan entered.

I ran to the bathroom and looked at myself in the mirror. I noticed a bruise on my neck from Jace. Tracing it with my finger, I was still damn turned on. It had never occurred to me just how hard up I'd been. Standing here crying, yet tingling between my legs, aching for Jace's dick, was a weird combination. But the need inside me was relentless. My weakness was pathetic. I licked my lips, still able to taste him, remembering the way he groaned when we'd kissed.

The muffled sounds of Jace and Nathan talking came into earshot, but I couldn't tell what they were saying. I wasn't sure if Jace planned to tell my brother about what happened with that James guy today.

After a few minutes in the bathroom, I snuck away to my room and applied some makeup to the mark on my neck before covering it with my hair. Looking at myself in the mirror, I vowed to act as nonchalantly as possible when I faced my brother.

When I finally entered the kitchen, Jace sat across from Nathan at the table. Both were holding beers.

"I told Nathan what happened today," Jace said.

Deciding to be a smartass, I tilted my head. "About what exactly?"

He glared at me. "About James stopping by."

"Oh yeah." I shrugged. "It was no big deal."

Nathan faced me. "Well, needless to say, it upsets me that you opened the door, and I hope you learned your lesson. You always need to check the peephole. At least this asshole won't come by anymore now that he has his money."

"He won't," Jace said. "But she still needs to be vigilant. Because this shit isn't exactly over yet. There are others."

I opened the fridge and downed some orange juice right out of the carton. That was out of character for me, but my head was still somewhere else.

I put the OJ back and turned to Nathan. "How's the new job going?"

"Pretty good." He grinned. "I actually came close to selling a car today, but then the guy's wife convinced him to go to the other dealership across town tomorrow before making a decision. So that sucked."

I frowned sympathetically. "Maybe he'll be back."

"Yeah. Hope so."

"That's cool, though, man," Jace said. "I'll cross my fingers that it comes through."

"Thanks. I could use the extra cash."

"I'm going for a stroll around the block. I need some exercise," I announced. I also needed a breather.

"Have fun," my brother called as I headed out the door without looking at Jace.

As the warm, early-evening breeze hit my face, I closed my eyes and took a deep breath. So much in my own head, I nearly ran into a woman walking her dog.

"Sorry!" I yelped.

Unable to manage my feelings anymore, I needed to tell someone about what happened today. The only person I trusted enough was Kellianne. She knew my history with Jace, and I wouldn't have to explain everything from the beginning.

Pulling out my phone, I dialed her.

"What's up?" she said when she answered.

"Jace kissed me," I announced. "And I'm all fucked-up."

"Oh my God. What?" she screamed, nearly blowing out my eardrum. "Start from the beginning, please."

I told her the whole story, backing up to the convo Jace and I had the night he drove me home from The Iguana, and ending on today's mouth mauling after the James incident.

"Oh my God, Farrah. That's so freaking hot. He totally lost control."

"I was honestly taken aback by it. I thought all hope was gone after what he said in his truck that night. But when he kissed me today, I realized how far gone I am. I would've done just about anything to keep kissing him. He shut everything down, though, insisting nothing more could ever happen between us. How am I supposed to just...forget?"

"This is a tough situation." She sighed. "But I don't think you have any choice. You know your brother would flip. Jace is really trying to do the right thing here. No matter what, you and Nathan will be fine. It's his relationship with Jace that would be on the line."

I stopped walking and looked up at the sky. "I must be a horrible person for wanting to sneak around behind Nathan's back."

She sighed. "No, you're not a bad person. You're just a little lovesick—and a lot horny—for a man you've crushed on since you were a kid. Even though sneaking around with him wouldn't be right, I'm sure the idea of getting to be with him is mind-blowing. I think the only chance you'll have of that is if Jace loses control again. Basically, he has to be thinking solely with his dick and not his brain. He won't *decide* to do it. It would just happen."

"I don't want Jace to have to carry around any guilt. I won't taunt him into losing control. I just wish things were different."

"Yeah, but they're not. Knowing where things stand, try to figure out how to walk away. It's not easy because he lives with you, but you need to make a conscious effort to move on."

"And how do I do that exactly?"

"You need to meet someone else, get your mind off Jace. Remember that fictitious online-dating story you gave him? Maybe we need to get you set up and make that a reality."

That sounded miserable, but I did need to find a way to shift my focus off the unattainable man who had been consuming my mind and heart for way too long.

After our conversation, I thanked Kellianne and continued my walk around the block.

When I got back to the house, Jace's truck was gone.

Inside, Nathan was alone in the kitchen, preparing dinner.

"Jace left?" I asked.

He banged a metal spoon against the saucepan. "Yup."

"Where did he go?"

"Not sure. Probably to that girl Alyssa's house."

Jealousy burned in my throat. "I see."

Nathan cocked a brow. "Why? You need him for something?"

Looking down, I shook my head. "No."

Returning to my room, I spent the next hour stewing until Nathan called me to the kitchen for some pasta that he'd made.

After dinner, I returned to my room and listened to music for the rest of the evening.

The worst part? Jace never came home that night.

Chapter 10

Jace

Since the day I lost control with Farrah, I'd spent every night at my parents' house. It was bad enough that I couldn't look Nathan in the eyes anymore, but it was obvious I needed to stay far away from Farrah, too. It had been two weeks, and I still didn't have the balls to return to my bedroom at their house.

I'd made up a story that my mother needed help at home with my dad, so I'd be living with them temporarily. Meanwhile, my parents didn't understand why I suddenly wanted to spend so much time with them. The good news was, even though my personal life was a shitshow, things at work were finally stabilizing. The bank had approved our business loan, so Muldoon would be able to pay off all of the money we owed. I'd also be able to put the twenty grand I'd given to James back in my bank account.

Dad's health was better than ever, too. After the last scan, the doctors were pretty sure his cancer was in remission. It was only a matter of time before he'd be returning to work. Then I could decide whether I wanted to find a job here or move back to Charlotte and try to get my old one back. The latter made the most sense; it was the direction I was leaning.

"How long are you going to be gracing us with your presence before returning to Nathan's?" my mother asked one morning over breakfast.

"I'm probably going back there tonight."

"Well, I'm not going to complain about this extra time I had with you, even if I don't understand it. You refused to move back in with us when you came home, so these bonus days were nice."

My mother had made me my favorite, pancakes, every morning. I didn't feel worthy of her spoiling. Instead, I felt like a dirty traitor. Nathan kept texting me random stuff, and it took every ounce of effort I could muster to respond with nonchalant comments. I felt guilty, not only because of what happened with Farrah, but because I still didn't trust myself around her despite knowing the consequences.

My mother placed another hot flapjack on my plate. "Everything okay between you and Nathan?"

"Yeah. Why do you ask?" I poured lines of syrup over the pancake.

"Just thought maybe that had something to do with why you've been here."

"Why does there have to be something wrong for me to want to visit my folks?"

"Because I know this isn't your favorite place, even if you love us." She walked back over to the stove, then turned around. "I forgot to mention that I saw Farrah."

My ears perked up. "Oh yeah?"

"She was with a guy. Looked like she was on a date."

I stopped chewing. "What do you mean?"

"Well, what else would she be doing sitting across from a handsome guy at Dean's?"

Dean's was a restaurant not far from my parents' house, which was also close to Farrah's job.

The syrup turned in my stomach. "When was this?"

"Yesterday."

Pissed at myself for feeling a jolt of jealousy, I exhaled.

"You look like that upsets you," she said.

"What?" I felt my face turning red. "No! She just... doesn't have the best judgment sometimes."

"How do you know that?"

Because she wants to fuck around with me, for one. I ignored her question. "What did this guy look like?"

"He was older."

My fork fell out of my hand. "Older?"

"Maybe around your age, possibly in his early thirties."

"Are you shitting me?"

"What's wrong with that? Your father is ten years older than I am."

"She's practically a kid. There's a huge difference between twenty-one and early thirties."

I felt like my head was going to explode. I wanted to jump in my car and go find her. But I shook that insane thought from my mind.

"What you just said about Farrah goes against everything you've told me before. I thought you felt she was mature."

I rubbed my temples. "She is...but that's because she's had to handle a lot from a young age. That doesn't mean she's ready to be messing around with a dude in his thirties. She hasn't had a lot of boyfriends."

My mother tilted her head and smirked. "You seem especially vested in her well-being."

"I am, because I care about her," I said, feeling caught with my pants down.

Mom wasn't dumb.

"Are you sure there's nothing more?" she asked.

One thing I could never do was lie to my mother's face. So I had to get the hell out of the situation. I wasn't about to admit I had inappropriate feelings for Nathan's sister, even if that was the truth.

"Breakfast was delicious." My chair skidded against the floor as I stood up. "Thank you."

"Ah, the famous eat and run. I remember that from back when I used to confront you about smoking pot in high school or whether you were having sex."

"Drop it, okay?" I dashed out the door to head to work.

Yeah. She knows.

• • •

That evening, I forced myself to show my face at Nathan's. I couldn't disappear from the house forever, so I'd suck it up and spend my first night back there tonight.

He had just gotten back from the dealership when I arrived. I hadn't seen Farrah's car outside, so I assumed she wasn't home.

He opened the fridge and grabbed a beer. "I feel like I haven't seen you in ages. How are things with your parents?"

A wave of guilt hit me. "Dad's doing much better now."

"Good to hear."

"How's the job going?" I asked.

"Really well. I sold an Escape today."

"That's amazing, man."

"Yeah. I never imagined I'd end up with something I liked better than my last job, but this proves everything happens for a reason." He chuckled. "Now I sound like Farrah."

The mention of her name made my pulse race.

I did my best to act casual. "How *is* Farrah?"

"I haven't seen much of her over the past week or so."

Hmm... "That's probably because she's going around town with some guy."

His forehead wrinkled. "What guy?"

It was wrong of me to rat her out, but my selfish side wanted Nathan to know about this. Aside from the fact that *I* was likely the most dangerous man Farrah had nearly gotten involved with, we needed to make sure she wasn't getting herself into trouble.

"My mother said she saw her with a guy at Dean's."

"Really? Well, she never mentioned it to me, but I'm probably the last person she'd tell."

"I'm only telling you so you can keep an eye out, make sure she's not running with the wrong kind of people."

"I appreciate that. You know I'll be on it."

I nodded. Despite my best efforts, I'd likely be on it, too.

Chapter 11

Farrah

Dr. Stein scribbled something on a piece of paper. "Why do you think you decided to talk to someone at this point in your life? It's been a while since your parents passed. Why not sooner?"

I wasn't sure how to answer, but I did my best to figure it out. "It's always been hard for me to open up to anyone, in general," I began. "But recently I've felt very out of control in terms of my emotions—and my actions. I feel like I need someone to keep me in check. I haven't ever felt quite like this—not even right after my parents died. I've come close to making some rash decisions that could've been very damaging to the people I love."

About a week after my last encounter with Jace, I'd decided to make an appointment with a therapist. It had been a long time coming, something I probably should've done right after my parents died. But I was always afraid of what would happen, that all of the raw emotions would be too overwhelming if brought to the surface. But after getting up at The Iguana, I had a newfound confidence.

Dr. Alicia Stein had been recommended by one of my co-workers. She had a nice demeanor and was very patient.

This was my third meeting with her. The first couple of sessions had been spent talking about my parents' death and working through some of those feelings. Today she'd shifted the focus to my current state of affairs.

"Tell me what's going on with you now. The last time we spoke, you had just met someone online."

"Yeah...Colton. He actually dropped me off here. He's really nice. I've only been seeing him for a couple of weeks, though."

"You've obviously grown close to him in a short amount of time if he's driving you to your therapy sessions."

"Actually, my car is a piece of crap and stopped working again, so he was nice enough to offer me a ride. It wasn't like I needed his support or anything. We're not at that level. But he's been very supportive, in general, and I did tell him I was coming to see you."

"How is the situation at home?" She looked down at her notes. "With your brother, Nathan, and...Jace? That's his name, correct? Your brother's friend?"

"Yes. Good memory."

"Well, I have it written down." She smiled. "Was just trying to read my own handwriting."

"Yes. Of course." I shifted in my seat. "I haven't mentioned this before, but there's a bit of a story there with Jace. Pretty sure it has a lot to do with why I came to see you when I did." I paused. "Something happened between us."

Her eyes widened.

I spent the next fifteen minutes telling Dr. Stein about my feelings for Jace over the years and ended at the part where we'd kissed. Aside from Kellianne, I hadn't talked about him with anyone—besides my mother before she died.

"So..." I said, "I have to wonder whether jumping into something with Colton is such a good idea, given how recently everything went down with Jace. The problem is, I know nothing can ever happen there. Jace made that crystal clear. There's no choice but to move on."

"Have you spoken to Jace about your feelings since the day you kissed?"

"No. In fact, I haven't seen him much over the past few weeks, and that's been intentional on my part. He stayed at his parents' for the first couple weeks after we kissed, and honestly, I know the excuse he gave Nathan was bullshit. He had said he needed to help his parents out, but he was just avoiding me. That's understandable. It was better that we didn't see each other for a bit."

"Is he back at your house now?"

"Yes, but I've still been avoiding him. I don't want to have to deal with any tension."

"Does he know you've been seeing Colton?"

"Apparently he does, though I wasn't the one to tell him. Nathan told me Jace had mentioned that his mother saw me out with Colton. So he knows I'm seeing someone."

"Why do you think your brother would be so opposed to something happening between you and Jace?"

It was hard to explain Nathan to someone who didn't know him. "My brother isn't close to a lot of people. He basically only has Jace and me. Before Jace moved back to town, Nathan was a bit of a loner. Jace is his only real friend. If something were to happen between Jace and me, and it didn't work out, Nathan would have to choose sides. Nathan and Jace have always been competitive, and as much as Nathan loves his best friend, I know he wouldn't think Jace was the right person for me. He thinks Jace likes to play the field. Nathan wouldn't trust him."

Dr. Stein nodded. "Jace is forbidden. That drives your attraction to him."

I shrugged. "My feelings for him go back to childhood. It's much more than the fact that he's unattainable. There are many things about him I'm attracted to—his vulnerability despite his rough exterior...his humor—from the moment I met him, when we were both kids, I was drawn to him. He came back to Florida after nine years of being away, and I've realized not much has changed in terms of my attraction, except that I admire him for additional reasons now. His desire to help his father, his hardworking attitude. Of course, the physical attraction has only grown—men get so much better with age, don't they?"

"I have to agree with you on that. It's quite unfair." She smiled and looked down at her notes again. "Okay, Farrah. From everything I can tell, you're on the right path. You know a relationship with Jace would be toxic, not only because it would hurt your brother, but because I think your feelings toward him border on obsessive. I think working toward developing something genuine with this new guy is the healthiest choice for you right now."

Her use of the word *obsessive* caught me off guard and made me wonder if I was coming across as a crazy person despite my best efforts not to. Kellianne had referred to my feelings for Jace as an obsession once, too.

The session lasted fifteen more minutes before Dr. Stein bid me farewell for now, and I left the office to find Colton waiting for me outside.

"Thanks again for picking me up," I said as I got into his electric blue Jeep.

"No problem." He leaned in to kiss me on the cheek. "How was it? I mean, you don't have to tell me what you talked about, but did you get something out of it?"

"Yeah... It's definitely been a good thing for me."

"I'm glad." He placed his hand on my knee. "Do you know where you want to go? I'm kind of hungry. Are you?"

My stomach growled. "I could eat. I just need to stop by the house real quick. I have to see if I got this envelope I'm waiting for. It's important, and I don't want it sitting in the mailbox."

"Mind if I ask what it is? Or is it private?"

"It's Shawn Mendes tickets."

He laughed. "You like him?"

"Actually, no. Well, he's okay, but the tickets aren't for me. They're for my next-door neighbor, Nora. She's eleven and is obsessed with him."

And I know a little about obsessions apparently.

"You bought them for her?"

I shrugged. "She doesn't have any money, and her mother is a single mom trying to make ends meet. I wanted to do something nice for her. I just hope her mother will let her go. She can be kind of strict, even though she leaves her alone every afternoon to fend for herself."

"Damn. It would be a shame if she stopped her from going. That girl is going to love you for those tickets."

I nodded. Just thinking about Nora's reaction made me giddy. "It's probably going to make her whole year. I've been counting on being able to snag tickets. Someone I work with is married to a guy who works at the box office and was able to get me two."

Colton reached over to pinch me on the cheek. "You're such a sweetheart, Farrah." His touch made my skin tingle. I was definitely attracted to him. With his blond hair and blue eyes, he was the total opposite of Jace, though. All things considered, that was a good thing. Jace was my forbidden dark knight, and Colton was more like an angel with open arms.

"It feels good to do something nice for someone."

"What you put out into the world will definitely come back to you," he said as he parked in front of my house.

"I'll be right back."

Sure enough, when I got to the mailbox, the tickets were sitting there, so it was a good decision to have come home. I checked inside the envelope to make sure everything looked alright before stuffing it safely inside my purse.

Just when I was about to turn back to Colton, Jace's truck pulled up. My heart began to race. His eyes met mine. Now that he'd spotted me, I couldn't just take off without saying hello. Unfortunately, saying hello also meant having to introduce him to Colton. This was going to be super awkward, but it had to happen eventually.

So I continued to stand by the mailbox and waited for Jace to exit his truck.

Wiping my sweaty palms on my shorts, I said, "Hey... how's it going?"

Jace slammed his door and his eyes darted over to Colton waiting in the Jeep. He inclined his head. "That your new boyfriend?"

“He’s not my boyfriend, but Colton and I are dating, yes.”

Without saying anything further, Jace walked over to the Jeep, prompting Colton to lower the window.

Jace stuck his hand out. “I’m Jace.”

They shook.

“Colton.”

“Where do you live?”

“Over on Hyacinth.”

“What’s your last name?”

“Sterns.”

Jace nodded once and walked back over to me. “Be careful.”

I exhaled. “I will.”

My heart ached. I missed him so much.

Jace disappeared into the house, and I went back to Colton’s Jeep and let myself in the passenger door.

After a bit of awkward silence, he started the car. “That was your roommate?”

I cleared my throat. “Yeah. That’s Jace—my brother’s best friend and our temporary roommate.”

“No offense, but he seems like an asshole.”

I could understand why he felt that way, but it still made me a little defensive. “He’s just protective of me. He’s no different than Nathan that way.”

“I can see why you haven’t brought me around yet.”

“Yeah, well, that needs to change. I have a right to bring anyone I want back to my house, and my brother is just going to have to live with it.”

But if I really meant that, why hadn’t I brought him over? Why didn’t I invite him over *tonight*? I couldn’t, of course, admit that the reason had to do more with the "asshole" he'd just met than my brother.

Colton sighed. "Well, if meeting that dude was so much fun, I can only imagine what it's going to be like to meet Nathan."

I frowned. "I'm sorry. It's not easy when the only family you have is your crabby older brother and his grumpy friend. Testosterone rules in my house."

I knew things would be different if my parents were around. Nathan would be less invested in my personal business. And my mother, in particular, would have loved Colton's sweet personality.

"It's okay. I can take the heat." He reached for my hand. "It's worth it."

• • •

That evening, Colton drove me home after we'd gone out to dinner.

I said goodnight to him at the door, and the last thing I expected when I entered the house was to find Jace sitting alone out by the pool.

I pushed the sliding glass door aside, prompting him to turn to me.

"Hey..." I said.

His voice was low. "Hey."

"Where's Nathan?"

"He went out for drinks with some guys from the dealership. I guess he sold another car today, and they were going to celebrate."

"Wow, that's awesome. I'm so thrilled for him."

"Yeah. No shit. Glad to see him happy."

I walked over and took a seat three loungers down from Jace's, hesitant to get too close. "I'm surprised to see you here. You're usually out."

"Nowhere to be today, I guess. Just sitting alone with my thoughts."

There was no amount I wouldn't have paid to know what thoughts swirled inside Jace's head.

"Nothing wrong with clearing your head."

"It's been a while, huh?"

"Yeah." I exhaled, surprised. "I'm glad we ran into each other earlier. It was a long time coming."

Jace stared at me for a few seconds. "You like this guy?"

I shrugged. "I do. It's too new to tell if it's more than just a casual thing. He's really nice, though. He's nothing to worry about, if that's what you're thinking. Totally innocent."

"I know. I ran a background check on him."

I smiled. "I figured that was why you got his last name."

"Damn straight." He stayed quiet for a moment. "You can come closer. I won't bite."

The thought of him biting me sent a chill down my spine.

I stood up and settled into the seat next to him. "I've missed you."

He nodded. "I've missed you, too."

"When you were staying with your parents, I wondered if you were ever coming back. But then when you did...I wasn't ready to face you, so I've been making myself scarce."

"I'm sorry to have put you in that position. This is your home. You shouldn't have to be uncomfortable."

"That's the thing... I *am* comfortable around you. I love it when you're home. But I guess I just assumed I make *you* uncomfortable lately."

"That's not it at all, Farrah. You make me the opposite of uncomfortable. My *feelings* make me uncomfortable. When I'm around you...I'm happy. That's what I struggle with."

This man definitely knew how to make my heart come alive. He also knew how to confuse the hell out of me.

I looked up at the dark night sky. "I started seeing a therapist."

"Really? That's a pretty big deal. Since when?"

"Since around the time you went to stay at your parents'. A co-worker gave me the name of someone a long time ago, and I decided to bite the bullet. She had the availability to take me, so I put my fears aside and did it."

"Good for you. I'm happy to hear that. Do you feel like it's helping?"

"It's always good to get suppressed feelings out, so I would say it's helping in that sense. It's still too early to tell what the long-term benefit will be."

"Yeah. I get that."

I hesitated. "She seems to think my feelings for you are...unhealthy. She called them obsessive."

He narrowed his eyes. "Do you believe that?"

"I don't know."

"That's bullshit, Farrah. You're attracted to me because it's human nature to be attracted to someone of the opposite sex who you also have a deep history with and get along with. There's nothing unhealthy about that. Don't let her make you believe it's wrong to feel those things."

"I'm surprised to hear you say that. I thought you felt what was happening between us was wrong."

He shook his head. "While it might be wrong to *act* on it, there's nothing wrong with how we *feel.* We can't help that. Wanting you feels very natural to me, even if nothing can happen."

While his words were validating, it also sucked to hear him once again reiterate the fact that nothing could happen between us.

"Colton thought you were a real douche today."

"Good. Let that be a warning to him. If he ever tries to hurt you, I'll be his biggest fucking nightmare."

We shared a smile.

"He's...really nice. I just can't seem to relax enough to let things progress." I paused. "We haven't...had sex or anything."

He swallowed. "You don't want to?"

"I guess my head isn't in the right place to start that with him right now."

He sucked some air in, then let it out. "Are you going to introduce him to Nathan?"

"I'm thinking about it."

"I'm gonna make sure I'm front and center with some popcorn when it happens." He chuckled.

"Thanks a lot." I laughed.

"Seriously, though, Farrah, if you're happy, I'm happy. Please don't think you have to avoid me, or that you can't count on me."

"I haven't felt that way. I know you care about me no matter what. And I respect you not wanting to risk hurting me or Nathan. I just wish..."

"Wish what?"

"That I didn't still have these feelings."

The moonlight shone in his eyes as he stared straight through me. "Can I ask you something?"

"Yes."

"Are your feelings for me..." He chewed on his lip. "Are they what's keeping you from moving forward with this guy?"

It was impossible to look him in the face and deny it. "I think so."

Jace closed his eyes briefly as he took in my admission.

"How come you're not with anyone tonight?" I asked.

"What do you think—that I'm with a different woman every night or something? That's not how it is."

"I honestly don't know."

"I'm not. I haven't been with anyone in over three weeks."

"Since we kissed?"

He nodded.

"Why?"

"Because you're not the only one who's fucked-up by it, Farrah."

"I guess I figured you'd still be out...doing what you do...regardless."

"Yeah, well, I guess I can't compartmentalize as well as you might have thought."

"Are you saying what you feel for me is *more* than just sexual?"

"Of course, it is. Why do you even have to ask that?"

"I don't know." I shrugged. "I don't really understand how you see me."

"You don't understand how I see you?" His voice grew louder. "I see you as kind, loving, caring, hardworking... and beautiful. There's absolutely nothing not to like about you, Farrah." He stared off. "I haven't been able to look Nathan in the eyes—even still. That's why I stayed at my parents' for a while. I don't know what to do with this energy between us. It's easy to say we're just going to forget about it, but it's not so easy when I'm around you."

"Tell me about it."

I couldn't believe he was opening up like this. But as he closed his eyes, again looking tormented, I had a hunch there was something more.

"Is everything else okay? You seem down, in general, tonight. When I came in, you were already deep in thought. Does it have to do with Muldoon?"

He shook his head. "Everything is great at work, actually. We got the loan. So that's not it." He paused. "I've been having to take Lincoln Road home every day because there's some construction going on. There's a detour."

My heart sank. "Oh..."

"Every time I drive by, the flashbacks hit me like a ton of bricks. But I refuse to find another way home because I have to face these feelings at some point. I've never been good at dealing with them."

It broke my heart that he'd been keeping this inside. "I've said it to you before, but you know you can talk to me about it anytime, right? I can handle it."

His eyes glistened. "If I can talk to *anyone* about it, it's you. Not Nathan. But I can't get myself there yet. That doesn't mean it's not constantly on my mind. You can't escape your thoughts. Part of the reason I didn't hesitate to move back here is because I felt it would do me some good to finally face all the things I've been running from."

"I'm proud of you for driving by there, even though it's painful."

He took a deep breath in. "Thank you."

He'd said he wasn't ready to talk about it, but there was something I needed to get off my chest.

"I sometimes wonder if you feel guilty that you were the only survivor. That kind of guilt can be quite toxic. You know it wasn't your fault, right? You had no control over any of it."

Jace placed his head in his hands. Was he about to cry? I hadn't seen him express this kind of emotion since he'd been back.

"I didn't mean to upset you," I said. "I just wanted to let you know that I understand. Even though I wasn't there...I understand."

He looked up at me. "It's okay."

I stood up. "I can give you some space if you'd rather be alone."

He reached for my arm. "No. I don't want that at all. Stay."

There was nothing I wanted more.

Chapter 12

Jace

She looked so beautiful under the moonlight. Sometimes it was hard to believe this was the same girl who used to chew on her hair. Farrah had turned into such a graceful and mature woman. As much as she had her quirks, her ideals and outlook were more in line with mine than most of the women I'd come across in my adult life. She wasn't judgmental, and I never felt uncomfortable around her, despite not being comfortable with my attraction to her. Right now, I absolutely loved hanging out with her.

"What do you want out of life, Farrah?" I asked.

She smiled and sat forward to look at me, her stare penetrating. "I think I want to re-create the peace I had before my parents died. I'm not sure how to do that, though. I don't know that I can ever feel normal again—completely safe. I don't want to have to rely on anyone for financial support, either. I want to feel secure, economically and emotionally. But I'm a far cry from that." She looked up at the stars. "So, my three answers are peace, happiness, and financial security." Farrah raised her chin. "I feel like you've accomplished so much. I would like to be in that same boat at some point—graduate from college and grad school and have enough experience to get a good job and take care of myself."

I shrugged. "I might have a good resume, but I'm far from where I want to be in life. A lot of that has to do with the fact that I ran away when things got tough and haven't dealt with stuff. So while I might appear to have my shit together, it's more of an illusion."

"Have you talked about your feelings with anyone?"

"That's what I'm doing now." I smiled. "This is the extent of it." I sighed. "I don't know what I'm supposed to be doing, to be honest. It's not like I can change anything that happened. Will talking about it *really* help? I don't know. I've always just buried myself in school and work."

"We have that in common—not dealing with things. I've been focused on my meaningless job and being there for Nathan, but I don't feel like I'm living my life the way I want to. Honestly, the past seven years have been a blur."

I nodded. "I also feel like I've had two different lives: before and after. You know what I mean?"

She nodded. "I know *exactly* what you mean."

Our eyes locked.

"I know you do."

"Despite how hard it's been," she said, "when you came back to Florida, it felt really good. It was like I got a part of the 'before' back. I didn't have much growing up. I had my parents, and I had Nathan, and honestly, Jace... I had *you*. Because you were always around. You coming back was the best thing that had happened to me in a very long time." She got a little choked up. "I know I complicated things by showing my feelings for you, but I hope you know that no matter what happens...I will always cherish you."

An unidentifiable feeling bubbled inside my chest—a warm sensation mixed with intense guilt.

I wanted so badly to lean in and kiss her. "You're amazing, you know that?"

"I think you're pretty amazing, too," she whispered.

"When my mother told me about seeing you with that guy, Colton, I guess she could sense a weird vibe from me. She asked if it upset me."

Even in the darkness, I could see her cheeks turn pink.

"You were jealous?"

I nodded. "You know the saying, if you can't take the heat, get out of the kitchen? That's what I did. I got the hell out of the kitchen—literally just got up from the table because I've never been able to lie to my mother."

"Why were you afraid to tell her?"

"I didn't want her to convince me to do the *wrong* thing. My mother is not a good influence. She's very much a romantic, and she freaking adores you. I think she would love it if we were together. She has a lot of respect for you."

Farrah's expression turned sad. "But she doesn't know Nathan like we do."

"Yeah," I whispered.

She cleared her throat. "Well, your mother is very sweet. I've always liked her. Both of your parents are great."

"When I spent those two weeks with them, it made me realize how lucky I am to have them." I immediately regretted saying that. "I'm sorry. That was insensitive. I just meant—"

"No, no, no. It's okay. I had my parents for as long as I did, and I was very fortunate for those fourteen years." She gazed out at the pool. "I can still sometimes hear my mother talking to me. It's like I know the type of advice she would give me for certain situations, even if she's not here. I don't have the same connection with my dad. He was a little bit harder to read. But the fact that I can sometimes sense my mother's presence when I need her is a good thing." She turned to me. "Anyway...I'm really glad you were here tonight. It's been forever since I had a chance to talk to you. I'm relieved you're not mad after the awkward run-in we had earlier."

"I don't have any reason to be mad at you. I just want you to be happy."

She shrugged. "I'm trying." She looked down at her hands. "Listen...that promise you made me a while back... about not bringing girls here—that's not really fair. If I'm going to bring Colton around, you should be able to bring whomever you want home."

The idea of him being here unsettled me. It wasn't going to be easy, but I had to support it because Farrah needed to move on from any ideas she had about being with me.

I arched my brow. "You sure about that?"

"Yeah... I can't guarantee I'm not going to hate her, but I have no right to tell you how to live your life. Besides, it would seem a little strange to Nathan if you never brought anyone by. Don't you think?"

Other women were the furthest thing from my mind right now. All I wanted was to taste Farrah's lips again.

"Are you going to bring this guy to the next movie night?" I asked.

She blinked a few times. "Maybe. I haven't thought about it."

Deciding to be a jealous wiseass, I raised my brow. "Where will you sit?"

Her face turned red. "What do you mean?"

I was a total asshole for bringing it up, but I couldn't help myself. "Are you going to try to sit next to me even if he's there?"

Her face turned even redder.

"You picked up on my little leg game. Congratulations."

"It was a bit obvious, yeah. Especially when your leg would *accidentally* press against mine."

"Yeah...but you didn't exactly move away when that happened, did you?"

"No, I fucking didn't. And I should probably go to hell for that."

"Well, we'll always have movie night." She winked.

My dick stiffened at the thought of being that close to her again. Farrah had no idea how much her leg presses had riled me up inside.

I moved the subject along before I got hard thinking about it. "Okay, so that's how we're gonna handle it? You bring your dude over, and I'll bring girls over. We'll pretend like nothing ever happened between us...move on from all the awkwardness?"

"I think so." She bit her lip, not seeming sure.

I nodded, still feeling jealous. "Right."

"Promise me something."

"What?"

"Promise me you won't avoid me from now on. I'll do the same."

I sighed, but I vowed to act like a damn adult moving forward.

I can do this. "That sounds like a plan."

• • •

My promise not to avoid Farrah was put to the test the following week when Nathan informed me that his sister would be bringing her new *boyfriend* over for a poolside barbecue. I didn't know why he used that term. Farrah had said things weren't serious. Had something changed? Why the hell was I so damn invested in knowing?

Nathan and I were hanging out in the kitchen, preparing the food, when he started grilling me for information before Farrah arrived.

He sprinkled some spices over a tray of chicken wings. "You said you met this guy briefly, right?"

"Yeah."

He wiped the excess seasoning off his hands. "What's he like?"

I rolled some ground meat into a ball and patted it down hard—well, more like *punched* it. "He seemed nice. Respectful. I think she can do better looks-wise, but that's me being shallow. I don't have any reason not to trust him. I ran a background check on him. Nothing sinister came up. Lives over on Hyacinth—with his parents, which is fucking lame."

Nathan rubbed the chicken. "He might be a loser."

"Possibly," I agreed.

"Thanks for looking into him. I'll try to not give him too much shit, I guess, unless I have reason to."

"I'm sure Farrah will appreciate that."

Nathan washed his hands and took a beer out of the fridge. "If this dude is a decent guy, I don't have anything to worry about, even if he does live with his parents. My concern with Farrah has always been that she's going to end up messing around with the wrong type of person. She's very fragile, even though she tries not to show it. After all the shit we've been through, she needs someone dependable. She couldn't handle being cheated on. That guy she dated in high school broke her heart—didn't cheat on her, but he dumped her before going away to school. Farrah needs to find someone who just wants to be with one person, someone who'll treat her right and be there for her when she needs him."

Exactly. The antithesis of me. "I agree. That's the type of person she needs."

Which is why even if she and I both weren't so damn scared of hurting Nathan, I still wouldn't be the right person for her. My track record sucked.

When the front door opened, I kept to myself in the kitchen, pounding the back of my hand into the meat mindlessly when I should've been forming it into burgers. Farrah and her little friend were talking out in the living room. I wasn't sure where Nathan had gone, maybe to change into his swim shorts. I really wished he'd get the hell back out here, though. He was supposed to be my buffer.

Footsteps approached the kitchen, and the next thing I knew, Farrah appeared, wearing a sundress so thin her nipples peeked through. Now that this guy was standing in front of me, I could see he was pretty short. That made me perversely happy.

"Hey, how's it going?" Farrah asked.

"Good," I said, moving to the sink to wash my hands. When I'd finished, I sucked it up and extended my hand to him. "How ya doing, man?"

"Good. Nice to see you again. Did you ever find any dirt on me?" he asked.

"No. You're clean as a whistle. Which is the only reason you're here."

"Good to know. I respect you looking out for her."

I stared him straight in the face. "I always will."

Farrah smiled at me, and our eyes locked. Then Nathan came in, and my focus shifted over to him.

"Nathan, this is Colton," Farrah said, her voice a little shaky. "Colton, this is my brother, Nathan."

Colton extended his hand. "Nice to meet you."

Nathan took it. "Same."

Farrah looked between them. "Nathan has assured me that he's going to be on his best behavior today."

"So long as no one gives me a reason to act otherwise," Nathan cracked.

Forcing myself to extend an olive branch, I said, "Can I get you a beer, Colton?"

"That'd be great."

"Miller or Heineken?"

"I'll take a Miller. Thanks."

As I walked over to the fridge, Farrah said, "What? No beer for me?"

I would've rathered Farrah not drink today. Her inhibitions would loosen, and then she might do something with this guy she wouldn't otherwise. I knew how that went firsthand. Nevertheless, I once again sucked it up. "You want a Miller, right?" I knew that was her favorite.

"Yes. And I was only teasing, Jace. I can get it myself."

The way she batted her eyelashes made me want to lift her up and take her the hell out of here. I had serious issues. I knew she'd rather be with me right now instead of this tool. And I got off on that in a strange way.

Forcing my eyes off of her, I walked over to the fridge to grab the beers.

After handing the bottles to Farrah and her *friend*, I popped mine open and took a long swig.

Farrah ventured out to the pool area with Colton, and I stayed in the kitchen, though my eyes were glued to her through the sliding glass door. When she slipped her dress over her head, my heartbeat accelerated. It took everything in me not to run out there and cover her up with a towel. I'd always known she had a beautiful body, but for some reason it looked ten times more perfect to me right now—probably because my jealousy was amplifying every thought and emotion.

What the fuck had my life become? A matter of months ago I was living in North Carolina, minding my own business with a thriving career. Now I was back in Florida, cleaning up messes my dad made and lusting after my best friend's little sister. Worse than that, I was unable to stop myself from *thinking* about her even when she wasn't around. And I criticized my family for having addictions? Being addicted to a human had the added risk of harming the other person.

Farrah jumped into the pool, and her boy toy followed suit. I continued to stay in the kitchen, slicing tomato and onion murderously as I stole glances out at the water. It was a wonder I didn't chop my finger off.

Nathan came up behind me. “He seems okay.”

I practically jumped at the sound of his voice. Damn, was I on edge.

“Yeah. Too early to tell,” I said as I maimed a tomato.

He looked out at the pool and turned to me. “Since we’re hanging out here all day, you should invite someone over.”

“Why would I do that? Wouldn’t you be outnumbered?”

“Actually…” He flashed a smile. “This chick from work is coming by. So…”

“A chick?” I grinned. “Who’s this? And why haven’t you told me about her?”

“Her name is Crystal. She works the front desk at the dealership. She’s cool.”

“Nice. It’s about damn time.”

“Whatever happened to that Alyssa girl?” he asked.

Alyssa was the last thing on my mind.

“Nothing. She’s been texting me a lot. I just haven’t seen her.”

“Why don’t you invite her over?”

I couldn’t think of one reason not to, even if the thought didn’t excite me. It might’ve seemed strange if I insisted on hanging out alone when Nathan had a girl coming over. I certainly didn’t want to be the fifth wheel. And I couldn’t bolt, as much as I wanted to skip this entire pool party.

Reluctantly, I took out my phone and texted Alyssa.

Jace: Hey. What are you up to this afternoon?

Her response was almost immediate.

Alyssa: Just doing some shopping. Why?

Jace: Would you want to come over for some burgers by the pool? We're having a little get together.

Alyssa: I would love that! Who's we?

Jace: Nathan, his sister, and a couple of their friends.

Alyssa: Ah. Yup. Sounds like fun.

Jace: Cool. Pick you up in an hour?

There'd been no doubt in my mind that she was going to say yes, considering she'd texted me almost every single day since we'd met, despite the fact that I hadn't shown much interest.

Alyssa: I'm heading home now. So that will be perfect.

If Alyssa could get my mind off Farrah for even a minute, inviting her over would be worth it.

Chapter 13

Farrah

She was so damn pretty that it made me want to pull my hair out—or maybe chew it like the old days. The moment Jace walked in with Alyssa, I regretted telling him he should resume bringing girls to the house. *What the hell was I thinking?* I'd said it to be fair, but the current situation was proof that it wasn't something I could handle.

Alyssa checked me out just as much as I did her. It was basically a staring contest. I caught her ogling my breasts. She caught me staring at her perfect nose and silky blond hair. Then she'd move her hand over to Jace's leg, and my eyes would follow as a form of self-torture. The fact that my attention had shifted so dramatically from Colton to what was going on between Alyssa and Jace was a real eye-opener. I'd thought maybe I was turning a corner, finding a way to move on with Colton. My jealousy-induced inability to focus proved otherwise.

Poor Colton. The guy could not have been any nicer. He just didn't do it for me the way Jace did. I didn't have an uncontrollable need to jump him, didn't feel the intense attraction through my core that I felt any time Jace was in the room.

Jace took Alyssa's empty bottle as he stood up. "You want another beer?"

"I'd love one," she said.

The fact that he waited on her and ignored me shouldn't have bothered me, given that I was sitting next to the guy I was dating. Colton looked at me adoringly as I stewed over my screwed-up feelings.

Nathan and Crystal played around in the pool while the rest of us continued to hang out on the loungers. I forced small talk with Colton while trying to control my feelings.

It was exhausting. I excused myself to the bathroom, promising to get Colton a beer on my way back. Once inside, I splashed some water on my face.

When I opened the door to exit, Jace was walking down the hall toward me.

He stopped. "I'm just...going to grab an extra towel."

His body was a few inches from mine, and I could feel its heat. My gaze traveled the length of his carved chest before moving to his face. We stared into each other's eyes for a few tense seconds as he towered over me. I finally forced myself to put one foot in front of the other and go back outside.

As I landed back in my seat next to Colton, my body still quivered from the encounter.

"Did you forget my beer?" Colton asked.

Shit. "I'm sorry. I did."

"No worries." He got up. "I'll get it. Want one?"

I wiped some sweat off my forehead. "No, thanks."

Later, after the sun went down, Nathan thought it would be a good idea if the six of us watched a movie. After much debate, we finally settled on one of the old Bourne films with Matt Damon, because Crystal had never seen that series.

Jace and Alyssa made popcorn in the kitchen while Nathan pulled the movie up on the TV. Nathan let Crystal have his usual spot in the chair, and he grabbed a pillow and sat on the floor by her legs. I had settled into a seat on the couch next to Colton, who had chosen to sit at the end. That meant there was a chance I'd be sitting next to Jace.

God. All I could think about was getting to sit next to Jace?

When Alyssa and Jace finally returned to the living room, I straightened in my seat and tried to seem nonchalant as Jace approached. Then he sat next to me, giving Alyssa no choice but to sit at the far end of the couch. Had he intended to do that? This would be my first time sitting close to him knowing what it was like to kiss him. Knowing that he was attracted to me. Knowing that he wanted me. Knowing that he'd been on to my last movie night leg game all along. With four of us sitting in a row, it was a tighter fit than normal, so I didn't even have to move my leg closer to his; we were naturally pressed together like sardines.

Nathan started the movie, but I couldn't concentrate. I enjoyed the heat from Jace's body and obsessed about how I was going to handle Colton later. How could I continue things with him when this entire day had solidified the fact that I was still completely and utterly obsessed with someone else?

About twenty minutes into the movie, I shifted my leg to the left so it leaned even more into Jace's. I must've been a despicable person, because Colton grabbed my hand at almost the same exact time, and I still didn't shift my leg away. I wanted every bit of the contact I was receiving from my left. My body was on fire. And if there was any doubt as to whether this entire thing was mutual, when I inadvertently moved my leg away, Jace leaned his leg back onto mine. It didn't even feel discreet anymore.

Lord.

This had to end. In that moment, I knew it was over with Colton, because this was just wrong. Even if nothing could ever happen between Jace and me, tonight was a testament that nothing much was happening with Colton either. I wanted to like him...but I couldn't fall for him hard enough.

As I pretended to be into the movie, I felt like I was going to explode. There was a chance Jace might go home with Alyssa tonight—or worse, that she'd sleep here. I'd do nothing but toss and turn thinking about it. I knew Colton was hoping I'd leave with him tonight, too. He'd proposed getting a hotel since he lived with his parents and never had any privacy. I'd been making excuses, because I wasn't ready to take that step. I knew now I never would be—not with him, at least.

After the movie ended, we all retreated to the kitchen. Alyssa sank into one of the chairs at the table and kicked her feet up. Her body language made it clear she wasn't anywhere near ready to leave. I was sure she had her heart set on staying right here, hoping to make her way into Jace's bedroom tonight. That drove me insane.

Colton wrapped his arm around me and whispered in my ear, "Want to get out of here? Take a ride? Maybe find a place?"

That was my cue. As hard as it would be to hurt him, I had to do the right thing.

"Can we take a walk outside?" I asked, my throat feeling parched.

He frowned, clearly sensing something in my tone. "Sure."

Colton followed me out to the front of the house. It was quiet on our street, aside from the sound of crickets chirping.

"What's the matter?" he asked. "You seem like something's bothering you."

Looking down at my feet, I said, "Colton...I'm really sorry. I know you've wanted us to be alone and take that next step, but I'm just not there. And...I don't think I ever will be." I looked back up at him. "This just isn't working out."

He looked at me strangely. "I'm sorry...did I miss something? You brought me here to meet your brother because we were getting more serious. We have a great day, everyone seems to be getting along, we watch a movie, and at some point during that time, you decide you don't want to be with me anymore? Am I understanding that correctly?"

"I know it seems sudden, but I've been struggling for a while." *Don't say it.* "It's not you...it's me."

Ugh. I said it.

I should be shot for that.

He bent his head back and looked at the sky. "Just fucking great. Feed me that damn line on top of everything?

You should've just told me to get out and slammed the door in my face. That would've been less painful."

Despite his belligerent tone, I felt bad for him. I deserved the attitude because I had misled him. "I'm so sorry, Colton. I really am. You're a wonderful guy, and you deserve the world. That's why I don't want to waste any more of your precious time."

He let out a long breath before looking me in the eyes. "You sure about this?"

Feeling terrible, I simply nodded.

It took him several seconds to process that. "Well... take care of yourself, I guess. Not sure what else to say."

"You too."

I stood on the sidewalk as he got into his car. A horrible feeling developed in the pit of my stomach as I second-guessed myself for a moment. Had I just made a mistake? He was such a stand-up guy. I shook my head, reminding myself that I needed to follow my intuition—and my heart. They were telling me to move on, and that I needed to talk to Jace tonight. Urgently.

When I returned to the kitchen, everyone turned to me. Jace's stare was particularly penetrating.

"What happened to Colton?" Nathan asked.

"He...went home."

My brother looked confused. "I assumed you were leaving with him."

"No, uh, he had to get some stuff done."

It didn't seem like the right moment to drop the bomb that I'd dumped the sweet guy they'd all met today. There was no explanation that would have made sense to them.

Alyssa put her arm around Jace, and I cringed. His eyes were still boring into mine, though. I turned and got a glass of water, busying myself in the kitchen, and after a moment, Alyssa got up to use the bathroom.

Relief washed over me. It felt like my one chance to communicate with Jace.

Once she was fully out of sight, I turned to him and mouthed, *Please.*

He swallowed hard.

I didn't know what my request meant, wasn't sure *exactly* what I was begging him for.

Please...put me out of my misery?

Please...don't take her back to your room tonight?

Please...let's just go somewhere?

It wasn't like Jace could ask me what the hell I meant, either.

Nathan stood and took Crystal into the living room. Now it was just Jace and me. I was about to say something more when Alyssa came out of the bathroom.

To my surprise, Jace suddenly stood. "I need to drive you home."

Alyssa seemed caught off guard. "Oh...you have somewhere to be?"

"I have an early morning tomorrow."

I didn't know where any of this was going until he turned to me. "You said you needed a ride to Kellianne's, right?"

Holy shit. "Uh...yeah. My car shit the bed again."

His eyes were piercing. "I can take you."

My heart beat rapidly as I nodded. "Okay...thank you."

Alyssa rolled her eyes. "Your car never seems to be running."

Jace went to the living room. "Nice meeting you, Crystal," I heard him say.

"Where are you going?" Nathan asked.

"Driving Alyssa home and dropping Farrah off at Kellianne's."

"You're going to Kellianne's this late?" he called to me.

"She's...going through some stuff. She just wants some company."

He seemed to buy it. "Oh...okay." Nathan was so into Crystal, I probably could have started a fire in the kitchen tonight and he wouldn't have noticed.

"Really nice meeting you, Crystal," I said.

"You too, Farrah. Maybe we can grab coffee sometime."

"I'd love that." I smiled and gave Nathan a discreet wink to show my approval.

Goose bumps peppered my skin as I followed Jace and Alyssa out to his truck. She climbed into the passenger seat next to him while I had no choice but to sit in the back. But I told myself to be patient. As soon as he dropped her off, I would have him all to myself. My body buzzed with excitement and nerves. I couldn't believe he'd taken me up on my vague *Please*. He'd translated what I'd asked for: alone time with him.

The ride was silent and uncomfortable. I could practically feel Alyssa's disdain seeping through the back of her seat. Jace turned on the radio, maybe to drown out the quiet.

"Are you dropping her off first?" she finally asked him.

"No. It makes sense to drop you off first."

When we got to her house, Alyssa turned to him after she let herself out. "Call me soon?"

"Yep," he said noncommittally.

She leaned her head toward the backseat. "Have a good night, Farrah."

"You too."

As a courtesy, I waited for her to enter the house before getting out of the backseat and moving to the passenger side. As I sank into the leather, I felt more relaxed than I had all night. Being next to Jace again felt like home.

He wouldn't look at me as we drove off.

"Where are we going?" I asked after a couple of minutes of tense silence.

He laughed almost angrily. "Beats the fuck out of me."

"Thank you for making time for me. I know my message was vague."

His eyes darted toward me. "I knew what you wanted."

That gave me chills.

My eyes fixed on his hands gripping the steering wheel.

"What happened with you and Colton tonight?" he asked.

"I told him I couldn't see him anymore."

His breath hitched. "I thought you liked him."

"Not the way I like you," I said matter-of-factly.

Jace sucked in some more air. "This is so messed up, Farrah. You were with that dude, and I was supposed to be with Alyssa, but all I wanted was to sit next to you during that goddamn movie just so I could fucking touch you."

His words made the muscles between my legs contract.

Jace finally stopped at the same desolate playground parking lot we'd visited once before.

He shut off the ignition. "You asked where we were going." After a pause that lasted several seconds, he said, "Pretty sure it's hell."

Then he leaned in and kissed me like I'd never been kissed before.

Chapter 14

Jace

My tongue was practically all the way down Farrah's throat; I'd never felt so out of control in my life. All of the reasons I knew I shouldn't have been doing this went out the window the second my mouth was on hers. The only thing that mattered right now was tasting her. I'd been starving all day, ready to lose my mind from jealousy. And this was my reward for the slow torture of having to watch her with him.

Every whimper that escaped her made my dick swell harder. I pulled her hair to bend her head back and suck on her neck, as if I were trying to draw sweet nectar out of her skin.

"Why do you have to be so damn beautiful?" I whispered, lowering my mouth to her breasts.

Farrah made an unintelligible sound as I sucked her tender nubs through the fabric of her dress.

She wasn't wearing a bra. I told myself I wasn't going to undress her, but as soon as she pulled the top of her dress down, I eagerly took her bare breast into my mouth. If I'd thought her neck tasted good, it was nothing compared to this. I knew there were other parts of her that were even sweeter—parts I really needed to avoid touching tonight before there'd be no turning back. I pried my mouth away from one tit and showed love to the other as she raked her fingers through my hair. With every tug of her hand, every moan that escaped her, I felt like I was spiraling. There wasn't an iota of control left in me.

"I want you, Jace. Please...I want you inside of me."

"No," I responded. I had to do everything in my power to resist.

What she said next nearly undid me.

"I want to taste your cock. Let me suck you."

"Jesus, Farrah." I pulled back, my dick throbbing in protest. "We're not having sex tonight. *Any* kind of sex. Don't say shit like that."

She looked flushed. "Okay."

I couldn't tell if she was embarrassed or disappointed or both. "We just...need to take this easy, okay?"

She licked her lips, and that's all it took. Despite my words, the urge to devour her mouth again won out as I pulled her back into me, this time kissing her angrily—angry at her for being such a damn cocktease, and angry at myself for my inability to resist.

"What am I gonna fucking do with you?" I muttered, my tongue halfway down her throat.

"Anything you want."

I bit her bottom lip gently. "Stop saying things like that."

"Why?"

"Because it makes me want to do it."

She smiled over my lips. "Good."

"You're evil, Farrah." I laughed a little. "You don't think I want to fuck you right now? I've never wanted anything more in my life."

"I don't care about anything else, Jace. I just want you. All of you," she begged. "Please."

Lowering my mouth to her neck again, I spoke into her skin. "Christ...stop begging for it."

Then, I just had to know. Lowering my hand, I slipped it under her dress. Her panties were soaked, and the warm heat of her pussy felt beyond incredible at my fingertips.

She panted. "It's crazy what you do to me, how wet you make me."

I moved my fingers in and out of her while my dick ached to replace them. At this rate, I knew I'd inevitably be inside of her. If it wasn't tonight, it would be tomorrow or the next day. Still, I remained adamant that it not be tonight. She deserved better than to be fucked in a parking lot. We were only here because we had nowhere else to go.

I needed to make her come so she'd stop taunting me.

Too far gone to stop this, I rasped, "Come on my hand." I pushed my fingers in deeper.

She slowed the bucking of her hips. "What about you?"

"Don't worry about me."

She repeated her earlier request. "Let me suck you. I want to taste your cum."

Those words nearly made my dick explode.

I kissed her harder. "I'm not letting you go down on me in my truck like a whore."

"Treat me like a lady if you want, but you can fuck me like a whore."

Fuck. “You’re relentless, Farrah.”

I pulled my fingers out of her and licked her arousal off. Her sweet taste sent me into a frenzy. I wrapped my hand around her head and pulled her close again, this time lifting her onto my lap so she straddled me. This was the biggest test of my resistance, because all I wanted to do was take my dick out and let her ride me as hard as I knew she would. But instead, I pushed her down onto my jeans where my cock was bursting through the seams. Her wetness seeped through her panties as she rode me over my pants while my dick throbbed. She moved her hips, pressing her clit against me while I held onto her back. Our eyes were locked on each other until the need to kiss her overtook my desire to see the need in her eyes. I sucked on her tongue as she continued to grind against me. I held on with all my might, trying not to explode.

Her voice was shaky. “I love the way you feel between my legs.”

“Show me how much you love it. Come on my dick.”

Farrah bent her head back and took a deep breath. It seemed like she was trying to prolong the inevitable, trying to hold back her orgasm—until she wasn’t able to anymore. She let out a loud sound of pleasure that anyone in the vicinity might have heard. Thankfully, we were in an empty parking lot. As she bore down on me, I couldn’t take it. I lost control, coming hard beneath her as my eyes rolled back. The grinding tapered down until there was nothing left.

As I looked up at her again, she gave me a snide smile—seeming pleased that she’d caused me to lose it.

Gripping her hair, I said, "Are you happy now, Farrah? I've never come in my damn pants before. That was a first for me."

"I'm glad you let go. I only wish it had been inside me."

"You're gonna be the end of me," I whispered, meaning that with all of my soul.

"What happens now?" She moved off of me and returned to her seat on the passenger side.

"Fuck if I know."

She looked so beautiful with her hair all messed up and her lips red from our kisses.

Still panting, she said, "Can we not try to figure it out for a while? I just want time with you."

"And then what? What happens when our time is up?"

"Then we deal with that when it comes."

"That sounds like a recipe for disaster." I rested my head on the back of my seat. "You deserve better than to have to sneak around with someone."

"I deserve what I *want*. And you're what I want."

This was dangerous. She didn't know what she was saying—even if she meant it.

"You're gonna get attached to me, Farrah. That's not healthy. I'm not right for you."

"You really think I'm not already attached to you? You're all I think about. Ever since the first moment you kissed me, you owned me. You fucking owned me, and these feelings are not going to just go away like magic because I tell them to."

Hearing her say I owned her did things to me. My mind raced to find a solution. I kept trying to put this on her when I knew damn well I couldn't stop it if I tried. I'd been instigating shit just as much as she ever had. The realistic side of me knew this was a dead-end road, yet my brain still tried to come up with any excuse to move forward with what my body needed.

Then I had a lightbulb moment that was likely brought on by my dick: Maybe it was better to give in and get it over with. Maybe there was a way to do this without Nathan ever having to know. I offered her a proposition before I could change my mind.

"The fact that we can't keep our hands off each other doesn't change the fact that we don't have a future together, Farrah." When she looked down, I placed my hand on her chin so she would face me. "Look at me. This will never work long term. If we choose to keep playing with fire, we have to do it with the understanding that there's an end point."

A look of concern crossed her face. "End point?"

"We have to end it before Nathan finds out. He'll never speak to me again, and he'll treat you like shit." I must have been crazy for what I was about to suggest. "Maybe we spend the next month...getting it out of our systems. After the month is over, I'll move out of the house, so we can have some space to really think about things. Now that Nathan has a job, I feel better about doing that. He doesn't need me anymore."

She looked hurt, and I couldn't blame her. But I didn't know how else to handle it.

Farrah finally spoke. "So...just be together on the down low for a month and then you leave? That doesn't sound like a good deal."

"We'll see where things are at that point. But either way, I move out of the house, since I think that's best for all of us anyway."

Farrah stared off for a bit. "I don't want you to move, but I understand. It's better to plan on that since we don't know how this will end up."

"I agree."

She looked out the window, seeming to contemplate my proposal.

Then she turned to me and nodded. "Okay. A month." She reached for my hand and looped her fingers in with mine. "Where are we going tonight?"

"I don't think we should be alone tonight. Nathan thinks you're at Kellianne's. What are the chances she'll let you sleep over there for real?"

"Pretty high...unless she has a male guest, which is rare."

"I'll go to my parents' house. Let Nathan think I changed my mind and decided to stay over at Alyssa's—pretty sure he wanted to be alone with Crystal anyway."

Boy, I seemed to have no problem lying tonight—lying to Nathan about my whereabouts, and lying to myself, because deep down, I knew there wasn't going to be any such thing as a clean break after a month's time. Someone was going to get badly hurt. Possibly two people I cared about. All because of my selfishness.

This felt like a runaway train. I just hoped it didn't crash and burn, taking all three of us down with it.

• • •

I thought maybe I'd get lucky and be able to sneak into my parents' house with both of them sleeping. All I needed was to somehow get to my dad's underwear drawer. But after I used my key to enter, I unfortunately found my mother sitting on the living room couch watching television.

She lowered the volume. "What are you doing here?"

Without saying anything, I rushed past her to their bedroom. Dad shifted in bed as I opened his drawer as quietly as possible to grab a pair of his boxer shorts. It was too dark to find pants, so I'd just settle for these. I couldn't let my mother know why I needed to change my pants. If she asked, I'd pull something out of my ass.

On my way back out to the living room, I dumped my dirty jeans in a corner of the guest room where I'd be sleeping.

My mother's eyes widened when she noticed me wearing only a T-shirt and Dad's gigantic boxer shorts. "What on Earth?"

I plopped down on the couch. "I'm spending the night."

"And you found the need to take off your pants the second you got here?"

"They have engine grease on them. I was fixing my truck. I wanted to be comfortable."

Her eyes narrowed. "What kind of trouble did you get yourself into?"

"I told you what happened."

"I'm not talking about your pants. I mean *why* are you spending the night?"

"I don't want to talk about it."

"This is about Farrah, isn't it?"

Fuck.

I put my feet up on the coffee table and ran my hand through my hair. "What do you want me to say? You knew from the last time you started to grill me that something was going on there..."

"Does Nathan know?"

I crossed my arms. "No. And he never will."

"What happened exactly?"

"What part of 'I don't want to talk about it' don't you understand, Mother?"

She smiled. "You know, when I was younger, I had an affair with your uncle Rod's best friend, Stephen."

That surprised me. "Really?"

"Oh yeah. I was only eighteen, and Stephen was a couple years older. Your uncle found us together, hiding in the shed behind Grandma's house."

"Well, damn. What did he do?"

"He beat the snot out of Stephen."

I chuckled. "That sounds like Uncle Rod."

"That was the end of their friendship."

"No surprise there. What about you and Stephen?"

"We continued to sneak around for a while. He was really sweet to me, but eventually my feelings waned, and it was too stressful to continue upsetting Rod when it didn't seem worth it anymore."

I rested my head on the back of the sofa and stared up at the ceiling. "This story is basically confirming what I already know. If Nathan were to find out about anything happening between Farrah and me, our friendship would be over."

"Well, that's the thing. It could be over temporarily. But years later, Rod actually admitted that he regretted his reaction. So, it was a friendship wasted. I understood that the way he found out was shocking. But if he'd allowed himself to get over that, and looked at it objectively, he would've seen two people who were crazy about each other, and who never meant to hurt anyone."

"There's one big difference between your situation and mine. You said Stephen was a nice guy—probably would've treated you like gold if you'd allowed him to. I've never been good at relationships. Farrah would end up getting hurt if I led her to believe there was a future for us."

That wasn't the only reason I didn't deserve her. But it was the only one I was willing to admit to my mother tonight.

"So if you're so sure about the way things should be, why don't you trust yourself? Why are you sleeping here tonight? You're feeling guilty about something that already happened, am I right?"

"I think we're done talking about this tonight." Kissing her on the forehead, I said, "I'll see you in the morning."

In the guest bedroom, I settled into bed and brought my fingers to my nose. I could still smell Farrah. *Holy shit.* My dick rose to attention as I replayed everything that had happened in my truck—the way she'd told me she wanted to suck me off, the taste of her lips and tits, the way she grinded her pussy on me until we both came. I was completely wired.

Maybe Farrah could sense my energy because a text came in from her a few seconds later.

Farrah: Are you still up?

My first instinct was to once again warn her not to think about me, not to get her hopes up. But ultimately, I relaxed into my pillow and typed out what I actually felt.

Jace: I can still smell you all over me, and it's keeping me awake.

Farrah: When can I see you again?

Jace: I think we need to pace ourselves. Let's give it a couple of days. Then we'll see.

We'll see. I knew those would be my famous last words.
The dots moved around while she typed.
In the meantime, I sent her another message.

Jace: Don't forget to delete this text.

A second later, her response came through.

Farrah: Goodnight.

I could sense her disappointment. She probably wanted a more enthusiastic text from me. Believe me, a part of me wanted to tell her I'd be picking her up in the morning to take her home, so we could finish what we'd started tonight while Nathan was at work. But the next time we gave in to our feelings, I knew we'd end up taking it too far. That would mark the beginning of me inevitably hurting her, which I was in no rush to do.

Chapter 15

Farrah

Two days after my encounter with Jace in his truck, I received a text at 5AM.

Jace: Nathan is leaving at 8:45. Can you call in sick to work?

I got chills.

My shift normally started at 7AM. It would have been ideal to give my boss more notice if I wasn't going to show up, but there was no way I could refuse the opportunity to be alone with Jace.

Farrah: Consider it done.

I sent a text to my supervisor, letting her know I was "sick" and apologizing for the late notice.

Over the next few hours, I couldn't fall back asleep. Tossing and turning, I stayed in my bed until I heard the sound of Nathan starting his car.

After he took off down the road, I got up to go in search

of Jace. Before I could even exit my room, he appeared at my doorway.

Shirtless, he gazed down at me.

I gulped. My eyes wandered down to the thin happy trail leading the way into his gray sweatpants. He was already hard.

"Hey," I breathed.

"Hey," he said, his chest heaving.

I stepped closer and asked, "What did you have in mi—"

His lips were on mine before I could get the words out. Jace's body pressed against me as he went in search of my tongue. I could feel his massive cock throbbing against me.

"Oh God," I whispered.

He lowered his mouth to kiss my neck. "I'm going to go to hell for this."

"I'll be right there with you."

He moved back, his eyes traveling the length of my body. "Take off your clothes," he said. "I want to look at you first."

My nipples stiffened as I tore off every shred of clothing, paying no attention to where I threw things on the floor. Nearly losing my balance, I kicked my shorts off before slipping my underwear down my legs.

Straightening my shoulders, I stood before him totally nude, the peach fuzz on my legs stiffening. Jace stared at me for several seconds, his pupils dilated. The look of hunger in his eyes alone made me wet. I'd never been stared at while naked before, but there was something so arousing about baring yourself and watching someone devour you with their eyes. My nipples practically turned to steel.

"Touch yourself," he demanded.

I lowered my hand. As I began to massage my clit, Jace lowered his pants and let them fall to the floor. His boxer briefs came off next. I watched as his gigantic cock sprung forward. It was perfect—huge and glistening—exactly the way I'd pictured it. I salivated, wanting to take it in my mouth.

"Holy shit," I muttered. "You're beautiful."

I hadn't seen anything yet because he started to jerk off as he stared at me. My fingers rubbed over my clit harder. I was incredibly turned on by the look of hunger in his eyes.

"I've thought of this moment every night for a month," he said.

We stayed in place for several minutes, facing each other and pleasuring ourselves. My level of arousal was unbearable.

"Lie on the bed and spread your legs apart."

My knees trembled as I moved to the bed and lay back, moving my knees as far apart as they would go.

He tugged on his dick several more times before moving onto the bed to hover over me.

"I found your pills in the bathroom once. You still on them?"

I nodded.

"Good. I want to fuck you raw, Farrah. Is that okay? I'm clean. I've been safe with everyone else."

There was nothing I wanted more. "Yes."

On all fours, he bent to take my mouth in his. "How

badly do you want me inside of you?"

"So badly," I breathed.

"Tell me. Tell me how badly you want me to fuck you right now."

"I've wanted you for as long as I can remember. There is nothing I want more than to feel you inside of me, and for you to fuck me harder than you've ever fucked anyone." I let out a long breath. "Please...please fuck me hard."

He bit at my collarbone. "You sure you want it hard?"

"Yes."

"I might hurt you."

"I don't care."

He moved back to look at me, and his eyes darkened with desire. It pleased me to know Jace had gotten to the point where all of his doubts and inhibitions were obliterated.

He spread my legs wider, and I felt his crown at my opening. "Put me inside of you," he said.

Placing my hand around his rigid cock, I felt how wet it was at the tip. I circled his crown around my opening, loving the feeling of his precum against my skin. It was validation. I began to stroke his shaft.

"Keep doing that and I'm gonna come in your hand and not in your beautiful pussy. Fucking put me inside of you, Farrah, before I explode."

I didn't know whether to prolong his agony or give in to my own need. Ultimately, I couldn't wait any longer. I rubbed his tip over my opening a few more times and pushed his cock inside.

A long groan escaped him as he sank into me. "Oh... fuck..."

I closed my eyes at the intensity. "Jesus Christ, Jace."

"Don't fucking move or I'm gonna come. I swear, I've never felt like this before." He shut his eyes tightly for a moment. He exhaled and began to move slowly in and out of me.

The fact that he seemed to be struggling for control made me almost *want* him to lose it. But I also wanted to stretch this for as long as possible.

We got into a groove as he began to fuck me in a rhythm that matched the eager thrusts of my hips. He couldn't have been any deeper inside of me.

"You're the first guy to do this to me without a condom, and you're gonna be the first to come inside of me."

"I can't wait," he rasped.

He moved faster, pummeling me so hard that my head banged against the back of the bed. Not sure how I'd explain to Nathan if a hole suddenly appeared on the wall.

My hands gripped his ass, my nails digging into his skin.

"Fuck me harder, Jace. Destroy me," I panted.

He thrust harder and laughed a little. "Watch your language, Farrah, or I'm gonna come."

"Good."

He sped up his movements, and I couldn't take it anymore. My clit began to pulsate as I lost control over my body. My voice echoed through the house as my orgasm tore through me. It was, bar none, the most intense feeling I'd ever had.

As soon as I reached my climax, Jace's body shook as he came. He let out a loud, unintelligible sound as I lifted my hips to meet each and every last one of his thrusts.

His body trembled as he came down from his orgasm.

My clit still throbbing, I could have easily gone for a second round, and it had only been a minute since I came.

I pushed his body deeper into me, wanting each and every ounce of his cum inside of me, never wanting to move from this spot.

"That was...everything." I exhaled.

Jace continued to breathe erratically. "I'm not sure I'll ever be able to walk away from you."

That filled me with immense hope, but I warned myself not to take anything said immediately after sex seriously.

"No matter what happens, I will never regret this, Jace."

He wrapped his hands around my face. "Neither will I, beautiful."

My heart clenched.

He held me for several minutes as the morning sun shone through the window.

Eventually, Jace got up and threw his pants on. He smiled. "Come have some breakfast when you're ready."

This felt like a dream.

After I cleaned myself up and put on a dress, I met him out in the kitchen. His gorgeous, carved back faced me as he stood at the stove frying eggs. I took a deep whiff of the buttery smell.

I couldn't help wrapping my arms around him while he cooked. A heavy wave of reality hit me in that moment. A month? A month and I was supposed to give him up? That was unfathomable. Now I felt more connected to him than ever. I could never sit back and watch him with another woman again.

"I lied..." I blurted. "I don't think I can do this. I can't just end things after a month with you. You're gonna break my heart."

His body stiffened before he turned around. "I don't want to break your heart, baby." He put the spatula down. "You're not the only one who's messed up right now."

He lifted me into his arms. I wrapped my legs around him and felt desperate to feel him inside of me again.

The sizzling eggs were about to burn.

"Can we forget about breakfast?" I spoke over his mouth.

He grunted and turned to shut off the heat. Jace pushed his pants lower while still managing to carry me. The next thing I knew, I felt his hot, wet cock at the tip of my already-soaked underwear. He moved my panties to the side and entered me in one hard thrust. Jace groaned as he jerked his hips and began to fuck me standing. It felt even better than the first time. As I raked my fingers through his hair, I savored the taste of his mouth, his breath, unable to get enough of him.

It was a wonder I didn't fall, given how hard he was thrusting into me while holding me at the same time. My nails dug into his back as I clung for dear life. The level of penetration this time was even more intense.

Unexpectedly, I climaxed, my muscles contracting around him. Looking deeply into his eyes, ripples of pleasure coursed through me. Midway through my orgasm, his body shook as he lost control. I decided there was nothing sexier than looking into a guy's eyes while he came inside of you. Nothing compared.

"You're gonna be the death of me." He buried his face

in my neck and laughed. “But I can’t think of a better way to die.”

Jace gave me a long kiss before he put me down.

I escaped to the bathroom, and when I returned to the kitchen, he was back at the stove, remaking the eggs.

The sight of a shirtless Jace cooking me breakfast gave me goose bumps. The coffee brewing smelled almost as good as him—almost.

“Hope you’re hungry...for food.” He winked.

“After the workout you gave me this morning, I’m starving.”

He served us eggs and toast. We ate in comfortable silence at the table, demolishing the food in no time.

“Do you have to go to work?” I asked.

“Unfortunately, I do...at least for a little while. But why don’t I meet you back here around four. That will give us some more time together before Nathan gets home.”

Nathan had been working at the dealership most days until six.

“I would love that.”

“If I can get here earlier, I will.”

He took my plate and his over to the sink. I grabbed the mugs and placed them in the dishwasher.

When I turned to him, I caught him looking at me. “What?”

He moved a piece of my hair behind my ear. “You’re so beautiful, you know that? I don’t even know how I’m supposed to keep my hands off you when he comes home later.”

“Well, then we have to find someplace else to go. I

don't care where it is, as long as I can be with you."

Jace looked a little lost for a moment, and then he kissed me on the forehead. "I want you to know that I don't take lightly what you gave me today. I know it's been a long time since you've been with anyone. I also know you trust me, and I won't take that for granted. This isn't just about sex for me, as much as I might have implied it when I suggested we...get this out of our system. My feelings for you go way beyond just the physical. I trust you, too. And I fully respect you. I haven't had that feeling with a woman in a long-ass time. Today meant a lot to me."

My heart pitter-pattered. As much as I'd enjoyed the sex, I needed to hear that. "I appreciate that, though I'm still not quite sure what the hell I'm supposed to do when our month is up."

"Let's try not to think about that right now." Jace lifted me in the air for a last kiss. Putting me down, he said, "Be here waiting for me at four, okay?"

"Of course."

He disappeared into his room to get dressed, and when he returned, he gave me a peck on the lips. "See you soon."

Watching from the window as he got in his truck, I let out an audible sigh.

I spent the rest of the day cleaning the house like a madwoman. I hadn't had a day off in the middle of the week in a long time, so I took advantage and gave our place the deep cleaning I'd been meaning to for some time. There was no better way to make use of the nervous energy running through my body.

When 3PM rolled around, I could hardly wait for Jace

to get back. I decided to kill the last hour by heading over to Nora's to check on her. Better yet, I decided to finally give her the Shawn Mendes tickets I'd been holding. After the euphoric morning I'd had, I felt like celebrating, eager to bring someone else the kind of joy I was experiencing.

I used my key to enter her house, then knocked as I always did on the inside of the door.

"Yoo-hoo! It's Farrah!"

It was quiet, and I wondered if perhaps she wasn't home, although that wouldn't have been good, since her mother always instructed her to come straight here after school.

Nora finally emerged from her bedroom. She looked a bit sullen.

"What's up?" I asked. "Is something wrong?" When she didn't immediately say anything, I pried. "Did something happen?"

She shook her head. "No."

"You look sad."

Nora hesitated. "I saw something today, and I'm afraid to tell you what it is. I don't want to get in trouble."

My pulse raced. "Okay...um...well, don't be. I can handle whatever it is you saw."

"I saw you and Jace."

Oh.

It hit me.

Oh no.

What?

I gulped. "Uh...me and Jace. You mean...what...what do you think you saw?"

"I had a fever this morning, so my mom let me stay

home sick. We ran out of stuff to put on the pita bread. I saw your car, but I wasn't sure if you were home or if the car was just broken down. So, I went to my yard and peeked through the screen thingy by the pool. I could see you and Jace in the kitchen through the glass door."

Shit.

I no longer had to wonder what it was she'd witnessed. I was absolutely mortified. "I'm sorry you saw us. I wish you hadn't peeked into the house, but it's not your fault." I finally looked up. "Do you want to talk about it?"

"Not really." She shrugged. "I know what it was. I ran into my mom and her ex-boyfriend once."

"Obviously I didn't know you were home at that time of day. I didn't even think you could see that clearly into my house. I'm sorry."

"I thought maybe you would be mad at me."

"No, of course not. You were looking for me. You didn't expect to see anything."

"Is he your boyfriend now?"

"We're...spending time together. My brother doesn't know, and it's important that it stays that way. I'll make sure to be more careful. Thank you for teaching me an important lesson today."

Several seconds of awkward silence ensued, and I wondered if perhaps this was no longer the best time to whip out the tickets.

I might've scarred you for life, but here are Shawn Mendes tickets to make up for it?

Ultimately, I decided the change of subject would be a good thing to take the attention off one of the most embarrassing moments of my life.

I took a deep breath in. "You know what would be

great?"

"What?"

"For us to both forget about that thing you saw and focus on something that's *definitely* for you to see."

"What do you mean?"

"I have a surprise."

"You do?"

"Yes. It's why I came by. I've been waiting for the right moment to give it to you." I reached into my pocket and grabbed the envelope.

Nora took it from me. "What is it?"

Rubbing my hands together, I smiled. "Go ahead and find out."

She opened it, lifting the tickets out, and when the words seemed to register, her eyes widened.

Then she started trembling. "Is this really happening?"

"It is." I bit my lip. "You're going to see him."

"Shawn tickets?" she cried. "How? When?"

"I have a friend at the ticket office," I said proudly.

Nora burst into tears before wrapping her arms around me. This distraction had indeed helped alter the mood, thank God.

"Oh my God!" She kept jumping up and down. "I just can't believe it! I'm going to be in the same room as him!"

"You think your mom will let you go, right?"

"She has to. I'll die if she doesn't."

"I'm sure she'll want to take you, but if for some reason she doesn't, I'd be happy to."

"Thank you, thank you, thank you, Farrah! This is the best thing that ever happened to me in my entire life!"

It felt amazing to make her so happy. I could certainly

relate to that feeling of giddiness after my morning with Jace—getting something you always wanted but never thought you would have. I was still in a state of euphoria, even if realizing that Nora had seen us put a damper on things.

"Put them in a safe place, okay? Make sure you let me know what your mom says, and if she wants me to take you."

"Okay!"

Grateful that the tickets had taken the tension in the air away, I hung out at Nora's for about twenty more minutes before heading back to my place.

Jace pulled in at four on the dot. Excitement ran through me as I watched him exit the truck. We'd only have a couple of hours in the house together before Nathan came home, but I planned to cherish every second. First, though, I'd have to tell him about Nora.

Before I could get the words out, he walked through the door and came straight at me, enveloping my mouth in his as if he'd been dying to kiss me all day. His heart thundered against mine, the intensity of those beats giving me hope.

I nearly lost my train of thought, but as good as the kiss felt, I needed to talk to him about what happened with Nora. Reluctantly, I pushed back. "I have to tell you something, and you're not gonna like it."

A look of alarm crossed his face. "What's wrong?"

"The girl next door, Nora, she saw us earlier...when we were in the kitchen."

His eyes widened. "She saw us...having sex?"

"Yes."

"What? How the fuck did that happen?"

"She was home sick from school today. She saw my car and figured maybe I was home. She peeked through the pool area and could see right into the kitchen through the sliding glass door apparently."

He closed his eyes. "Fuck." Shaking his head, he said, "That's not good. It's the first day we've snuck around, and someone already caught us?"

"I know."

He bit his lip. "Can you trust this girl not to say anything?"

"She won't. Don't ask me how I trust an eleven-year-old...but I do."

"You'd better be right." Jace scrubbed his hand over his face. "Well, this is a fucking wake-up call. Did we mess her up?"

"I hope not. She claims she'd walked in on her mother and an ex-boyfriend once, but obviously that's not the right way for a kid to learn about sex."

"I can't believe I wasn't more careful—taking you like that in the middle of the kitchen in broad daylight. What the fuck is wrong with me?" He held out his palm. "Wait, don't answer that. I've been letting my dick make all the decisions lately."

"I can relate. I couldn't wait for you to get home. It's why I went next door. I was feeling so damn restless."

"I thought about you all freaking day. I practically got into an accident driving so damn fast to get back here." He exhaled. "Did you eat lunch?"

"No. I've been too wired to eat."

"Me too. Why don't I make us something?"

If he was hungrier for food than he was for me, Jace clearly wasn't in the mood to have sex. Now that I'd unloaded the news about Nora seeing us, I couldn't say I felt any differently.

We ended up making sandwiches and taking them out into the living room. After we ate, Jace held me on the couch for a while as we watched TV. Even though he was silent, I could somehow feel the thoughts floating around in his head. He was worried—worried about his decisions, worried we were going to get caught. We had a clear view to the front of the house from the living room window, in case Nathan were to walk in early.

I looked at the clock. "Nathan should be home in a half hour."

As much as I knew it was risky, I'd still sort of hoped Jace would initiate sex. But he never did. The closer it got to the time that Nathan normally returned, the more of a smart decision that became.

When my brother's car finally pulled in, Jace got up from the couch like a bat out of hell. I had to laugh at how swiftly he disappeared to the opposite side of the house. Was this how it would always be when Nathan came home now? Jace and I would act like a couple of scrambling birds?

"Hey..." my brother said as he entered, throwing his keys on the small table near the front door.

I stretched as I stood up from the sofa. "Hey! How was your day?"

"Good. Sold another car."

"Oh my God. Really? That's freaking awesome!"

"I know. I've been on a roll."

"What happened with you today?" he asked.

That was kind of a weird way to phrase the question. Riddled with guilt, I said, "Nothing much. Work was boring."

He drew his brows together. "No, it wasn't."

I thought I might pee my pants. "Hmm?"

"You weren't at work today."

My stomach sank. "What are you talking about?"

"I hit the drugstore on the way home and ran into that chick you work with. Denise, I think her name is? She said you were out sick and asked if you were okay."

My heart hammered in my chest.

"Oh." I looked down at my shoes, feeling so freaking guilty for lying. And he didn't even know the half of it.

"Why did you lie to me?"

My brain scrambled for an answer. "I...took a mental health day."

"Is this about that guy? Did he do something?"

Blinking, I had to think for a moment. "Colton? No. We're not seeing each other anymore, but that was my choice. This has nothing to do with him. I just needed a break today and didn't tell you because I didn't want you to think badly of me for lying to my boss."

His expression softened. "You know I wouldn't think that. Is everything okay? You struggling or something?"

As his genuine concern for me grew, so did my regret for having to lie to him. "No. I'm fine. I just felt weird admitting to you that I skipped out on work."

His brows drew together. "Well, I find that kind of troubling, to be honest."

"I'm sorry, Nathan. Okay?"

Jace walked in at that moment. "What's going on here?"

"My sister thinks it's okay to lie to me. That's what's going on."

Jace's face turned practically white.

I spoke before he could freak out too much. "Nathan ran into one of my co-workers at the drugstore. She asked him about me, since I called in sick today. I told Nathan I went to work, because I felt funny about playing hooky. I shouldn't have lied."

Jace's eyes moved between Nathan and me. He looked as guilty as I felt.

"Yeah. I agree. It was dumb to lie," he finally said.

Nathan turned to me. "It's not the fact that you stayed home from work. I could give a shit about that. It's that you thought it was okay to look me in the face and lie. It makes me wonder what the hell else you're lying to me about."

Jace swallowed. "Alright, man. Go easy on her. Everyone tells white lies from time to time."

I knew he felt the need to defend me because he felt bad for not taking some of this wrath. I smiled, but paranoia started to seep in. If my lie about work got my brother this upset, I could only imagine how badly he would lose it if he knew the real reason I'd stayed home today.

Nathan suddenly stormed out of the living room. "I'm going to get a beer."

As he left, Jace and I just looked at each other. There were no words necessary. We both knew we were fucked.

Chapter 16

Jace

Fifteen days.

For fifteen days I'd been sneaking around behind my best friend's back, sleeping with his sister and afraid to say I was loving every minute of it.

It had also been fifteen days since I'd given up my morals to be with a girl I wanted with every inch of my being, even though I knew I was wrong for her.

And it only took fifteen days for me to wonder if I was actually falling in love with Farrah. What I'd once assumed was infatuation felt stronger than ever. Would you die for someone you were infatuated with? There was no doubt in my mind that I'd die for Farrah. *Infatuation* didn't seem like the right word to describe what we had anymore.

She was the first thing I thought about when I woke up, and the last thing I thought about at night. I also found myself depressed whenever I thought about my self-imposed one-month time limit, at which time I was supposed to just forget about everything that had happened between us and move out. How was I supposed to give up these feelings and pretend they'd never existed? Yes, I wanted to protect Nathan. But at what cost?

Meanwhile, Farrah and I had been meticulous about not getting caught. No more skipping out of work or doing anything out of the ordinary that might tip Nathan off. We went to our respective jobs each day, but at night, she'd say she was hanging out with Kellianne. Her friend was the only one who knew about us, so she acted as our alibi. Farrah would even park her car at Kellianne's house in the event Nathan happened to drive by. I'd meet her there and scoop her up in my truck. Then we'd drive at least an hour away—somewhere we wouldn't be recognized—and go to a hotel. At some point close to midnight, I'd drive her back to her car at Kellianne's, and she'd head home. Then I'd go back to the hotel and spend the night there, or return to the house later, depending on the night, to change things up. We'd repeated this pattern every day for over two weeks.

Tonight was a little different, though. Nathan had scheduled family movie night. I would have preferred to be alone with Farrah and not under Nathan's microscope, but we couldn't exactly cancel. Nathan had invited Crystal, so that would serve as an extra distraction from any inappropriate looks or vibes Farrah and I might emit toward each other.

Crystal had cooked pasta for all of us, and after dinner, we hung out by the pool before we were set to watch the movie. Farrah and I were careful to stay at opposite ends of the patio, but I couldn't stop looking at her. When she'd emerge from the pool, I'd marvel at her beauty and wonder how I'd been able to have my way with her every night. Then I'd catch her staring at me from afar, and I'd smirk. She'd blush, and it would take everything in me not to race over to her and kiss her senseless. I felt like a teenager again, without a care in the world. I didn't want this feeling to end.

How was it fair that Nathan got to be openly affectionate with his girl, and I couldn't be with mine? The realization that I'd internally referred to her as *my girl* didn't even surprise me. She *was* my girl, wasn't she? Even if I couldn't announce it to the world.

At one point, while Nathan and Crystal were sucking face on one of the loungers, Farrah got up to go to the kitchen. She gave me a *come-hither* look before escaping into the house. I knew what she was trying to pull. I normally wouldn't have taken the risk right under Nathan's nose, but I was dying to kiss her.

I waited several minutes after she went inside to follow. Taking one last look at Nathan and Crystal immersed in each other, I finally got up and headed toward the house.

My dick was hard as I went to find Farrah. Like a game of hide-and-go-seek, I searched each room until I finally found her in my bedroom, which was at the far corner of the house. She leaned against the bureau. Her eyes were heavy, filled with lust as her chest rose.

My erection was already bursting through my swim trunks. I pressed my body into hers so she could feel how hard I was, wanting her to know what her behavior out there had done to me. Then I kissed her so hard I thought I might bruise her lips.

When the sound of the sliding door registered in the distance, Farrah ripped herself away and ran out of the room. There was no way I could reemerge sporting this stiffy, so I decided to walk across the hall to the shower.

The water rained down on me as I jerked my swollen cock, imagining everything I'd wanted to do to her. My eyes shut tightly as I came hard, shooting all over the tile wall.

I washed my hair and body, plotting how I was going to escape with Farrah later.

After I got dressed in my room, I found Farrah in the kitchen, still wearing her bikini. I got hard again at the sight of her. Our eyes locked, and she flashed me a wry smile. I was sure she knew why I'd taken so damn long in the bathroom.

Nathan and Crystal were already in the living room setting up the movie, leaving Farrah and me alone in the kitchen.

"How was your shower?" she asked.

"Very...imaginative."

"I bet."

"You were there in spirit." I smiled.

She looked down at herself. "I'd better change into some clothes before the movie."

My eyes fell to her mouth. "Do you have to? I kind of like it just the way you are."

"I'd better—for your sake."

I looked out toward the living room to make sure Nathan was still engrossed in conversation and whispered, "I'm gonna fuck you so hard later."

She licked her lips. "I don't expect it any other way."

I loved how fast she got turned on, how wet she always was for me the second I touched her. And there I was, hard as a rock again. *So much for that shower.*

When Farrah left to go change, I opened the refrigerator to try to cool myself down—literally stuck my head inside.

I eventually went to the living room and offered to make popcorn for everyone—you know, to try to make up for the fact that I was fucking Nathan's sister behind his back. Popcorn ought to atone for that kind of betrayal, right?

Back in the kitchen, I got to work popping and placed it into four individual bowls.

Farrah was already curled into one corner of the couch when I returned to the living room. I handed out the bowls and sat at the opposite corner of the sofa. It would have seemed too obvious if I planted myself right next to her. I tried to focus on my popcorn and not on the fact that I wanted to feel her body next to mine.

Throughout the movie, inch by inch, Farrah moved closer to me. As much as it pained me, each time I moved a little farther away. Then she'd move a little closer again. It was like a game. In Nathan's eyes, there would be no reason why I'd need to sit right up against her if there wasn't a third person on this couch. There was plenty of room for us to stretch out. Farrah smiled over at me, her eyes glinting.

Finally, she stopped, and we paid attention to the movie for a while. It was almost the end when my eyes veered in her direction. Farrah watched the final scene intently, but all I could focus on was her beautiful innocence and delicate profile. As risky as the past couple of weeks had been, these days had been the best of my life. It wasn't just the phenomenal sex; it was the fact that I felt like I could tell her anything. We could relate to each other. We wanted the same things out of life. We just wanted peace. We wanted to be happy. And we wanted to be together.

Having lots of sex.

My stare must have lingered on her a few seconds too long, because when my gaze moved over to Nathan, his eyes met mine.

• • •

That night, Farrah took off a half hour before I did to head to Kellianne's.

Later, I met up with her in the parking lot outside her friend's apartment.

As soon as she stepped into my truck, I confessed what had been weighing on me the entire ride over.

"Your brother caught me staring at you tonight."

She closed the door and put on her seatbelt. "What do you mean?"

"I was looking at you toward the end of the movie, just thinking about how beautiful you are, how happy you make me...and I got lost in thought. I looked over at Nathan, and he was glaring at me. He'd been watching me, watching you. God knows how long I'd been doing it. He gave me a look. It was obvious. He knows something, Farrah. He probably thinks I just have a crush. I don't think he suspects anything more. But still. I felt like he was on to me. And you know the most surprising thing?"

"What?"

"How little I cared." I grabbed her hand. "I'm starting to feel resentful. There he was today, enjoying his life with a woman he cares about, and I can't be with the one I care about because it might...what? Hurt his feelings? Meanwhile, he's happy, and I'm miserable."

Farrah squeezed my hand tightly. "What are you saying?"

I looked down at our joined fingers. "I'm saying... maybe we need to tell him."

Her eyes went wide. "Really?"

"I don't know. What do you think?"

"I think...the past two weeks have changed things. I feel closer to you than I ever imagined, and can't see myself walking away from this. I don't want to hurt my brother. But...I don't want to lose you more."

I nodded. "There's no way I can give you up, Farrah. No way. Nice try on my part, attempting to convince myself of that long enough to bite the bullet with you, but it was all bullshit."

Her eyes filled with hope. "Never thought I'd hear you say that. I feel the same way."

I finally started the truck and took off down the road. Still lost in my head over how to handle what felt like an impossible situation, I hadn't been paying attention to where I was going and ended up driving down the road where Farrah's parents had been killed.

She shocked me when she said, "Can you stop here?"

It had been a long day, and all I wanted was to get to the hotel. But I couldn't deny her request.

I slowed down. "Are you sure?"

She nodded.

The road was adjacent to an empty field. I pulled over onto the grass, and we both got out.

"Show me the exact spot where it happened," she said.

Every muscle in my body clenched. Reliving the most traumatic moment of my life wasn't something I'd expected to have to do tonight. But I'd do anything for her, even if it meant having to suffer through it.

She held my hand as I led her to where I remembered her father's truck being parked that day.

Feeling nauseous, I stopped. "It was right about here."

We stood together at the side of the road as a few cars whizzed by. I watched Farrah close her eyes and fall into an almost meditative state. So many emotions swirled through me. Most of all: guilt. She didn't know the full story of what had happened. In fact, if she did, she likely wouldn't want to be with me. Being here was a reminder of why the right thing to do would have been to let her go. It was too late for that, unfortunately.

"I can feel them here," she said. "I can feel their presence. It's amazing." She opened her eyes and looked at me. "I feel like they can see us, too."

My stomach churned. I knew in my heart that Farrah's parents wouldn't want us together if they were able to see us right now. I could only hope they were somehow able to forgive me. And I hoped I could garner the courage one day to tell Farrah exactly what had happened.

She reached for me, pulling me close before placing her head on my racing heart.

"I want you to let go of the pain, Jace."

I let out the breath I'd been holding since practically the moment we stopped here. "I don't know if I can do that."

"I know you live with survivor's guilt. It's time to work on letting it go. I want to help. I think we need to come here often, spend time and habituate to the pain. We can get each other through it. My therapist actually recommended this very thing, but I don't think I can do it alone. I want you with me."

Coming here repeatedly sounded like torture, but maybe her suggestion made some sense. Maybe I could get through it if I had her by my side.

It started to rain, so we walked back to where my truck was parked and got in.

I was about to start the ignition when Farrah placed her hand on my arm. "Let's just sit here for a while and listen to the rain."

Looking at the time, I tried to convince her otherwise. "It's past midnight. You sure you don't want to just get to the hotel? Maybe we can do this another day."

"Just for a little bit? I'm not ready to leave."

I nodded. If this was what she needed right now, I wasn't going to argue with her.

Over the next several minutes, I settled into a relaxed state while listening to the rain pelt my truck. Farrah leaned against my chest as I kissed the top of her head.

"I've never been this content in my life," she said. "I know I should feel the opposite, considering we have to sneak around with each other, and that's sort of dangerous, but I feel very safe when I'm with you."

"Why do you like me so much?"

Her answer was immediate. "I don't."

"You don't?" I chuckled.

She turned around. "I don't like you...I love you."

My heart felt like it was in a choke hold.

She repeated in a whisper, "I love you, Jace."

I should've told her I loved her back, but I froze. I didn't want her to think I was only saying it because she had.

Farrah straightened up to look me in the eyes. "Don't feel like you have to say anything back, okay? I just wanted you to know how I feel."

"I don't feel like I deserve your love," I said. "Even years ago, after I found out you had feelings for me, I always noticed the way you looked at me and felt undeserving of that admiration. When I came back here after all these years and found that you still looked at me that way, I felt even less deserving." Placing my hands around her face, I tried my best to tell her exactly how I felt. "You said I make you feel safe... Well, you make me feel the same. When I'm with you, I don't want anything or anyone else. I've never felt this way in my life. I—"

The sound of banging interrupted me. Then came a flash of light that hit me in the eyes. At first, it was hard to see through the raindrops. I thought it was a cop. But when I got a look at his face after lowering the window, I immediately wished to God that it *had* been the police. I turned to her. Regardless of how freaked out I was, there was nothing worse than having to witness the fear in Farrah's eyes.

She trembled. "Oh no."

How could this be happening?

How the hell did he know we were here?

"It's gonna be okay," I said, hoping that was true.

Vowing to be strong, I opened the door and got out. Farrah did the same.

"What the fuck is going on?" Nathan shouted in my face.

Trying my best to remain calm, I asked, "Why are you here?"

Nathan looked almost possessed, his eyes bugging out of his head and filled with rage in the pouring rain. "Why am I here? That's a damn good question. How about...I'm not as stupid as you think! Both of you gone every single night from the freaking house? The way you make googly eyes at each other? I didn't want to believe it for a long time. Then tonight it just hit me, like 'how stupid can you be, Nathan?'" He turned his attention to Farrah. "I put two and two together, especially after you lied to me about staying home from work that day. I decided to drive by Kellianne's after I dropped Crystal off tonight. Of course, your car was there, but no one was home. So, fine... I thought maybe by some chance I was wrong. I gave you the benefit of the doubt—figured maybe you were out with her in the middle of the goddamn night. So I decided to go home, and what do I see on my way back but a truck that looks an awful lot like Jace's parked on the side of the road—in *this* spot of all places?"

Farrah's voice was shaky. She wiped rain from her face. "We were going to tell you, Nathan."

"Oh really? That's easy to say now that I caught you, right? You've spent half your life throwing yourself at him. It finally worked for ya, huh?"

"Don't talk to her like that." I put my arm around her protectively.

He nearly spit on me when he said, "I have nothing to say to you. You can have any whore you want in this entire town, and you mess around with my sister? Seriously, how much lower can you get? You move in with us to help me out, and this is how you do it? By banging my sister, when you know damn well you're not staying in Palm Creek?"

"I'd stay for her," I immediately said.

"What? You can't be serious."

"I'm dead serious, Nathan. I wasn't expecting it to happen, but I fell in love with your sister."

Farrah's eyes met mine, and the fear in them seemed to ease a little. That wasn't the way I'd wanted to unleash those words, but here we were.

I love her.

"Love?" Nathan scoffed. "You've got to be kidding me. You don't know shit about love," he screamed. "Lust, maybe..."

Raising my voice, I yelled back, "I get that you're angry we kept this from you, but we needed to figure things out in private before throwing it on you."

"There's nothing to figure out. Because this ain't happening." He turned to her. "Not if you give two shits about your relationship with me, it ain't."

Farrah got in his face. "You're really going to sit here and say I have to choose him or you?"

Nathan flashed me a diabolical look. "You don't have any clue who you're really getting involved with, little sister."

His words were a punch to the stomach. Fear rose within me. And I knew. I knew what was coming. My instinct was to look down at my feet so I didn't have to see the pain in her eyes when she found out.

Farrah continued to defend my actions. "Of course, I know him! I trust Jace more than I trust most people. He's your best friend, for Christ's sake. You should trust him, too."

"Really. Tell me then, did you have a clue that the guy you're screwing is probably the reason our parents aren't here?"

Farrah gripped my side, my shirt now drenched. "How dare you say that!"

She had no idea what she was defending.

"Nathan, stop," I demanded.

She couldn't find out like this.

She looked at me. "Why would he say something so cruel?"

I felt the world closing in on me. The right words were nowhere to be found.

"Why would I say that?" Nathan replied. "Because it's true. The only reason the gunman fired at our parents that day was because *Jace* decided to charge at him. The guy never would have shot Mom and Dad if Jace hadn't provoked him." He looked me in the eyes. "He's the reason our parents aren't here."

He'd unleashed those words in the most terrible way, leaving me speechless to defend myself.

Farrah, though? She didn't even flinch, nor did she hesitate to stick up for me.

"How the hell do you know that, Nathan? You weren't even there."

"I didn't have to be. Jace told me."

Her eyes glistened as she turned to me. "Is that true?"

I could hardly get the words out. But I tried for her sake. "Yes...I...thought I could tackle him. I tried to... and..." My voice shook as I found myself unable to explain my rationale that day.

As I watched the pained expression on Farrah's face, I regretted the day all those years ago I'd decided to open up to Nathan about what happened. He would've never known if I hadn't told him. But about a year after the accident, the truth had been eating away at me. The fact that I'd charged at the assailant never made it into the police report because I'd never told anyone. The decision to try to get the gun from him continued to haunt me every day of my life. And now, my secret was ripped open for what felt like all the world to see—or at least my entire world: Farrah.

To my absolute shock, rather than cry or come at me with hatred, Farrah wrapped her arms around me again. "It's not your fault, Jace. Whatever you did...you thought you were protecting them."

But Nathan wouldn't leave it. "If he really thinks he didn't do anything wrong, then why did he not tell you? He hid the most important thing from you so it didn't deter his chances of taking advantage of you."

My fists tightened. "That's not fucking true, Nathan." I knew he was hurt, but I wanted to punch him right now.

"You're just another notch on his belt, Farrah."

I didn't know what was worse: the fact that Farrah had to find out this way, the fact that Nathan was hurt, or the fact that deep down, I worried he was right about me, about all of this. Farrah sticking up for me only solidified the fact that she was too easy on me. It hadn't even taken her a full minute to put all of her faith in me. I didn't deserve the huge pass she was giving me right now.

Nathan pointed his finger at me. "I thought I could forgive you for that huge mistake you made because it was unintentional. But this? Sneaking around with my sister? This was calculated. You crossed a line. I won't forgive this, and I won't *forget* everything else, either."

Farrah still hadn't let go of me. "Nathan, please. Can we all just go home and discuss this?"

"Home? He's not coming home. And you can decide whether you want to go with him or come home with me. Because you can't have it both ways."

"You've got to be kidding," she cried.

"I'm not kidding in the least." He glared at me. "You can come tomorrow when I'm at work and pack up all your shit."

Nathan said nothing else as he got back into his car and sped away, tires spinning in the wet gravel as he pulled out.

We continued to stand in the rain, both of us in shock. As I pulled Farrah into my arms, I felt helpless. Quickly, I ushered her back into my truck. We were both soaked.

This moment was my biggest nightmare: Farrah having to make a choice between her brother and me. Moreover, I knew it *wasn't* a choice. She would choose me, if I let her. If I took her with me tonight, things might never be the same between them. I wasn't sure I could live with that guilt. I already blamed myself for their parents' death, and now I was going to rip apart their family in another way?

Kissing her forehead softly, I said, "I'll drive you to your car. Then I'll go to my parents'. He needs some time to cool down, but if you leave with me tonight, this situation will get ten times worse."

She looked conflicted. "Okay...maybe you're right."

I was relieved she didn't fight me on it.

"Maybe in the morning he will have calmed down a little, but I can't go back there with you tonight."

"I'm so sorry this happened." A tear fell down her cheek.

I wiped it away. "Me too, baby. Me too."

The ride back to the house was eerily quiet. My guilt felt suffocating. What I'd done clearly hadn't hit Farrah yet. When the shock faded and it finally did, things would get ugly.

Chapter 17

Farrah

Almost a week went by before I saw Jace again. He had come to the house to get all of his things the day after Nathan caught us, but he'd done it while we were both at work. He'd called to check on me a few times, but that was the extent of it. He said it was best to stay away from each other for a while. This felt like a nightmare.

At first, I'd just assumed he was avoiding Nathan, but with each day that passed, I worried he was also avoiding *me*. I didn't want to lose my brother, but the fear of losing Jace trumped all.

In our numerous arguments over the past week, Nathan had made it clear that he wasn't backing down about Jace's betrayal. Not only could he not forgive Jace for dating me, but he'd opened a major old wound. That explained so much about why the robbery was always so difficult for them to talk about. But even with the knowledge that Jace might have caused the gunman to shoot, I couldn't blame him for everything. And I didn't understand how Nathan could. It made me sad that Jace had been living with that guilt all this time. I worried that he'd spent the past week beating himself up about what happened all over again. I was worried for us—but I was more worried for him.

When I got out of work Friday afternoon, my prayers were finally answered. Jace's truck was parked outside my office building.

Finally.

He got out and shut the door before walking over to me.

I expected him to reach out and kiss me, but he didn't. An unsettled feeling developed in my stomach.

"Can we take a walk?" he asked.

Something in his voice made my heart sink. Hope turned to dread pretty fast. We walked down the block, past a row of stores, and then around the corner to a residential neighborhood.

"I can understand why you haven't come around Nathan, but why have you been avoiding me?" I asked.

"I needed time to think—not just about what I want, but more importantly, about what's best for you. Those two things are unfortunately not one and the same." He stopped walking for a moment and looked into my eyes. "I had no right to keep that information about what really happened the day your parents died from you. I allowed you to fall in love with me without divulging something you had every right to know—something that quite frankly *should* have changed your opinion about me."

"Why? Why should it have changed my opinion? You were acting in self-defense. You thought you were doing the right thing. How could I blame you for that?"

"Farrah, there's a very good chance that the choice I made led to the outcome. Don't you see that?" He looked up at the sky, then back at me. "You might not blame me now, but when this love fog you're in subsides, it will eventually hit you. You'll wake up one day, look at me, and see nothing but the man partially responsible for your entire world being taken away."

I shook my head. "I'm sorry, but I'll *never* see it that way."

"Even if you don't, Nathan made it clear that *he* does. He can't see past it. That was something I hadn't realized until the other night. I didn't know he still harbored so much anger and blame toward me. Knowing that changes a lot."

I felt jittery with panic. "What are you saying? Get to the damn point, Jace."

"I'm saying I don't want to be responsible for you losing the only family you have left when I already feel responsible for you losing your parents. I can't live with that." He closed his eyes. "As much as I want this to work, and goddamn it, Farrah, as much as I love you, I can't put you in this situation. It would be the ultimate act of selfishness." Jace placed his head in his hands. "Walking away from you is the hardest thing I've ever had to do."

Walking away? He'd nearly knocked the wind out of me.

"Walking away..." I repeated.

The pain in his eyes was palpable. "I need to leave, Farrah."

A rush of blood traveled to my head as I pleaded, "This is a mistake."

"It's the last thing I want, but it's what's best for you, even if you don't realize it right now."

I wanted to cry, but shock prevented me from doing anything. "Where are you going?"

"Back to North Carolina. Honestly, that was always the plan. I don't belong here."

Always the plan?

My devastation turned to anger. "So that's it? You were going to leave all along? And now you're just going to pretend nothing happened between us? That you didn't fall in love with me?"

Jace covered his face with his hands. "I didn't say that. I won't forget any of it. Ever." He looked up at me. "For as long as I live, Farrah. I'll just be hoping you can forget *me*. This is not a decision I want to make. It's the decision I *have* to make. There's a difference."

I felt betrayed. And more than that, I felt disappointed in him for not fighting harder, for not being willing to risk everything to be with me. Despite that, I was still tempted to beg him not to leave. But then what? This wasn't just about Nathan anymore. It was about the wound Nathan had opened when he dropped that bomb, and Jace's inability to deal with it.

Jace was back to running from his guilt like he always did. Being with me would mean having to face it, something he didn't seem willing to do. I, on the other hand, had been willing to give everything up for him, but only as long as it brought us happiness. Right now, he was miserable and running scared. That was clear. If he wasn't willing to let the past go to allow himself to be happy, how could this ever work?

"I don't know what to say, Jace. I'm in shock."

"You don't need to say anything. There are really no words for this. The whole situation sucks. I swear to God,

I never meant to hurt you. I just feel like I need to stop this before I do irreparable harm to both of you."

I didn't want to break the news to him that he'd already done that. His leaving would never be something I'd just "get over." If he thought that, he sure as hell had underestimated my feelings for him. And I didn't know that I could ever forgive my brother for putting us in this situation.

He placed his hand on my chin. "Farrah, look at me. I need you to hear this." He exhaled. "I can't...live on the pedestal you've always put me on. I don't deserve it. That's the truth. If I stay and ruin your relationship with your brother, I'll never be able to forgive myself. I'm still working on forgiving myself for everything else. I'm nowhere near there yet. Aside from all that, I have never been capable of holding on to a relationship. There are just too many damn ways to hurt you."

Didn't he realize he'd already hurt me?

"You're really leaving?" My voice trembled.

He nodded. "Yeah."

"When?"

"Tonight."

"Tonight?" I wiped a tear and shook my head. "Jesus. I'm surprised you even bothered to say goodbye."

"I'm leaving tonight because I can't be here another minute if I know I'm not staying. It's too painful. I can barely look at you right now."

I mustered up the courage to say one last thing. "I want you to know that even though you think you're protecting me, you're making the wrong decision. I don't need you to protect me. I need you to trust me, to listen to me. Because

I would love you no matter what. All of this—all the pain, all the shit with Nathan—it all would have been worth it. But I don't know how to convince you of that."

His eyes were watery, but he didn't cry. "Please just go on with your life. I will always remember this time with you as my happiest days."

As much as I wanted to return the sentiment—because it was true—I refused to say another word. Empty inside, I had nothing left. I couldn't bear to look at him anymore.

I turned to walk back toward my building where our cars were parked, and he walked a couple of feet behind me.

When I got to my car, I stopped in front of it and turned around to meet his eyes one last time.

"I'm so sorry, Farrah."

With tears streaming down my face, I got in and started my car. As I stepped on the gas, I looked in my rearview mirror and noticed he'd stayed in the same spot, watching me drive away. Jace shrank farther and farther into the distance, but the pain I felt grew bigger and bigger. What if now I had nothing else left?

Three Years Later

Chapter 18

Jace

My girlfriend, Kaia, seemed understandably upset when I returned to our table at the Japanese restaurant. Her eyes shot daggers. "Do you mind telling me what the hell that was all about?"

There was no easy way to say it. "That was her."

"That was..." She blinked. "That was...*Farrah*?"

"Yes."

Her face turned red. "Of all places we could eat lunch, you take me to the restaurant where she works? What the hell, Jace?"

"For Christ's sake, Kaia. I didn't know. I had no idea she worked here. You think I would have put you through that intentionally?"

Kaia's eyes softened. "You swear you didn't know?"

"Of course not."

This restaurant didn't even exist the last time I was in Palm Creek. To the best of my knowledge, Farrah hadn't waitressed a day in her life, so the fact that she worked here made no sense. I'd been looking for a peaceful lunch after a horrendous week. Instead, I got the shock of my life.

Still reeling from my run-in with Farrah outside, I wiped sweat from my forehead.

"She's beautiful," Kaia said. "You know, like, you've heard that saying—the face that launched a thousand ships? Helen of Troy, I believe? That girl is the face that drove Jace out of town."

There was no safe way to agree with that. Kaia was a ticking time bomb as it was. So I stayed silent.

"Well, it's not like I didn't think she would be beautiful," Kaia continued. "Why else would you have risked everything for her?"

I couldn't disagree with that, either. Once again, this was an appropriate moment to shut up. Farrah had looked as beautiful as ever, albeit with a coldness in her eyes I didn't recognize.

Kaia fluffed out her cloth napkin almost violently. "What did she say to you?"

"We didn't talk much. She basically...left the building. I caught up to her along the main road after she crossed the parking lot. She asked me what I was doing in town, and I told her my mother had died. She seemed upset to hear that. She gave me her condolences...asked how my father was. Then she said she had to go and kept walking. That was the end of it."

"Why the hell did she run away in the first place? She couldn't say hello?" She laughed angrily. "Or at least she could've done her job and taken our order."

It killed me that Farrah had run like that. But she'd never expected to see me sitting there. Fleeing was a knee-jerk reaction. I should know. "I think she was just in shock and didn't know how to handle it."

"Boy, you must have really fucked her up to make her run like that."

I hoped Kaia wasn't right. I hoped Farrah had gotten over what I'd done to her by now. But all signs pointed to the fact that she hadn't. In any case, I once again chose not to address my girlfriend's comments.

This entire thing sucked. Kaia wasn't supposed to see Farrah. Heck, I wasn't even supposed to see her. Kaia and I had been in Palm Creek for a week. She was leaving tomorrow to fly back to Charlotte, while I stayed to help my dad after the sudden loss of my mother to a heart attack.

Kaia and I had been together for a year. She never understood why I wouldn't come home, why I wouldn't ever take her back to Florida with me to meet my parents. My mother and father had come to Charlotte a couple of times to visit me that first year after I left, but that had been before I met Kaia. So she'd never had a chance to meet my mother.

All Mom ever wanted was for me to come home to Florida again, and I couldn't grant her wish—until she died. No one had seen that heart attack coming. I couldn't remember my mother being sick once. It wasn't supposed to happen like this. My father had been the one with cancer. Now Dad was fine, and my mother, who was the glue that held our family together, was gone. Fifty-nine years old. Not that I wished my almost seventy-year-old father had died instead, but life was so damn unfair. Losing Mom was probably the only thing that could have deflected my attention from all the other reasons coming home was traumatic. The pain of her death cut so deep that nothing else could compete with it.

Up until the past week, my life had been pretty good. After a couple of years of feeling lost, I'd pushed myself to move on, and I'd managed to escape into a comfortable life with Kaia in the past year. She and I had met through a mutual friend. I cared for her, but it was getting to the point where she wanted more of a commitment from me, and I'd yet to take that step. We'd been discussing moving in together, but I kept putting it off.

After Dad called to tell me about my mother, Kaia insisted on coming to Palm Creek with me. When she sensed my extreme discomfort, she grilled me until I finally came clean on the circumstances under which I'd left town three years ago. I told her about everything—from the shooting to my relationship with Farrah and the fallout with Nathan.

The drive down here from Charlotte had been tense. Kaia kept wanting to talk, analyzing everything I'd confessed. Meanwhile, I was numb because—for fuck's sake—my mother had just died; I didn't have the mental energy to analyze anything.

Kaia believed I must have unresolved feelings for Farrah. It didn't take a scientist to figure that out. Still, I refused to acknowledge how I felt, because from the day I left, I'd done everything in my power to block out the mess I'd made, which meant trying to forget Farrah. I hadn't *felt* anything in three years. And now with my mother gone, I had bigger things to do than dig up old pain. But damn if my chest didn't ache after seeing Farrah again. All of the feelings I'd buried seemed to smack me in the face at once.

My mind was all over the place as I stared blankly at Kaia from across our table at the restaurant. Someone finally figured out our waitress was MIA and came around to take our order. She brought us two waters and placed a pot of hot tea in the center of the table. Kaia ordered the teriyaki chicken. My brain was too fried to think about what I wanted—not to mention that I had no appetite—so I told the waitress to bring me the same thing.

Kaia poured some tea, and instead of drinking it, she stared down into the steaming cup. She tapped her fingers along the porcelain. "Listen, I've been thinking a lot about this...and after what happened just now, I feel even more strongly about it."

I'd started to pour some tea but stopped. "What?"

"I think we need to take a break."

"You're breaking up with me..."

"No. Not exactly. I just think you need to figure out all the shit that's keeping you from being able to move on. And I think you need to do it without being tied down." Her eyes became watery. "I love you. But I realize now that there's a lot you haven't dealt with. Until you do, I'm not sure you can ever be the man I need."

"You don't think that sounds like you're breaking up with me?"

"Well, it's not a breakup. But it's a break. A separation. I won't blame you for anything that happens while you're figuring shit out here. Do what you need to do. But if you come back to me, your baggage can't come with you."

What exactly did she want me to figure out? "There's nothing for me to figure out here other than taking care of my father for a while."

"That's not how I see it. Especially not after what happened just now." She took a long sip of her tea.

"Look, you can't even tell me when you're coming back to Charlotte. I understand you need to stay here for a while for your dad, but I also think you need to deal with the other stuff you're running from." She paused. "As much as I love you, I have to let you go right now."

I wasn't sure how to feel. Disappointed? Relieved? I was basically numb.

Kaia's last boyfriend had left her to go back to his ex-wife. So I could understand her fear when it came to unfinished feelings for an ex.

I nodded. "If that's what you feel you need to do, I'm not going to try to stop you."

Our food arrived, interrupting the conversation at the worst possible moment.

We began to eat in silence.

Even though taking a break had been her decision, she seemed upset. I think she might've expected me to put up more of a fight. But that was never gonna happen. This week had sucked the fight right out of me.

• • •

My father sat alone in the living room when I returned to the house that night. He had only a small lamp on, so the majority of the house was dark. So goddamn depressing.

"Old man, it's me." I threw my keys down on a table.

"You're back sooner than I thought. You said you weren't coming back until tomorrow."

"Kaia left. She booked an earlier flight. I just took her to the airport and checked out of the hotel to come stay with you."

Kaia hadn't felt comfortable staying at my dad's house this past week, so we'd gotten a room at a hotel nearby.

"She seemed like a nice girl."

"She was—until she dumped me." I chuckled.

"What?" My father straightened in his brown recliner.

"She thinks we need to take a break while I'm here."

"She wants to date other people?"

"No. I think it's more about protecting herself because she thinks I might not be coming back to Charlotte for a while."

"You don't have to stay here, son."

I didn't want my father to feel bad about this. "It's not up for debate, Dad," I explained quickly. "It's what Mom would've wanted. It's the least I can do."

"She wouldn't want you to let a nice girl go so you could babysit me. She only ever wanted you to be happy. She always felt horrible about why you left. It's why she never gave you shit about leaving so abruptly three years ago. She understood. When you told us about Kaia, she was happy—even if she wished things would have worked out for you and Farrah."

As soon as he mentioned Farrah's name, my nerves spiked. "Speaking of Farrah...I think Mom might have been playing some games up in heaven today."

"Yeah?"

"I took Kaia out to lunch at that Japanese restaurant on Seminole Highway. Farrah works there now, apparently. She was assigned to our table and bolted when she saw me."

"You're shitting me. She works at the Japanese restaurant?"

"Evidently...yeah. I ran after her and spoke to her briefly. I told her about Mom. The whole thing was unbelievable."

"Well, that explains the flowers from her that came today."

That jolted me. "Are you serious?"

"Was just about to tell you." He pointed. "Right over there on the table."

I walked over to a bouquet of white roses mixed with other flowers and lifted the note.

Dear Mr. Muldoon,

I ran into Jace today, who told me about Faye. I'm so very sorry for your loss. Her warm smile and kindness will always be something I'll remember. Please accept our deepest condolences and know that you are in our prayers.

Fondly,

Farrah and Nathan Spade

Continuing to stare down at the card, I said, "She must have ordered these the second she ran away from me."

"Well, it was a very nice gesture."

I had to agree. It touched me that Farrah had done this, despite how I'd treated her. It spoke volumes about the type of person she was.

I hadn't been able to stop thinking about her all day, despite the drama of my girlfriend dumping me... or forcing a break—whichever it was. It was a relief that Kaia wasn't here, though, to continue analyzing my every expression and reaction to the mention of Farrah's name.

Farrah's running away haunted me. I kept replaying the scene in my head—not only the way she ran, but how fast all the feelings I'd harbored for her came flooding back the moment I looked in her eyes. It was unnerving, but not surprising, considering I'd only ever buried my emotions instead of dealing with them. That was my MO.

I finally put the small card back in the envelope and placed it on the table. "Have you eaten, Dad?"

"I'm fine."

"You haven't, then?"

He hesitated. "No."

My poor father was like a fish out of water. I wasn't sure if he hadn't eaten because he wasn't hungry, or because my mother was no longer here to cook for him.

I opened the cabinet. "Want some pancakes?"

"Only if you're making them for yourself."

"I'm actually getting kind of hungry again, yeah," I lied.

Dad moved over to the table and sat with his head in his hands. I grabbed the nonstick pan and turned on the heat. It broke my heart to see him so sad and helpless. I found a bowl and started mixing the ingredients. As I poured the batter into the pan and watched it sizzle, tears formed in my eyes. For the first time since coming home, I let them fall. It was the only time I'd cried since the moment I pulled onto I-95 heading north three years ago.

This simple thing—making pancakes—was something I'd watched my mother do hundreds of times. I'd been going through the motions all week, and in this ordinary moment, staring into a pancake pan, it finally hit me that she was gone.

• • •

Over the next week, I spent each day helping my father go through Mom's things, deciding which items to keep and which to donate. Sifting through a dead loved one's belongings, which still smelled like her, was the purest kind of torture. Dad broke down multiple times in the process.

One afternoon, I needed respite from that routine, so I decided to go to the grocery store and run some errands. I hadn't been planning to drive by Farrah's house, but somehow I ended up passing the road I needed to take to get home. Before I knew it, I was approaching her and Nathan's neighborhood and decided to turn down their street.

My heart raced at the sight of a small child playing out in front of their house. The little girl was in one of those red-and-yellow plastic cars. A rush of adrenaline hit. *Whose kid is that?* Nathan's? Farrah's? I'd specifically asked my mother not to seek out information on them, and to the best of my knowledge, she'd never run into them in the three years I'd been gone; she would have told me if she had. I had no idea what had transpired with them because I'd made a conscious effort to stay out of their lives.

Totally freaked, I got out of my truck and approached the driveway.

Jesus Christ.

The more I looked at the little girl, the more worried I became. She couldn't have been more than a few years old, maybe younger. I did the math in my head, and a terrifying thought occurred to me. Could she have been *my* kid? Her hair was almost black like mine. Maybe that thought was crazy, but it wasn't out of the realm of possibility.

Before my nerves had a chance to explode into full-fledged panic, a woman rushed out and took the child into the house through the garage. She turned around once and flashed me an alarmed look. Apparently, I'd gotten a little too close and had been mistaken for a perpetrator.

Who is that woman?

The mother? A sitter?

A friend of Farrah's, maybe?

I went from possibly having an illegitimate child one second to just dazed and confused the next.

As I continued to stand in front of the house staring at it blankly, a voice to my left said, "Hey, I know you."

I turned to find a teenage girl who looked vaguely familiar. Then it hit me. *Nora.* The eleven-year-old who lived next door was now a teenager.

Well, I'll be damned. I felt so old. "Hey." I moved toward her. "Nora, right?"

"Yeah. You're Jace. I remember you. You used to live there." She tilted her head. "Were you looking for Farrah?"

"Um...no. Not really. I was just driving by and... stopped."

"They don't live here anymore."

My eyes widened. "They don't?"

"No. They moved about two years ago."

My stomach sank. "Where do they live now?"

"Off of Tamarind."

That was sort of a crappy neighborhood compared to this one.

"Are you still in contact with Farrah?"

She frowned. "Unfortunately, no. I lost touch with her after she moved. She was always so sweet to me, though. I miss her a lot."

Yeah. I can relate.

Nora grinned. "I'll never forget the time she bought me Shawn Mendes tickets. I'm over him now. But back then? He was everything." She laughed. "I remember going next door one day to tell her my mom said it was okay if she took me to the concert. I was all excited to ask her to go with me. I caught her at a bad time, though. She was crying and upset. I asked her what was wrong, and she said you had left town. I'll never forget that. She didn't want to talk about it. After that, I was afraid to ask her to go with me because I thought she wouldn't be in the mood. I ended up going with my mother, but I would've rather gone with Farrah."

Jesus. I needed to get away from this one before she told me something else I didn't want to hear. "Thanks for letting me know they moved."

"No problem." She disappeared inside her house.

My pulse continued racing as I stood on the sidewalk. It would take a while to get over that long-ass minute where I thought I might've had a daughter. How fucked-up would that have been?

I returned to my truck and rested my head on the back of the seat to calm down for a few minutes before heading home.

Thoughts of Farrah tormented me the rest of that night. I had questions. Lots of them. Why the hell did they move to a shitty neighborhood? Farrah had loved that house, that pool. I suspected it wasn't her choice to leave.

• • •

The following afternoon, Dad napped while I got some work done on my laptop in the living room. I was fortunate that my property management job allowed me to handle a majority of my duties remotely. I needed to delegate more while away, but managing everything from here had been doable so far. I'd probably have to fly to Charlotte once or twice during my stay here if they needed me on site, though. Between my job and helping Dad out at Muldoon Construction, I was plenty busy.

The doorbell rang, interrupting my work. I got up to see who it was—probably yet another neighbor coming by with a casserole. Or maybe it was someone from Mom's church checking in on my father. It had been a couple of weeks now since my mother died, but people still trickled in from time to time.

When I opened the door, I froze.

Shit.

Standing before me was the last person I ever expected to see.

I blinked several times. "Nathan..."

His eyes were piercing. "Hi, Jace."

I swallowed. "Hey."

"Long time no see."

My body was rigid. I didn't know whether to hug him or brace myself for a punch.

"Can I come in?" he asked.

Still in shock, I nodded several times before the answer came out. "Uh...yeah."

Moving aside to let him enter, I immediately noticed he was limping. One of his legs was pretty much dragging the other. Nathan had also gained some weight and looked...rough, for lack of a better word.

"What happened to you?" I asked.

Still struggling to make it to the other side of the room, he said, "I got into an accident two years ago."

I tensed. "Accident? What kind of accident?"

"I was drunk and got behind the wheel. Stupidest thing I ever did. I was lucky, though. Didn't kill anyone. But I fucked myself up, and I've been out on disability ever since."

Damn. Things started to add up. My chest hurt. It pained me that I'd had no idea what he'd been through.

"Man, I'm sorry."

"It's my own fault. Nothing to be sorry about." He looked around. "Anyway, I came to tell you that *I'm* very sorry about your mom. I was shocked to hear."

"Thank you. We're still in shock, too."

He walked over to the couch. "Can I sit?"

"Yeah. Of course."

As cordial as he was, I waited for the bomb to drop, waited for him to lose it on me. Although, this person didn't seem like the same Nathan who'd raged at me the last time I saw him.

After he sat, I took a seat on the chair across from him. I stayed silent until he spoke.

"Where's your dad?" he asked.

"He's napping."

Nathan nodded, rubbing his palms together.

A clock ticking in the corner of the room was the only sound. This was awkward as fuck.

"I'm sure you're...surprised that I'm here," he finally said.

"That's an understatement."

"When Farrah told me she ran into you, I couldn't believe you were back in town, and when she told me why, I felt horrible." He shut his eyes. "Well, I've felt horrible when it came to you for a long time." He let out a long breath and started to bounce his knees up and down.

"Take it easy. I'm not going anywhere," I said.

He stopped bopping his legs. "I handled everything all wrong with you, Jace. I messed up big time, and I need to apologize."

Wow. I didn't know how to respond. My first inclination was to tell him it was okay, because he'd apparently been through more than enough to make up for whatever he did to me. But another part of me wanted to tell him to fuck off. I'd never been more confused in my life.

"Nathan, I don't know—"

"Hear me out," he interrupted.

"Okay..."

"I never should've used what happened to my parents against you the night I caught you and Farrah. I'd promised you I would never tell anyone what you confessed to me, and instead I used it as ammunition. I was angry at you for messing around with my sister. What I did was downright cruel. I want you to know that I don't blame you in any way for what happened to them."

Again, I didn't know whether to be angry or relieved to hear him say that. It felt like too little too late. "It would've been nice to know that three damn years ago," I said loudly. It seemed the anger had won out.

"It wasn't clear to me then. It took a while for me to see things the way I do now. My biggest fear back then was losing Farrah. I was sure you'd end up hurting her—or worse, taking her back to Charlotte with you. I was selfish more than anything else. When I caught you sneaking around with her, I felt betrayed. But over time, I've realized my anger was a reflection of my own struggle, not a reflection of you or anything you might have done."

"When did you figure all this out?"

"Unfortunately, being out of work for so long, I've had a lot of time to think and reflect on my life. I started going to church, believe it or not."

"Really? You'd never stepped inside a church, from what I recall..."

He chuckled. "I know. I was depressed and desperate. Just walked in one day in the middle of the week. It was me and a bunch of old people. But they were friendly, and I kept going on Sundays after that. There's this counselor I met through the parish who volunteers his services. I've had a lot of meetings with him. He's not a doctor or anything, but he's become a good friend and helped me realize that all of my actions came down to a fear of being alone, of abandonment. My dependence on Farrah wasn't healthy, and neither was my attitude toward you. It was more than just being angry at you for sneaking around behind my back. That shit went back to childhood."

He lost me a little. "What do you mean...childhood?"

"I've always envied you—your ability to excel at everything that you tried, your ability to get girls, your ability to make something of yourself. In my mind, you had it all. It felt like you were taking the one thing I cherished, the only family I had left, when you could've had practically any other thing in the world. I didn't understand why you needed Farrah, too. It was years of jealousy and envy coming to a head. That—along with never having dealt with my parents' deaths—I just...snapped."

I rubbed my temples. My head felt like it was going to explode as my emotions wavered between relief and anger over having wasted the past three years.

Through my silence, he continued. "It took me nearly getting killed in that accident to work on myself enough to see things clearer," he said. "I've wanted to contact you so many times, but I never had the guts because I was ashamed of how I handled everything." He exhaled. "But when I found out about your mother and that you were back, I knew I couldn't put it off any longer."

I sighed. "I get why you were disappointed that Farrah and I went behind your back, but I never meant to hurt you. My feelings for Farrah were genuine."

"I don't think I realized how deep Farrah's feelings for you were until you left. It fucked her up. I understand that it was more than just a fling between you two. It had nothing to do with me, but I *made* it about me."

My heart lurched. I didn't want to hear how badly I'd devastated Farrah, even if I'd always known that was the case.

"She was messed up," he said again. "But after a while, things changed. I don't know how to explain it. She seemed to get over it, but at the same time, she sort of hardened. And she's been that way ever since." He shook his head. "I blame myself."

"How is she handling things with you...after your accident and everything?" I asked, though I wasn't sure I wanted to know. "How is she overall?"

"The accident happened about a year after you left. I was in a rehabilitation center for a while. When I was released, Farrah had to take care of me before I built my strength back up. There were several months where I could hardly walk. She'd come home from work and have to deal with my shit. It was a wonder she didn't lose her mind."

"All of this...it's why you guys moved..."

"Yeah. How did you know?"

"I drove by. Saw another family living there. The girl next door confirmed you didn't live there anymore."

"I had to stop working and started collecting disability. We couldn't afford that mortgage. I knew if we sold the house and bought a smaller one, there'd be some money left over for Farrah's education."

"She's not working at the law firm anymore, I take it?"

"She finally started school last year." He smiled. "Because a lot of her classes are in the morning, she quit the old job, and now she waits tables at Mayaka. We used the last of our savings—the money we got from the big house—to pay off the shitty place we live in now. So the money she makes can go toward school."

It made me proud that Farrah was finally in college. It seemed like the only good thing out of any of the stuff he'd just told me.

"I'm sorry things have been tough."

"Enough about me," Nathan said. "How have you been? How long are you here?"

"I don't know. At least a month or two. Maybe more. When Mom died, my father was in the process of selling the company and getting ready to retire. He has a buyer, but it hasn't changed hands yet. It's not set in stone. I don't know what to do with him—whether to help him sell the house and take him back to North Carolina with me or what. He's lost without her."

"I can only imagine. Your parents were the poster children for a happy marriage."

I took a few moments to soak in the sight of Nathan in front of me. "I have to say, it's pretty surreal, sitting here having an actual conversation with you. I didn't think I'd ever experience this again."

"I may be in the worst physical shape of my life, but mentally I see clearer. The problem is, I've already fucked up so much—my relationship with Farrah included. I don't know how to fix things." He shook his head. "Three years ago, I wouldn't have ever thought I'd say this, but I wish she'd ended up with you, rather than the asshole she's dating now."

My entire body tightened. "Why? What's the story there?"

"He's a condescending jerk. His family owns the Bianchi chain of liquor stores. He thinks just because he has money, he's better than everyone."

Blood rushed to my head. "Really..."

"Remember Crystal?"

"Yeah..." I wished he would've elaborated on Farrah's situation a bit more.

"That didn't last long at all. I haven't had a serious girlfriend since her. Kind of hard to impress the ladies when you're limping around like I am." He sighed. "I can't complain, though. I'm lucky to be alive."

I nodded.

Nathan stayed that afternoon and chatted with me until my father woke up. He gave Dad his condolences, and before he left, he gave me their new address and told me I should stop by the house sometime.

I didn't know how I felt about that. I didn't want to upset Farrah. But she was just about the only thing on my mind.

Chapter 19

Jace

A week after Nathan's surprise visit, I still couldn't get over his change of heart. Between work and dealing with Dad, I'd managed to stay busy enough not to do anything rash. As the days passed, though, the need to see Farrah became more urgent. But given what I'd learned and the way our first encounter had gone, I had no idea what to expect if I showed up at her house.

However, Nathan's putting aside the past and reaching out motivated me to grow some damn balls and make the first move. I texted Nathan to ask if he'd be okay with me coming by to talk to Farrah. He responded that he had physical therapy this morning, but Farrah didn't have class today. He said she would probably be home until she went to work at three this afternoon. I asked him to tell her I would be stopping by around two. He confirmed, but he didn't say anything about her reaction. I took that as a cue that she was okay with it. At least I hoped so.

As I drove to their house, I had no idea what I was going to say to her. Instead of rehearsing something I would likely mess up anyway, I'd spent the day ruminating. Nathan's new outlook on everything still made me somewhat angry. What was the point of my leaving, of breaking his sister's heart, only to have him be so forgiving in the end? It was amazing what a brush with death could do to someone. I supposed there was no way of knowing exactly how things would have played out if I'd stayed; things could've ended up worse than they were now.

My palms were sweaty as I pulled up to their small property. This house was easily a third of the size of their last one. It hurt me that Farrah no longer had the pool she used to love so much. But at least they'd paid this house off and didn't have to worry about a mortgage.

I exited my truck and walked to their front door. With stiff knuckles, I knocked.

After a moment, Farrah opened the door. My heart clenched. I'd hoped for a smile but got nothing but a blank stare. Even so, she was somehow more beautiful than ever. Draped over her breasts, her chestnut hair was longer than I remembered. She'd lined her eyes in a way that brought out their gorgeous hazel color with gold speckles.

Feeling instantly unwelcome, I lifted my hand. "Hey."

She swallowed and, in a barely audible voice, said, "Hi."

I looked over my shoulder briefly. "Are you gonna run from me again? I've got my tennis shoes on this time. I came prepared."

"I really do want to run, to be honest."

Ouch. I fiddled with my thumbs. "Can I come in?"

She stepped aside. "Sure."

Looking around, I noticed some of the furniture was the same, like the old couch where we used to sit for movie night. It was about the only thing that felt familiar right now.

"How are you?" I asked.

"I've been better."

"I get it."

She looked down at her flip-flops, and I did the same, noticing the red color painted on her toes.

Farrah finally looked up at me. "I ran the other day because my reaction to seeing you scared me a little. Your leaving hurt me badly, but I've come a long way from three years ago. I don't ever want to be held hostage by my emotions like that again. I would've done anything to be with you. It was pathetic."

"Pathetic? I don't remember you that way at all."

Her voice grew louder. "Why did you want to see me, Jace?"

I ran my hands through my hair. "I just want to know you're okay."

"For what? So you can feel better about the decision you made to leave? What's done is done. Life goes on. I survived. I've moved on. I don't like being reminded of a time I'd rather forget."

The pain was reflected in her eyes. As much as she'd tried to sell me on the fact that she'd moved on, that certainly wasn't the vibe I got, even if she did seem different from the girl I'd left behind.

There was so much I wanted to say, but all that came out was, "I'm sorry."

She deflected. "How is your father?"

"Pretty lost."

“I’m sorry to hear that.” Her eyes softened. “I know how much she meant to you. It was devastating to hear that Faye passed so suddenly.”

“Thank you.” I took a few steps toward her, noticing she moved back the same number of steps. “And thank you for the flowers.”

Her voice was low. “Of course.”

Farrah’s rigid body language told me not to get comfortable, so I opted not to sit, instead continuing to stand across from her while keeping my space.

“I was shocked that Nathan came by to see me,” I said. “It meant a lot. I never expected that he’d want to talk to me again, let alone initiate a visit.”

“Yeah. Well, he’s changed a lot since his accident... finding Jesus and all.”

“I can see that.”

“In many ways, it’s like he and I switched places. He’s much more apt to forgive and forget now. Whereas I’m less trusting than I used to be.”

Well, that was a clear message. For a moment, the silence was deafening. Every time she looked me in the eyes, she’d catch herself and look anywhere else. My eyes, however, stayed fixed on her.

“Who was the woman with you that day at the restaurant?” she finally asked.

“My girlfriend...well, my ex-girlfriend now. I don’t really know where she and I stand. We’re taking a break while I’m here.”

Farrah fidgeted. “I see.” She looked over at the clock. “Well, I actually have to go. I’m going to be late for my shift.”

Shit. I'd barely had a chance to speak to her, and with her being so cold, I didn't feel comfortable pushing things.

"Do you...need a ride?"

"No."

That was a dumb question, but I was desperate for more time with her.

"Okay. You were walking home the other day. I wasn't sure if you had a car."

"I chose to walk that day for exercise. I have a car." She pointed out the window. "That's my Focus parked across the street."

Turning around, I spotted the small, blue vehicle. It was a heck of a lot better than the piece of crap she used to drive.

"Okay...well...I guess I'll let you get going."

Farrah wrapped her arms around herself. "Yeah..."

Feeling defeated, I forced myself to walk away. The superficial conversation we'd just had left me unsettled. This wasn't how it was supposed to go. I hadn't said everything I'd wanted to say to her. She'd had her guard up. I'd often wondered what a reunion with Farrah would be like. This was nothing like I'd imagined.

A nagging feeling persisted as I got back in my car and drove off. I'd finally had an opportunity to face her, and I completely blew it.

The farther I drove, the more I felt like I needed to go back and pour my heart out—tell her how sorry I was for leaving, how much I regretted hurting her. It wouldn't matter if she said nothing. I should've said more.

Unable to accept my cowardice, I turned my car around and drove back toward her house. Slowing down, I could see her getting into her car in the distance. I stopped short of where she was parked. Farrah didn't see me because she had her head on the steering wheel. I watched as she sat for a moment, looking distraught.

This changed things. It was proof that her cold demeanor was a façade, that she was affected by my visit. Anything more I might have to say would only further upset her, though. She had a right to this private moment, and it felt wrong to disrupt her, especially since I was the cause. As much as it pained me not to comfort her, I did what I knew she'd want—I drove away slowly so she'd never know I'd come back.

• • •

A few days later, I was surprised to see Nathan's name pop up on my phone.

I answered, "Hey, man."

"Hey. Are you busy?"

"No." I scratched my head. "What's up?"

"I was wondering if you had time to stop by. My car won't start. I don't think it's the battery. Something else is up. I was hoping you could take a look. I could take it to the mechanic, but I don't really trust him. The last time I went there, it cost me a pretty penny for a shit job."

I suspected he might've been looking for an excuse to get together to gauge where things stood with us.

"Yeah. Sure. I can come by."

"Doesn't have to be right away. I know you must be working at this time of day."

"It's no big deal. My job is pretty flexible. I could use a break from staring at the computer screen."

"Cool."

There was one thing I needed to know first, though. "Is Farrah home?"

"No. She's in class, and she has a shift at the restaurant tonight. She usually goes there straight from school. She won't be home at all."

"Okay, good. I don't want to upset her." I paused. "Did she mention anything after I came to see her?"

"I asked her how it went, but she said she didn't want to talk about it. I didn't push."

"Yeah. It was tense. I didn't stay long." I exhaled. "Anyway...I can be there in a bit."

• • •

After two hours, I was able to get Nathan's car running again. He mostly stood around, watching me as I worked. We reminisced a little about old times, though certainly not about anything that happened three years ago.

He went into the house at one point and returned with a small paper menu.

"I'm ordering a pizza, if you're hungry," he said.

"I'm starving, actually. Sounds good."

Twenty minutes later, the pizza and breadsticks arrived. He paid the delivery guy, and we took the food inside.

Nathan set the pizza box on the coffee table in the living room and brought a couple of sodas from the kitchen. While I was fixing his car, Nathan had told me he'd been sober since his accident, so I figured he wouldn't offer me a beer. He had the latest Formula One race from this past weekend on DVR, and he pulled it up after I'd told him I hadn't had a chance to watch it yet. Watching Formula One together used to be one of our favorite things to do.

Even though this resembled old times, I knew things would never be the same again. But maybe this was the start of a new normal.

Halfway into the race, I looked out the window and saw a car pull into the driveway. "You expecting someone?"

"No," he said before leaning his head out to see better. "Shit."

"What?"

"It's Farrah and her dumbass boyfriend."

My pulse sped up as my fight-or-flight mode kicked in. "I thought you said she wasn't coming home."

"She told me she wasn't."

Damn it.

I'd never in my entire life wished for the power to magically disappear until now. I would've left if I'd known this might happen. Standing up from the couch, I braced myself. My heart felt ready to jump out of my chest as the door opened.

Farrah was the first to step inside. When she spotted me, she froze in her tracks.

She glared at Nathan as she spoke to me. "What are you doing here?"

"Nathan needed help fixing his car. I didn't think you'd be home."

"Why aren't you in class?" Nathan asked.

"My professor was sick. They canceled it. Niles met me at school and took me out to lunch."

When her boyfriend walked in, all of our heads turned toward him in unison. No one said anything. He was tall, with brown hair and a Roman nose—average-looking, at best. No one would ever be good enough for her in my mind, but after what Nathan had said about him, I disliked him before he'd even opened his mouth.

"What's going on?" he said. Before anyone could answer, he bent to take the last slice of pizza from the box.

What a dick.

Farrah broke the ice. "Niles, this is my brother's friend, Jace."

"Hey," he said with his mouth full. "That your truck parked outside?"

"Yeah."

"You must love your fuel economy in that thing." He snorted.

This dude can't be serious.

I squinted at him, not even dignifying his rude comment with a response. I could immediately see why Nathan hated this guy. Even if he wasn't condescending, I'd probably hate him no matter what. But now, I *really* hated him.

Farrah disappeared into the kitchen, but Niles—*what a pompous name*—decided to stay in the living room.

"So, Nate, have you given any thought to my job offer?"

Nathan and I gave each other the eye. He hated being called *Nate*. Something told me he'd corrected this douche plenty of times in the past.

"I already told you why I wouldn't be taking that job."

"Because you'd rather mooch off the government?"

Whoa. My fists tightened. If I didn't think it would piss off Farrah, I might've actually punched him.

"You know I don't drink alcohol. Why the fuck would I work in a liquor store?"

"Because you should put aside your weaknesses for a good opportunity. I told you, I could get you a managerial job."

"And I told you I don't want one. Why do you keep asking me?"

Farrah returned, looking annoyed. "Stop bugging my brother."

He spoke with his mouth full again. "I'm only trying to help him."

Farrah's eyes locked with mine. The urge to get her alone, to talk to her, to make sure she was okay—especially given this asshole—overwhelmed me. All the things I'd needed to say to her the other day felt like they were choking me.

So, I did something I hoped she would understand, mouthing a message she had once given me. *Please.*

Farrah blinked. I was crazy for hoping she would entertain it. Several moments of silence passed.

But then...

She turned to her boyfriend. "Niles, I think I'm gonna take a nap before work. I'm not feeling that great."

"You want me to lie down with you?"

The pizza turned in my stomach.

"No," she said. "You should go help your grandmother with that thing she called you about anyway."

Yeah. Go on and help your grandmother, dickhead.

"Okay." He stood up, dumping his pizza crust in the box. "Have a good night at work, babe."

When he walked over to give her a kiss, I had to turn away.

Relief washed over me the second the door closed behind him.

Chapter 20

Farrah

"Jace and I are going to talk."

Nathan looked between Jace and me like he'd missed something. He had, of course. Because there'd been no conversation, just a secret message he had no clue about.

My brother stood. "Want me to leave? Give you some privacy?"

"No," I said. "We'll take a walk." I looked up at Jace. "Come on."

He followed me out the door. A gentle breeze blew my hair around as I took a deep breath in, feeling so gosh darn nervous and unprepared to be alone with him.

"Where do you wanna go?" he asked.

Moving some of my hair behind my ear, I said, "Around the block is good."

We set off down the street.

Jace slipped his hands into his pockets. "Thank you for figuring out what I was asking."

"Well, you stole my line." I forced a smile.

"I did." He grinned, seeming relieved.

As much as I tried to fight my feelings, the physical reaction I had to being next to him was no different than it used to be. Which was exactly why I needed to nip this in the bud.

"Nathan's not crazy about your boyfriend," he said. "And now I can see why."

"Nathan's not crazy about anyone who takes my attention away from him."

"I think it's more than that in this case. But as long as you're happy." He searched my eyes. "You *are* happy, right?"

I wasn't sure how to answer that. I wasn't unhappy, but true happiness wasn't something I'd felt for a very long time. Neither was it something I strived for or expected anymore.

"I'm at peace. Peace is more important to me than happiness. I made a vow to myself after you left that I wouldn't allow my happiness to depend on other people. It has to come from within. I'm still working on it. But I don't expect anyone else to make me happy—least of all a man."

"So, you're saying that guy doesn't make you happy, then..."

I sighed. "Niles is not perfect. But he's what I need right now. It's easy with him. I don't want to be with someone who'll leave me devastated and take my heart and soul when he goes."

Jace's breath hitched. "So you're saying you're with this guy because you don't care one way or the other if things work out?"

"It feels safe." I shrugged. "It is what it is."

Jace searched my eyes. "Listen, I didn't ask you to make time for me so I could undermine your decisions. I just want to say what I needed to say to you the other day before my nerves got the best of me."

I stopped walking. "What is there left to say? Nothing is going to change what happened."

As we stood face to face, the sun reflected in Jace's blue eyes. "I just...want you to know that if I could do everything over again, I would've stayed. I know that's not what you want to hear. And it's too little too late. But I still want to explain myself." He kicked the ground a bit, looking tormented. "My guilt was off the charts back then. I let it rule my decisions. And of course, I thought Nathan didn't have the capacity to forgive me. Everything I see now, in retrospect, makes me even more sorry I didn't follow my heart and stay with you. There was no part of me that wanted to leave. At the time, I felt like I was doing you a favor. I know it's too late to change the past, but I want you to know how damn sorry I am that I hurt you."

His eyes were filled with regret. I did believe he was sorry. It just didn't change anything for me. I could forgive him, but I couldn't *trust* him.

"I know you didn't mean to hurt me, and I don't harbor any ill will toward you, Jace." I rubbed over my arms and gazed out at the street before looking back at him. "But I've worked really hard to come out of the darkness I fell into after you left. I was lovesick. The way I overcame that was to train myself not to feel anything. When you practice being numb for long enough, it actually sticks. That's sort of where I am right now."

"That breaks my fucking heart," he said.

"Well, mine broke a long time ago. But whaddya know...I've figured out that you don't actually need one to function."

Jace shook his head. “Nathan told me how tough things were after his accident. The way you got him through that and managed to land on your feet is commendable. I’m proud of you for that and for enrolling in school, too.”

“There’s nothing commendable about starting college late.” I chuckled. “But thanks.”

Jace exhaled, seeming frustrated. “Farrah, tell me what to do. Tell me what you need from me. Is it to not come around again? I only agreed to come over today because I thought you weren’t going to be here. I don’t want to upset you.”

There was no simple answer to that question, but telling him to stay away wasn’t right.

“I don’t want you to stop being there for Nathan, even if it’s hard for me to see you. My brother needs you. He needs that friendship back.” I paused, thinking back to Nathan’s accident and how I’d thought I was going to lose him. My voice trembled. “He almost died. And as much as you say you’re proud of me, I’m ten times prouder of *him*. I’ve forgiven him for what he did to me—to us. And I forgive you for leaving, too, okay? But one thing I can’t do is be the girl I was when you left. She’s gone.”

He looked at me for the longest time as he processed my words.

“Fair enough.” He nodded as he looked down at his shoes. “I understand, Farrah. Thank you for saying you forgive me. That means more to me than you realize.”

When he met my eyes again, the intensity of his stare caused me to look away. “You still don’t know how long you’re staying?” I asked.

“I don’t feel ready to go back. My father is not in a good place mentally. He needs my help. Honestly, anything I’d be going back to in Charlotte is more in shambles than what's here. And that's saying a lot."

I had so many questions about that girlfriend of his—about his life over the past few years. "You said your girlfriend...broke up with you?"

"She thinks I have unfinished business here. She says I won't be able to move on with my life until I've settled it. She chose to give me the freedom to do that."

That made me anxious. What was left to settle? I needed to get out of this conversation. "I'd better get back," I said. "I'm going to be late for work."

"Yeah. Of course. I've got to get home and check on Dad anyway."

We walked back to the house in tense silence. When we stopped in front of Jace's truck, once again he looked deeply into my eyes. I was terrified that he might try to hug me, and I prayed he didn't, because I didn't want to feel all of the emotions I knew being touched by him would elicit.

He kept his distance and simply said, "Have a good night at work."

"Thanks."

Turning around, I walked to the house without looking back.

Inside, my brother was still sitting on the couch.

"What was that all about?" he asked.

"Nothing you need to be concerned with. Jace and I haven't seen much of each other since he's been back. We needed to talk. He mainly wanted to make sure I was okay with his coming around here to see you."

"What did you tell him?"

"I told him it was fine. I'm not going to stop you guys from rebuilding your friendship. I know how much he meant to you at one time, even if you did single-handedly ruin that relationship."

A look of genuine sadness crossed Nathan's face. "Listen...I know how much he meant to you, too. And I fucked that up. I've told you countless times how sorry I am about the way I reacted. But watching you today, I realized how much Jace being here is affecting you. If it upsets you, I won't bring him here anymore."

My muscles tensed. I didn't like that Nathan had noticed how *affected* I was—almost as much as I didn't like the fact that Jace still had an effect on me at all.

"What's done is done, Nathan. You rebuilding a friendship with him isn't going to change anything between him and me." *I'm determined to make sure of it.*

"Will you at least promise to be honest with me?" he asked. "I don't want to fuck anything up for you again. Shit, if you told me today that you wanted to pursue something with Jace, I'd be a hell of a lot happier to see you with him than that asshat you're dating."

It surprised me to hear him say that. It also made me a little bitter. Actually, *a lot* bitter. But I wouldn't acknowledge it.

Instead, I said, "Can you not call Niles an asshat? I realize he's not always on the mark, and he certainly doesn't understand what you're going through, but he got me out of a dark place. No one's perfect."

• • •

Three weeks had passed since my walk with Jace. I hadn't seen or heard from him, even though I knew he and

Nathan had hung out a few times. They'd specifically done so when I was working or otherwise not home—not that I was keeping track, but I'd expected to run into him at least once in all this time.

The hiatus from Jace ended one evening at work. It was a particularly busy night at Mayaka, and we'd had to seat people from different parties together at the same hibachi tables. One minute there was a family with three kids at table ten; the next minute I looked over to find Jace and his dad sitting at the far end next to them. Jace looked extremely out of place, sandwiched tightly between his father and a little girl who was trying to get him to show her how to use chopsticks. Despite my sudden nerves, the sight warmed my heart a little.

Putting on my big-girl panties, I moved my shoulders back and headed over to them.

"Mr. Muldoon, it's so good to see you."

"Likewise, gorgeous." Jace's dad smiled. "And please call me Phil."

Jace patted his shoulder. "Pipe down, old man."

Blowing a breath up into my hair, I asked, "What brings you two here?"

"My son said he was in the mood for some Japanese, but I think he was really just in the mood to look at your pretty face."

"Jesus..." Jace rolled his eyes. "I can't take this guy anywhere."

As much as them being here made me uncomfortable, I had to laugh at how red Jace's face turned after that comment.

I took the order of the entire table and gave it to the chef, and I appreciated the respite returning to the kitchen provided as I got waters for everyone.

When I returned to the dining area, the chef had begun chopping vegetables and working his usual magic: tossing an egg into the air before it landed on the grill, searing all of the meat and seafood with beautiful precision. Beyond the shooting flames, I could see Jace's smile, which made my chest ache. His dad was smiling, too, and I was happy to see that. The little girl seemed to be egging the chef on. She volunteered Jace to catch some food in his mouth. Jace complied. After three tries, he finally caught a piece of chicken before lifting his arms in victory as the entire table cheered. Then he high-fived the little girl. My heart fluttered, because I'd never seen Jace interact with a child before. It made me wonder what he'd be like as a father, whether that was even something he wanted. We'd never discussed it. I wondered how close he'd come to getting married to that girlfriend he had back in North Carolina, what might have happened had he not been forced to return here. I shook the thoughts out of my head, reminding myself that these questions were irrelevant. I shouldn't have been so concerned with the answers.

Although he stole glances in my direction, I didn't stop to make conversation with Jace and his father. I was glad we were so busy tonight. Eventually, though, the other family at Jace's table paid their bill and left. Jace and his dad lingered, so I forced myself to go over there to see if they wanted anything else.

"Can I get you some dessert?"

"My son would definitely like a piece of your pie, but he's too proud to ask."

Jace shut his eyes, looking mortified.

I cleared my throat. "You mean apple pie a la mode?"

"Whatever you have." Phil winked.

"Coming right up."

In the kitchen, I prepared a piece of pie, putting extra whipped cream on top, remembering that Jace used to eat it straight out of the can when he'd lived with us.

I walked it over to their table and placed it in between them with two forks.

"Hope you enjoy." I also set their check down. "And no rush. Just wanted to leave this here for whenever you're ready."

Before I could escape again, I felt Jace's hand around my wrist. It sent what felt like shockwaves through my body.

He looked into my eyes. "Thank you."

Jace released my wrist gently. I nodded, wishing it were the nearby flames that had made me so damn hot. I felt unbalanced as I walked to the other side of the dining room.

After that, I focused so intently on serving another table that I didn't notice Jace and his father leave. Looking over at their empty seats, I felt a mix of relief and strangely...emptiness. Maybe his departure reminded me of another sudden exit three years ago. Either way, I was better off now that he was gone. I could concentrate on my job.

When I went to their table to retrieve the bill, I noticed Jace had left cash, along with an unreasonably large tip.

That didn't surprise me. But the message written on the receipt did.

You're so beautiful it hurts.

Chapter 21

Farrah

Nathan caught me in the kitchen after I came home from class. "What are we doing for Thanksgiving?"

"The usual. You know, I make a turkey, and we order sides from Regina's. I placed the order a while ago. Then you eat so much dessert that you're rubbing your stomach for the rest of the night. Why?"

He patted his belly. "Well, I fully intend on keeping up with tradition in that respect, but I was wondering if we had extra room at our table this year?"

I arched my brow. "For who?"

"For Jace and his dad. This is their first Thanksgiving without Faye. Neither of them can cook anything but pancakes. I asked him where they were eating, and he said he was planning on taking his dad to a restaurant. I thought it might be nice if they could have a homecooked meal with us—or at least a homecooked turkey."

My mind began to whirl. I'd been looking forward to a low-key day of eating my feelings without any added stress. But how could I say no when I knew how difficult this holiday would be for Phil and Jace? Thinking about that brought back memories of my first Thanksgiving without our parents. Nathan had tried to cook a turkey for us and burned it. I'd broken down in tears, and we ended up having McDonald's because it was the furthest thing from Thanksgiving food. That turned out to be what we both needed—to just forget the holidays altogether that first year.

I didn't have the heart to say no. "I suppose it would be okay if they joined us."

"Are you sure?"

"Well, obviously you know it's going to make me a little uncomfortable, but not enough to say no."

Nathan's mouth curved into a smile. "You're the best. Thank you."

"I won't even have to order more food from Regina's. We just won't have a week of leftovers like normal."

"You didn't invite Niles, did you?"

"He's having the main meal with his parents. They invited us to their house, but I knew you wouldn't want to go. He'll come by after dinner for dessert."

"I guess I can deal with that."

I smiled and suppressed a sigh. Now I'd just have to deal with this unsettled feeling in my stomach until Thanksgiving was over.

• • •

In the early afternoon on Thanksgiving Day, the doorbell rang. Showtime. I'd have to get my act together and *keep* it together for approximately three hours, maybe more.

When I opened the door, Jace and his dad were standing behind a gigantic bouquet of yellow and orange flowers.

"Wow. You didn't have to do that," I said, taking the arrangement from Jace.

He slipped his hands in his pockets. "Well, I had nothing to offer in the potluck department, so I figured flowers were safe."

Intentionally avoiding looking Jace in the eyes, I hugged Phil before going to the kitchen to put the flowers in water.

Once I returned, I got my first good look at Jace. He wore a muscle-hugging, brown sweater rolled at his sleeves and smelled like musk and leather. His cologne brought back a plethora of memories, causing my body to come alive in an unwanted way. I willed my damn hormones to calm themselves.

Phil wandered the house a bit and peeked into the small dining room before making his way to the table. "Cute little setup you have here."

I smiled. "Thankfully it's just the four of us. I don't think we could fit many more people at our table."

His eyes looked glassy, as if he might cry. "I can't thank you enough for having us. I couldn't bear to be in our house. My wife always invited friends over and made a big to-do about this holiday. Today...the silence was deafening."

It was hard to know the right thing to say. "I'm sure she's with you in spirit. I always feel my parents with us during the holidays, even though they're not physically here."

He nodded. "You certainly do know what we're going through, don't you? So many people pretend to understand loss, but if you've never lost someone who was your entire world, you really don't."

Don't I know it. I flashed a sympathetic smile.

Jace and Nathan walked into the dining room.

"Put my son to work, Farrah," Phil told me.

"Actually, there's not much to do. I'm only making the turkey and gravy. All the fixings are coming from Regina's."

"Well, I'm sure Jace will be happy to taste-test your gravy." Phil smirked.

"I hear the senior center is putting on a free lunch today. Maybe I should drop you off?" Jace cracked.

We all laughed. At least having Phil here broke the ice somewhat.

Feeling flushed, I went toward the kitchen. "I made some appetizers. Let me grab them."

About a minute later, Jace's deep voice caused me to jump. "Can I help?"

When I turned, he was way too close for comfort. *God, he looks so good.*

"No. Thank you."

Moving past him, I carried out a cheeseball covered in slivered almonds and a plate of raw vegetables and dip. I set them on the coffee table in the living room.

"It wouldn't be a holiday without my sister's cheeseball," Nathan said as he reached for a cracker.

"Well, I love cheeseballs." I smiled. "After all, I've lived with one all my life."

Jace joined his dad on the sofa.

I turned to Phil. "Can I get you something to drink? We don't keep alcohol in the house, but I have pretty much everything else. Soda, seltzer, sparkling cider?"

"I'd love a sparkling cider," he said.

"We get wild in this house with the sparkling cider, thanks to me," Nathan said.

Jace shrugged. "It's fine."

I returned to the kitchen to pour Phil's drink.

When I returned, I checked the time on my phone. "I actually need to pick up the side dishes from Regina's. I timed it so the turkey would be ready by the time I got back."

Jace jumped up from the couch. "I'll drive—help you carry everything."

What am I supposed to say...no?

I shrugged. "Sure, if you want to."

Jace tossed his keys into the air. "Nathan, take care of the old man while I'm gone, will ya?"

Phil lifted his glass. "I plan to get inebriated on this stuff."

Jace and I walked out together. He disarmed his truck, and the moment I stepped inside, déjà vu set in—the smell of his cologne, the leather against my back, his closeness as he sat next to me. The only thing missing was the hint of cigar. This wasn't the same truck from three years ago, but it might as well have been. It seemed like just yesterday when I'd been a lovesick twenty-one-year-old, lusting after my brother's twenty-seven-year-old friend. Now I was twenty-four, trying with everything in me to fight the same feelings of lust for the same man, who was now thirty. It seemed the only thing that had changed was our ages.

"Put your seatbelt on. How many times do I have to tell you?" He winked.

"I'm a little distracted by the memories of being in your truck."

"Most of them good, I hope." In a seductive tone, he added, "I know we had some good times in my old truck."

"All except for one."

"Yeah," he whispered.

The night Nathan caught us was one of the worst memories of my life.

He turned the key and backed out of the driveway.

About a half mile down the road, he glanced over at me. "I can't tell you much I appreciate you having us over. I know I make you nervous. Even if you're trying not to show it, Farrah, I see it in your body language. You've given up a peaceful holiday out of the goodness of your heart. I should've said no, but I couldn't pass up an opportunity to distract Dad." He paused. "And to see you."

I fidgeted in my seat. "It's my pleasure. It means a lot to Nathan, too."

"I feel really lucky to have him as a friend again. He's always felt more like a brother, though."

"He's a good brother, despite all of his faults."

Jace nodded. "Where's your boyfriend today?"

"Having dinner with his family. He's coming over for dessert later."

He swallowed. "I see."

My eyes lingered on his Adam's apple, wandered up to the cleft in his chin...then his lips.

"How long have you been dating him?" he asked.

"A little over a year."

"How did you meet?"

"He struck up a conversation one day at his family's liquor store. I was buying wine to bring over to a friend's house—since I don't drink anymore around Nathan." I cleared my throat. "Nathan and Niles don't get along that great, as you know. I don't push the issue about him coming to our place. I could've gone to Niles's family's house today, but I'd rather spend Thanksgiving with my brother. It's tradition."

"I know traditions are important to you. Do you and Nathan still have movie night?"

"Actually, that's the one thing we've faltered on. It's more like every couple of months now."

"Well, at least you try."

As we approached the catering place, he slowed the truck. "Is this it?"

"Yup."

Jace parked, and we both exited the vehicle.

After I gave my name to the woman at the counter, she informed me that my order wasn't ready yet, that they were experiencing a slight delay due to one of their ovens breaking down. She suggested we return in thirty minutes.

"I guess we have to kill some time," I said. "We'll be cutting it close with the turkey. I might have to ask Nathan to take it out. But it's not worth going all the way home and coming back."

"No biggie. It looked like there was a café open next door. Let's grab a coffee or something."

Jace and I ordered two hot chocolates and took them to his car. The weather in Florida was finally cool enough to warrant a hot drink.

He put the music on low as we quietly sipped. I gazed out the window, but could feel his eyes on me.

He eventually broke the silence. "Do you still go to that bar for those confessionals?"

I shook my head. "I stopped going to The Iguana a while back, but from what I hear, they still do it once a week."

"Whatever happened to your friend, Kellianne?"

"We're still good friends. She's married now, and she just had a baby girl."

"Wow. That's wild."

"Yeah."

"Do you still write at night liked you used to?"

I looked down at my cup. "I haven't written for myself in some time. And even if creativity struck, I don't have a lot of time now between school and work."

"I know we never spoke about it, but Nathan told me you're majoring in criminal justice. I think that's badass."

I nodded. "For the longest time, I couldn't figure out what I wanted to do. But when it came down to making a decision, criminal justice felt right—probably because of what happened to Mom and Dad."

Jace's eyes seared into mine. He swirled the liquid around in his cup. "You think you'll go on to law school?"

"I haven't ruled it out. There's a lot I still haven't decided."

"Figuring out what you want to do with your life is no small decision. I'm still figuring it out, too. I've been wavering back and forth a lot lately."

"How so?"

"Well, my father's decision to sell the company had a lot to do with my mother. They were supposed to be traveling the world together in their retirement. Now that she's gone, he doesn't think he wants to retire quite yet. He needs something to focus on."

"He's thinking of backing out on the sale?"

"Yeah. But the thing is, he can't handle it all alone anymore. He hasn't asked me to help, but I feel like that's what he wants—for me to stay here and run the business with him."

An anxious feeling came over me at the prospect of Jace staying in Palm Creek. "Is that what *you* want?"

"I know I don't want to leave Florida right now. He needs me. I'm also a little worried, to be honest. With my mother gone, he might fall into old habits."

"The gambling, you mean."

"Yep." He sighed. "He never went back to it, and I'd like to keep it that way."

"I can understand that fear."

"So, I'm pretty sure I'm staying—permanently this time." His eyes lingered on mine.

I sat there stone-faced, unsure of what to say. The thought of him leaving again scared me even more than his staying. I wasn't about to analyze what that meant.

"What about your life back in Charlotte?" I asked.

He sighed and placed his cup in the holder. "There's not much to go back to. Kaia and I had an okay relationship, but I'm not in love with her. Being away made me realize that even more. I've had a lot of time to reflect. That relationship was something I should've ended before it got too serious. But I was comfortable with her, and that was good enough for a while." He turned toward me. "Maybe you can relate. You said you felt...safe...with your boyfriend. That's sort of how it was with Kaia." He paused. "Feeling safe doesn't always mean it's right, though."

I took a deep breath in as I continued to look out toward the street, refusing to look in his eyes so he couldn't sense my weakness.

"You know," he said. "When I first came back, I nearly had a heart attack when I drove by your old house—before I knew you guys had moved."

My forehead wrinkled. "Why?"

"There was a little girl playing outside. She had black hair like mine. For a moment, I thought I'd left behind more than just my heart when I took off."

It took me a few seconds to realize what he meant. "You thought I had your baby?"

"Only for, like, two minutes—the longest two minutes of my life. Then her mother came out and snatched her, thinking I was some kind of weirdo for staring at her little girl from the sidewalk."

My mouth hung open. "Wow. I guess I can see how you might have thought that." I looked at my lap. "After you left...my period was late."

His eyes widened. "What?"

"I thought I was pregnant."

"Shit," he said. "That must have been scary."

"It was."

"You *weren't*...pregnant, though?"

"No. It was probably stress or something. That can mess with your cycle. But I can relate to your little heart attack. Although, mine lasted for over a week."

"Fuck." He laid his head back and looked at me. "If that had happened, I would've come back. You know that, right? I would never have let you go through that alone."

"At the time, I certainly wouldn't have believed that."

Jace turned his body toward mine and closed his eyes, readying himself to say something. "I made a huge mistake, Farrah. I left believing you would be better off without me because of my feelings toward myself. I felt so guilty for my involvement in what happened to your parents. I'd never dealt with any of it. And when Nathan unleashed my deepest secret like that, it caused me to spiral. Leaving you was a form of self-punishment. I ran so I didn't have to face my guilt and shame. If I could go back, I would stay, endure the pain. I would've stood up to Nathan and for myself. I would've done everything I could to keep us together. But that's a realization that's only possible through hindsight. I'm paying for it now, because it hurts me to look at you and not see the joy you used to have in your eyes. It hurts me even more to feel like I took it away."

As much as he was partially right, it wasn't fair to let him feel like the entire burden was his to bear.

"I'm a stronger person for it," I told him. "I needed to lose you to find myself—my inner strength. I'm tougher than I was. And I won't let anyone destroy my heart like that again."

Jace's expression darkened, my words seeming to hit him where it hurt, though they weren't meant to.

Feeling a need to escape, I looked at the time. "The food has got to be ready by now."

He looked out toward the building. "Oh yeah. You're right. It's been way over a half hour."

Jace and I went back inside to retrieve two pies and five aluminum trays of food—sweet potatoes, green bean casserole, mashed potatoes, corn bread, and stuffing. I carried two trays back to the car, and Jace piled the rest into his arms.

The ride home was quiet. The tension in the air was still thick, but I felt more at ease around him after the conversation we'd had. It had felt good to let some of that out. As hard as it was to talk about what happened between us, in a strange way, I still felt like I could tell Jace anything.

Back at the house, the turkey was ready to come out of the oven. Jace volunteered to lift the heavy bird out for me. After that, he carved it and helped me set the table while Nathan continued to entertain Phil in the living room.

Later, Jace reached over me to place silverware at one of the settings near where I was arranging the sides. The contact gave me goose bumps. I'd been fighting my physical attraction to him all day. It was easy to convince myself he wasn't right for me since he'd broken my trust. It was another ball game trying to stop my body from reacting anytime he was in the vicinity.

When the four of us finally sat down, Nathan and I were on one side of the table facing Jace and his dad, with Jace sitting directly across from me.

Nathan made an announcement. "Before we eat, we should all say what we're thankful for. Mom would be disappointed if we didn't."

"I think Faye would have agreed," Phil said.

We each took turns. Nathan spoke about how thankful he was to have reconnected with Jace, for his continued recovery from the accident, and as always, he was thankful for me. Phil went next and admitted it was hard to be thankful for much this year. But he *was* thankful for his belief that his wife was watching over him and the fact that he was sharing a meal with good people today.

Next it was Jace's turn.

My eyes were fixed on him as he began to speak.

"This year brought a lot of unexpected things to my life. I lost my mother, who meant the world to me. That was definitely the lowest point. It was also a huge eye-opener about how life can change in an instant. You don't have forever to make amends or to tell people you love them." His eyes met mine for a moment before they traveled over to Nathan. "I never could've imagined that coming home during one of the darkest points in my life would have brought me unexpected peace and a second chance at friendship. The past three years away weren't easy, but I learned a lot about myself, how I'd let guilt and fear take over my life for so long. I've made mistakes... but I never meant to hurt anyone. I've been working on forgiving myself." He looked toward my brother again. "Nathan, your ability to forgive me so freely has helped in that process." He paused. "So, what am I thankful for? I'm thankful to have my brother back." Jace's eyes traveled around the table. "I'm thankful to be sitting here with the three people who mean the most to me in the world." He looked at Phil. "Dad, you've taught me a lot about strength since Mom died. You get up each day and push forward, even though I know that's not easy for you." He turned to me. "Nathan and Farrah, you've taught me about humility and putting aside pride in favor of forgiveness. Thank you again for opening your home to us. No matter what's happened in the past, I will always be here for you, if you need me."

A conflicted mix of emotions tore through me. I hated that I could feel the wall I'd put up starting to come down. That terrified me.

When everyone turned to me, my heart pounded, and the first thing that came out was, "I'm thankful for Xanax."

Everyone laughed.

"Seriously, I'm thankful that even though it's always been just Nathan and me, today we get to experience a sense of family through our mutual losses. No matter what's happened in the past, I'm grateful for this day and for this peaceful moment in time with you." I smiled shyly. "That's all."

Nathan grabbed my hand and squeezed it. "Lord, bless this table and this family. Thank you for everything you've given us."

"Amen," the four of us said together.

I let out a breath and began to relax now that Nathan and Phil were digging in. Jace, however? He hadn't touched the food yet. I could still feel his eyes on me, even though I pretended to be focused on serving myself.

Chapter 22

Jace

Despite my nerves earlier, Thanksgiving had turned into a pretty calm day. After dinner, Nathan, Farrah, and I cleaned up while Dad watched football in the living room.

When Nathan left to join him, Farrah and I were alone in the kitchen. I knew for sure now that my feelings for her were just as intense as they'd been when I left. I tried my best not to get caught staring, but I couldn't take my eyes off her. Farrah looked amazing in a form-fitting, tan dress and high heels that made her even taller than she already was. Her long brown hair was almost down to her ass. And what a beautiful ass it was—the perfect size. I had a lot of good memories with that beautiful ass.

I noticed her humming something. It was familiar. Squinting, I listened intently, determined to recognize the song. Then it hit me.

"That's an Evanescence song."

"Hmm?" She seemed startled by my interruption as she abruptly stopped wiping the counter.

"The song you're singing."

"I didn't realize I was humming."

"You were. It was that Evanescence song. What's it called?"

She looked away. "'My Immortal.'"

"Yeah. That's right. It's beautiful."

She didn't acknowledge my sentiment. Instead, she turned and continued what she'd been doing.

How the hell was I supposed to stay in Palm Creek and keep these feelings inside? The pressure to tell her how I felt was immense. When I was away, it was out of sight, out of mind. But tonight? It took everything in me not to unleash my feelings. The words were still at the tip of my tongue as I piled the last of the food into a Tupperware container.

Let me make you happy, Farrah. Give me another chance to be the kind of man you deserve. I promise I would rather die than hurt you again.

When the doorbell rang, my stomach sank. I knew she was expecting her *boyfriend* for dessert. I'd hoped he wouldn't show.

Farrah left the kitchen to answer the door. Reluctantly, I followed her into the living room.

Nathan had already let Niles inside.

"Hey, how was your dinner?" she asked him.

"It was good," he said. "I missed you." When he leaned in to kiss her, I had to look away. It hurt more than the last time.

Seeming nervous, Farrah turned to face me. "You remember my brother's friend, Jace." Then she gestured over to my father. "And this is his dad, Phil."

He offered his hand to my father. "Nice to meet you, sir." Then he lifted his chin toward Nathan. "What's up."

"Hey," Nathan droned, seeming just as happy to see this guy as I was.

Niles didn't even make eye contact with me. That made me wonder if Farrah had mentioned our past. Either way, that didn't stop me from glaring at him. I couldn't help it. I wanted him gone.

He wrapped his arms around her from the back, which made me cringe.

"Hey, good news..." he told her. "Over dinner today we decided to spend Christmas in North Carolina. You'd better take some time off. You're coming with us."

Farrah blinked, seeming like she didn't know what to say about that. So nice of him to offer her a choice about going.

"Whereabouts in North Carolina?" I asked, forcing him to acknowledge me.

"North. The mountains. We have a house there." He looked over at Nathan. "You need to come, too. I know she's not gonna want to leave your ass alone."

"No, thank you," Nathan said. "I'll be just fine here. Don't worry about me, Farrah, if you want to go."

Farrah chewed on her lip. "I don't know. I'll have to think about it."

I knew it had to be difficult for Nathan to concede to her leaving over Christmas. I was certain the idea of her spending the holidays out of state with this guy bummed him out.

"You won't be alone anyway," I said. "Dad and I will need a place to crash again. Christmas will be no easier for us than Thanksgiving. You're stuck with us."

Nathan's expression brightened. "Sounds like a plan."

Farrah thumbed in the direction of the kitchen. "I'm gonna get the desserts ready."

After she left, Niles turned to Nathan. "Can I talk to you outside for a minute?" His voice was low.

Nathan shrugged and reluctantly stood up. "Uh... sure."

What the hell is that about?

He'd better not have been bullying Nathan into taking that damn liquor store job again. It was interesting that he'd waited until Farrah went into the kitchen, like he didn't want her to know he was accosting Nathan. My fists tightened. I wanted to punch him.

I watched them talking out the window. Nathan looked tense as he listened to whatever Niles had to say. Tempted to go out there, I refrained.

After a few minutes, they came back inside. I'd known Nathan long enough to see that something Niles had said out there definitely irked him. As soon as I got the chance, I'd have to ask him what happened.

Niles sat down next to Dad, and they started shooting the shit about the game.

I could see Farrah in the dining room setting up the dessert plates. I'd been so preoccupied that I'd neglected to see if she needed anything. No other lazy asses in this house had offered to help.

"What can I do?" I asked, popping my head in.

She didn't look up at me. "Nothing. Go sit. I'm just warming the pies. I'll call everyone when dessert is ready."

Farrah looked around, as if she'd forgotten where she'd put something. She seemed rushed and tense. I wanted to hug her, take all of her stress away. Rather than leave the doorway, I continued to watch her. I don't think I realized I hadn't moved until she said, "What?"

"What do you mean?"

"You're looking at me like you want to say something."

I shook my head. "I'm sorry. No. I'm just..." I said nothing else.

All of the unspoken words continued to bubble in my chest. But if I couldn't say them earlier in the truck, now was certainly not the right time with Niles in the next room.

Once everyone gathered around the table, it was clear that someone was going to have to stand, since there weren't enough chairs. Niles was the fifth wheel who'd disrupted our peaceful family gathering of four, but I quietly volunteered by taking my pie to the corner of the room and leaning against the wall. I watched Niles like a hawk as he turned to speak to my father.

"So, Phil, what is it that your company does?"

"I own Muldoon Construction."

"No shit? You guys handled the renovation of the old strip mall into apartments, right?"

My father nodded proudly. "Yes, indeed we did."

"My cousin lives there. He's always complaining about the cheap particleboard in the kitchen."

Farrah's eyes narrowed. "Niles..."

What the fuck?

It was a miracle I hadn't punched him yet.

Dad's response couldn't have made me any happier. "Well, you tell your cousin that unless he wants to pay more rent to live in the best section of town, he'd better kiss the ass of that particleboard."

Niles stuffed his face with apple pie, and thankfully, he shut up after that.

What the hell does she see in this guy?

"Hey, Jace. You mind if I show you that thing with my car I was telling you about?" Nathan suddenly asked.

I squinted before realizing he was bullshitting just to get me alone. Placing my plate on the corner of the table, I said, "Yeah." I patted my dad on the shoulder. "Be right back."

"Is it so urgent that you have to leave the table in the middle of dessert, Nathan?" Farrah asked.

"Yeah. I don't want to forget. Sorry. It's been bugging me. It won't take long."

Once outside, I made sure we stood away from the window so Niles couldn't see us.

I kept my voice down. "What's up, man?"

"We have to do something about him."

"About Niles?"

"Yes."

"What happened?"

"He's trying to convince me to go up to North Carolina for Christmas with them because he doesn't think Farrah will leave me alone here."

"So just tell him no."

"The reason he wants to make sure she goes is because he's planning to propose to her there."

I suddenly became conscious of the Earth spinning. Running my hand through my hair, I muttered, "Fuck."

"Jace, be honest with me, okay?"

Swallowing hard, I nodded. "Alright."

"Are you still in love with my sister? I see the way you look at each other..."

That was a question I hadn't addressed aloud until now. But I knew the answer. "I never stopped loving her. I only ever tried to forget about it."

"I just want her to be happy." His voice cracked. "If I felt *he* made her happy, I wouldn't try to fight this. But it just seems like she's...I don't know...comatose with him. Just going through the motions. I don't believe for a second that he truly makes her happy. He gives her a sense of security, maybe. But there's a difference."

"I don't know if Farrah could ever trust me again after what I did, Nathan. You don't just forget about someone leaving you like that."

"I know the hand I played in that. I can't let my sister marry someone she doesn't love because she's too damn scared to get her heart broken again."

The door suddenly opened.

Farrah put her hands on her hips, looking pissed at both of us. As much as I didn't want her to be mad, the spark in her eyes was better than the emptiness I'd seen before. I'd gladly take any emotion from her right now—even annoyance.

"What are you guys doing?"

"Nothing. We're done. We were just coming in," Nathan said.

Her eyes moved between us before she went back inside.

I was on edge the rest of the night. I never finished my dessert, and although everyone moved to the living room to watch a movie, I couldn't tell you one thing that happened in it.

There was only a month between now and Christmas. What if Farrah decided to go to North Carolina and accepted his proposal?

I had to at least try to get her back, to regain her trust. But that wouldn't be possible until I learned to trust myself.

Before Dad and I left that night, Farrah stopped me in the driveway. "That song I was humming in the kitchen earlier tonight? Listen to the words. I played it a lot after you left. It reminds me of you...and of them...of everything."

She ran back inside before I could ask her to elaborate. I thought about it the whole ride home, but didn't want to play the song with Dad in the car, in case it made me lose it.

The second I got back to the house, I went to my room and pulled up the lyrics to "My Immortal," desperately trying to decipher them as I played the song. It's about feelings of abandonment and anger—unconditional love for someone who can't return it. Depending on how you interpret it, the song could be about someone who died or someone who left unexpectedly.

You and them.

Me and her parents.

I played the song on an endless loop, and it haunted me the entire night.

Chapter 23

Farrah

Bouncing Kellianne's baby in my arms, I looked down at her sweet face. Little Karma had just turned three months old. I'd only previously seen her in the hospital. It was the first time I'd visited my friend at home since she'd given birth. It was also the first time I'd filled her in on Jace's return to town.

"How long is he staying?" she asked.

"Well, that's the clincher. After all that, he went back to North Carolina a few days after Thanksgiving. He's there right now."

"Already?"

"Nathan said he wasn't sure when or if he'd be back. Jace wasn't specific."

He'd been gone for a week. And he hadn't bothered to say goodbye, although he'd called Nathan to tell him he was leaving.

"Are you upset?"

Adjusting the baby in my arms, I said, "I don't know how I feel, Kellianne. I've been fucked-up ever since he returned, but his leaving so abruptly brought back some bad memories."

"How do you know he's not returning?"

"I don't, but the bigger problem is...*why* am I so damn concerned? His coming home was my biggest nightmare for so long. I guess I was just getting used to the idea of having him back in town. I've loved the fact that he and my brother found a way to renew their friendship. That made the stress of his return worth it."

She folded some of her daughter's clothes from a basket of laundry. "Have you told Niles about your past with Jace?"

"Yeah. A while ago. That was a mistake. He was the biggest asshole to Jace's dad over Thanksgiving."

"What made you tell him?"

"He kept calling me out for acting strangely. He thought I was cheating on him. I'm done lying about stuff. Life is too short. Nothing is ever gained from hiding the truth. I told him everything, and I assured him it didn't mean anything anymore, that it was a long time ago. But I think it made him insecure. To make matters worse, I've been a mess ever since Jace left. Niles can sense that, too."

Kellianne sighed. "You still have feelings for Jace. That's all I know."

There was no denying it. "His coming back made me realize that no matter what happened between us, first and foremost, Jace is still my family. And even though his return wasn't easy on me emotionally, it's felt like getting a piece of my family back. That's where I feel safest with Jace at this point—keeping him in that space and not..."

"Not giving him your heart."

"He broke it. But I still care so deeply for him. Just not enough to trust him *that* way again."

"Yeah. I get it." She took a fidgeting Karma from me and placed the baby on her breast as she grabbed a Boppy pillow.

The baby immediately latched on.

I smiled at the sight of my friend breastfeeding her little one. "She's so precious, Kel."

Kellianne looked down at Karma. "Someday you'll have one of your own."

"Hopefully not any time soon. I need to finish school once and for all. But yeah...someday." I sighed "I want to give a child the kind of life I had as a kid. I want to experience those days again through the eyes of my children. I just need to get my shit together first."

She smiled. "You will."

My thoughts veered to what Jace had told me about thinking that little girl outside of my old house might have been ours. I wondered for a moment what life would be like if that *had* been true. I wondered a lot of things as I fell into a daydream. Was Jace reconciling with his ex back in Charlotte? Furthermore, why did I care so damn much?

On the ride home, U2's "So Cruel" played on the radio. I listened to the words, and it made me wonder if being so cold to Jace since he came back had finally driven him away.

• • •

As the days wore on, I became obsessed with the idea of Jace never returning to Palm Creek. I managed to act as normally as possible around Niles, but he wasn't happy with me, because I'd yet to commit to going to North Carolina with him for Christmas.

One Friday night, he was particularly miffed because I'd told him I was too tired to hang out. That was the truth. I had a night off from work, and I just wanted to chill at home.

Nathan and I were watching TV when the sound of a car pulling into the driveway brought my attention to the window.

"Who's here?" I asked as I stood up.

"I don't know. I'm not expecting anyone."

It was an all-too-familiar black truck.

My heart began to race.

He's back.

I opened the door before Jace had a chance to knock.

He wore a black leather jacket and smelled like sandalwood. The Christmas lights adorning the front of the house sparkled in his gorgeous eyes.

I got choked up. "You're...here."

"I am." He searched my eyes, undoubtedly noticing something I'd hoped he wouldn't.

But it's too late.

Jace took a few steps inside the house, then reached out and gently wiped the tear that had fallen from my eye.

"Good to see you, man," Nathan called as he stood up from the couch. "You know, I'm craving a calzone from Berretti's. I have a half hour before they close at nine. Either of you want anything?"

"No, thanks," Jace said, never taking his eyes off me.

"I'll be back, okay?" Nathan limped past Jace, out of the house.

Silence filled the room.

"Why are you crying?" he asked.

"I just..." My voice trembled. "I didn't think you were coming back."

Without hesitation, he pulled me into his arms, enveloping me in his warmth. I resisted for a moment, but it felt like...home. Feeling his heart beat against my cheek caused me to break down. I let everything out—everything I'd been keeping inside for the past three years. I'd tried so hard not to feel anything, but right now I failed miserably. In this moment, I felt *everything*. Every moment of longing, every skipped heartbeat, every iota of pain...and love seemed to hit me all at once.

He whispered over my hair. "It feels so damn good to hold you."

I moved back to look at him. "I couldn't imagine why you left so abruptly. I thought you'd changed your mind about staying."

Jace wrapped his hands around my face. "I told you I was moving back here. How did you think I was gonna get all my stuff? I had to bring it back somehow."

Feeling stupid, I wiped my eyes and laughed. "I don't know. I never thought about it."

"Clearly." He pinched my cheek lightly. "I had a lot of loose ends to tie up."

I swallowed. "Did you see Kaia?"

"I had to formally end things with her, yeah. She'd already broken up with me, but I needed to talk to her and properly close that relationship—apologize to her."

"How did she take it?"

"She said she knew she'd made the right decision once I let her leave Florida so easily after Mom died. She's accepted for some time that it was over, so it was no surprise to hear me confirm I wasn't coming back."

"Well, I'm sorry...for her. I know how it feels."

He nodded. "I know you do." He looked down at his shoes. "Fuck."

Wiping my eyes, I said, "I'm pissed that I couldn't control my emotions tonight."

He shook his head. "I'm not. It's allowed me to see how you really feel." He leaned in. "You know...I was thinking about you the entire drive here. I know you're with someone, but I couldn't help feeling like every mile closer to you I was closer to where I'm supposed to be. It's kind of messed up that even if I can't be with you, I still want to be where you are. At least here I know I can protect you." He placed his hand on my chin. "Look at me." He brought my eyes to his. "I will never leave you again. Do you understand?"

Just then, a banging on the window startled me. It stopped and then started up again even harder.

Niles's voice came through the glass. "You're a fucking liar!"

My heart dropped to my stomach. I looked up at Jace. "Oh no."

He stayed cool as a cucumber. "It's okay. We weren't doing anything."

Absolutely dreading it, I knew I had to open the door. When I did, I was met by Niles's heated stare.

"What the fuck, Farrah?"

"It's not what you think," I pleaded.

"Really? I came by to surprise you because you said you weren't feeling well. I spot *his* truck outside. Nathan's car is nowhere in sight. Then I look in your window and see him practically kissing you, and you're trying to tell me nothing is happening? You think I'm that stupid?"

"We didn't kiss," I insisted. "We were talking up close. That's all."

Jace intervened. "She didn't ask for any of this. She didn't know I was coming tonight. I just got here."

Niles looked between us. "I don't know what to believe right now. All I know is what I saw. And it looked like you didn't exactly mind having him in your face."

I chose to be honest. "I'm sorry. I'm very confused right now."

He ignored my comment and turned to Jace.

"You think you can weasel your way back into her life? She told me how you manipulated her when she was younger and then left. Now you came back and saw she'd moved on, so you're playing games with her again."

Jace remained calm. "I never meant to hurt her, but don't you claim to know anything about our history. You don't know shit."

Niles pointed to the door. "Can you please leave us alone?"

"Actually, no," Jace said. "I'm not leaving her alone with you when you're this angry."

That didn't surprise me, especially after Jace's promise to protect me.

"Niles, let's go to my room and talk in private for a minute, okay?"

With his arms crossed, Jace stayed in the same spot, standing guard as I walked away with Niles.

I closed the door to my room, and my raging boyfriend laid into me.

"I can't believe this. What the fuck, Farrah?"

"Nothing happened beyond what you saw. We were talking, and things got a bit intense. I hadn't expected him to come here. Jace had nothing to do with why I stayed home tonight. I didn't lie to you."

Niles made no effort to lower his voice. "I don't get it. This guy tore your heart out. Why are you even talking to him, let alone allowing him to manipulate you?"

"My history with Jace isn't something I expect you to comprehend. But it's a part of me I can't erase. He lives here in Palm Creek now. He's Nathan's best friend, and that means he'll always be in my life."

He slammed his hand on my bureau. "There's no way I'm going to live in the shadow of some guy you used to fuck."

"What are you saying?"

"I'm saying it's him or me. I won't accept him coming around and brainwashing you under my nose, pretending he's trying to protect you when he's just trying to get in your pants again."

I cocked my head. Maybe this was the catalyst I needed to take a break from Niles. Things hadn't been perfect between us for a long time, even before Jace returned.

Forcing the words out, I said, "I think we need to take a break."

Niles rubbed his temples. "I can't believe this." He shook his head, looking down at the ground. After a long silence, he looked up at me. "I was going to propose to you on Christmas. I hope you're happy. Now you can stay in this shithole with your loser brother forever. I would've given you a good life. You never would've had to worry about another damn thing for as long as you lived."

My head was spinning. Forget the proposal bombshell, but the nerve of him to call my brother a loser.

He'd always patronized Nathan, and that should have been reason enough to leave him months ago. But now? I wouldn't stand for him being so blatantly disrespectful. Not when my brother had worked so hard to turn his life around.

I smiled coldly. "Well, now you've just made my decision a hell of a lot easier."

He opened the door and stormed out. "Call me when you come to your senses, but don't ever speak to me again if you let him touch you."

I followed him to the front door and watched him slam it as he left.

His tires screeched as he sped down the road.

Like a protective statue, Jace stood in the same spot where I'd left him. "He didn't lay a hand on you, did he?"

Shaking my head, I rubbed my arms. "No, but he wasn't happy."

He came closer. "That's my fault. But I'm not fucking sorry, Farrah. He's not right for you. Not to mention, he's a dick. I heard every word he said, and it took everything in me not to go in there and pop him one. Do you know how many times I've had to stop myself from punching that guy since the moment I met him?"

I nodded. "I needed a break from Niles."

"Are you okay?"

"I've been unsure of things with him for some time. I don't think I should continue to be in a relationship if I'm so confused. Him calling Nathan a loser was the last straw. I need to be on my own—not in a relationship—for a while."

Jace let out a relieved breath. "Follow your gut."

"I don't know if you heard...but he said he was going to ask me to marry him over Christmas. I'm not ready for that. So I'm glad this happened because I would've had to tell him no. That would have been a disaster, especially if he proposed to me in front of his family."

"Yeah." Jace gritted his teeth. "I knew about his plan to propose to you."

"You knew? How?"

"He took Nathan aside over Thanksgiving, trying to convince him to go to North Carolina so you would go."

That made me feel a tad sorry for him. "I know Niles can be an asshole, but I'm sure he's very hurt right now."

Jace's stare burned into me. "Never mind how he's feeling. Think about yourself, Farrah. You don't owe anyone anything—not me, not Niles. When you decide to be with someone, it should be because that's what *you* want. All I want is for you to be happy. I mean that with all of my heart. If he made you happy, I would support you being with him a hundred percent, even if I did want to kill him half the time."

My exchange with Niles had depleted any energy I had left tonight. When I rubbed my temples, Jace took it as a cue.

"I should go."

"No." I put my hand on his arm. "Nathan will want to see you when he gets back."

He placed his hand over mine and squeezed it. "Can I ask you a favor?"

"Okay..."

"Will you let me be your friend? I promise I won't cross any lines—unless you beg me to." He winked. "But seriously, I just want to be able to see you."

I smiled. "I would like that."

"I miss our conversations at night by the old pool. I miss everything about those days."

Nathan interrupted our moment when he walked in holding a pizza box.

"Everything still kosher in here?" he asked.

"It is now," I said. "You missed some major drama, though."

He put the box down on the coffee table. "What?"

"Niles came by and threw a fit when he found me with Jace. He gave me an ultimatum, and we basically broke up."

"Are you kidding?" Nathan's face lit up like a Christmas tree. "This is, like, the best news ever." His smile faded. "Uh, I'm sorry, though. Are you okay?"

"I think it's for the best." I sighed. "I've been needing space from him for a while." Tilting my head, I said, "You knew he was going to propose to me, huh?"

"Yeah. I'm not gonna lie. I've been freaking out about that."

"I don't like how he treated you, Nathan. I turned a blind eye to it for a long time. I'm sorry I did that. Ultimately, he never truly made *me* happy either."

"I'm sorry, sis. I mean that."

Jace smacked Nathan on the back. "Listen, I'm gonna leave you two be. I've caused enough trouble for one night."

"Good trouble, though, brother. Good trouble." Nathan beamed.

"Dad has been eagerly awaiting my return anyway. Pretty sure he's been living on Pop Tarts and pancakes the entire time I've been gone."

He gave me a warm smile, and then he was out the door.

I went to bed feeling like a weight had been lifted. Only now I was anxious about what tomorrow would bring.

Chapter 24

Jace

If I was going to earn Farrah's trust again, I had to start from the ground up. Three years ago, sex had first fueled our relationship. I had no doubt that intense attraction was still there, but it couldn't solve this. If I wanted to earn her trust, I'd have to open up about difficult things just as much as I'd wanted her to do the same. With each year that passed, holding everything in had become more toxic for me. So I'd recently started seeing a therapist for the first time in my life. It was too early to tell, but I hoped it would help.

Farrah had been busy with school as the semester came to an end. I spent the majority of my time working on the transition to my new role heading up Muldoon Construction under my dad's tutelage. I'd planned not to see Farrah until Christmas, although every night I'd been tempted to text her the song "No One's Gonna Love You" by Band of Horses. I wished she understood that no one would ever love her as much as I would. *Yeah, I'm doing a great job of handling this "let's just be friends" thing*. Still, I vowed to give her space, keeping all of that shit inside for now.

A few days before Christmas, imagine my surprise when I opened the door one afternoon to find a gorgeous brunette standing there—one I'd missed like hell.

"Hey." My mouth spread into a wide smile.

"Hope it's okay for me to drop by."

My father spoke from behind a newspaper. "Trust me. You just made his day."

"Thank you for outing me, old man."

"Hi, Farrah." Dad waved.

"Hi, Phil."

Without me having to ask, my father folded up his paper and winked before heading to his bedroom to give us some privacy.

She stepped inside. "I just thought I'd come by and see how you're doing."

"I'm glad you did. I'd been trying to give you space after the drama that went down the last time we were together, but I've missed you."

"How are things going with work?" she asked. "Nathan told me you gave your job notice in North Carolina, and you're diving into the construction business headfirst."

"Yup. Now that I've formally made that decision, I feel good about it. And things are in a much better place at Muldoon than they were three years ago. No real messes to deal with this time."

"Good."

Lowering my voice, I said, "I really need to get my own place. I love my dad, but I miss my privacy."

"Are you planning to buy something?"

"Eventually." I felt a desperate need to take her away somewhere. "Want to get out of here? Go for a ride? I'll drive you back to your car after."

She took a moment to answer. "Yeah. Sure."

Yes. "Okay. Let me grab my keys."

We ended up driving to a lake I'd discovered recently. It was about a half hour away. I went there a couple of times a week to clear my head in the middle of the day. I took her to my favorite spot under a shady tree, overlooking the water.

Farrah sat atop a rock and looked around at the gorgeous scenery. "This is really nice."

"It's my secret hideaway—not so secret anymore."

"Thank you for sharing it with me." She took a deep breath of the fresh air. "You guys are coming over for Christmas, right?"

"If you'll still have us."

She smiled. "Nathan is counting on it."

I lifted my brow. "And you? Counting on it or dreading it?"

After a short delay that had me on edge, she answered, "I want you there, too."

I smiled.

We took some time to enjoy the silence, no sounds but birds chirping and leaves rustling.

"So...I've been working on myself lately," I eventually announced. "Finally seeing a therapist, which I know is long overdue."

She reached for my hand. I didn't realize how much I'd been starving for the contact until she touched me.

"That's wonderful, Jace. You know, I stopped seeing mine a couple years ago, but I need to go back. Are you finding it helpful?"

"So far, yeah. I've only had two sessions. But we started with the tough stuff. We talked about how my leaving town three years ago wasn't about fear of Nathan or hurting him. It was my own guilt that made me feel I didn't deserve you because of the blame I'd placed on myself. Until I'm willing to face those memories and face my role in everything, I won't begin to heal."

She let go of my hand. "Why do you think you're able to face it now and not three years ago?"

"Ironically, it took the loss of one of my own parents to make me realize I don't have forever to work it all out."

My therapist had encouraged me to talk to Farrah more about some of the things I'd been keeping in—specific memories. As hard as it was, I decided to put that into practice.

I looked up at the sky. "Your mother was holding my hand that day. I think on some level she felt like she needed to protect me the way she would her own son." My eyes shut tightly. "It was in those seconds, holding her hand, that I decided I needed to protect *them*. The guy was pointing the gun at your dad, and I counted to five before lunging forward. The gun slipped out of his hand, but he grabbed it before I could. And that's when he..." I couldn't finish the sentence.

With tears in her eyes, she reached for my hand again. "It's okay."

"I have to accept that I may have caused what happened. But when I made that decision, I felt like he was going to pull the trigger. I didn't want your mom to have to witness that. I don't know what would be different today if I hadn't lunged. I don't know if it would've changed the outcome or just the circumstances. But keeping it all inside, trying to block it out, has been toxic. When you don't deal with something like this, it grows inside you like a cancer. And eventually, it will kill you. Guilt and negative emotions *can* kill you."

"You're so right," she said. "I spent the majority of my teen years trying to hold it together, never wanting to show my pain or burden others with it. But the truth is, sometimes, even today, I'm so angry at the world, I just want to scream."

I looked around at the vast lake. "This looks like a pretty damn good place to lose it. There's no one in the vicinity." I arched my brow. "I'll scream if you scream."

"Are you serious?"

"I am." I grinned. "On the count of three, okay?"

"Okay." She squeezed my hand.

"One...two...three..."

We screamed together at the top of our lungs like a couple of lunatics, our voices echoing in the open air. It might have seemed like a crazy thing to do, but it was beautiful. We were letting go—together. Each time we'd stop, one of us would do it again. We probably screamed for three minutes straight.

When we finally stopped, an indescribable calm came over me. It felt like what I imagined a race car driver felt when he finally stopped his car and got out. I sensed the same calmness in Farrah as we resumed sitting in silence again, staring out at the lake.

About five minutes later, our peace was interrupted when a police car pulled up on the gravel road behind us. The cop got out and headed toward us. We both stood. Farrah brushed some grass off her butt.

"Everything okay, officer?" I asked.

He ignored my question and headed straight to Farrah. "Are you okay, ma'am? Someone reported screaming coming from this area. Was it you?"

I guess this lake wasn't as private as I'd thought.

• • •

Christmas Eve at Farrah and Nathan's was low-key and just what the doctor ordered. I'd refused to let Farrah bear the brunt of all the food preparation this time, so I'd insisted on handling everything. I placed an order for an entire ham dinner with all of the fixings from Regina's. Dad and I picked up the food on our way to their house.

We had a nice, drama-free meal. Farrah and I had a blast telling Dad the story of how we'd nearly gotten arrested for causing a public disturbance down at the lake. The best part of the night? When Farrah announced that she'd officially closed the door on any reconciliation with Niles. She'd met with him to exchange some items and made it clear that things were over between them for good. That news was the best damn Christmas gift. Even if she never wanted to be with me again, at least I knew that asshole wouldn't be the one to have her. She deserved so much better.

The only thing keeping me from totally relaxing tonight was the constant need to tell her how I felt. It was like Thanksgiving all over again, but ten times worse. I still didn't know if she'd ever be ready to give me another chance. Did she prefer to keep me in the friend zone forever and not risk getting hurt again? She'd just gotten out of a relationship, so it wasn't exactly an ideal time to start anything with someone else anyway. The uncertainty of it all left me unsettled and unable to totally enjoy the evening. I needed to unleash these feelings, but I didn't want to hear her tell me there would never be another chance for us. So keeping my heart to myself for now felt like the safest thing.

After dinner, we all went into the living room to watch *It's a Wonderful Life*. My parents had always insisted on playing that movie every Christmas. This year it was even more important to keep that tradition because it had meant so much to my mother.

Dad sat on the end of the couch, I was in the middle, and Farrah was on the other side. I reminisced a little about our leg games back in the day, but I didn't make a move. About halfway into the film, though, something incredible happened: Farrah rested her head on my shoulder. It might have been a casual thing, but to me, it was a sign of comfort and trust. This was a huge deal—it meant everything. Still, I warned myself not to take it as a sign to push for more anytime soon. I decided to enjoy it without trying to figure out what it meant for the future. Leaning my head into hers, I took a deep breath of her scent.

Once the movie ended, Dad seemed eager to go, though I was nowhere near ready to leave.

My father put his jacket on. "Farrah and Nathan, it's been a pleasure, but this old man needs his beauty rest."

"Thank you for tonight," I said, pulling Farrah into a hug and savoring every second of her soft breasts pressed against my chest. Feeling her heart beat against mine was a bonus. "This was the best Christmas Eve we could have hoped for."

I leaned down to kiss her cheek and noticed the changing color of her skin. She still reacted as strongly to me physically as she ever had. Yet I knew I couldn't act on that.

"Be careful driving," she said.

"Sweet dreams, beautiful," I whispered in her ear.

Dad and I each hugged Nathan goodbye and went on our merry way home.

Later that night, back at the house, Dad got a second wind and refused to go to bed just yet. Instead, he decided to make some tea and confront me about my feelings for Farrah.

He steeped his teabag. "Now that the bonehead boyfriend of hers is out of the picture, when are you gonna go in for the kill?"

"That's not how it works, Dad. I broke her heart. I can't just move in the first chance I get. I haven't earned her trust back yet. To be honest, that may never happen."

My father took a sip of his tea. "I'm still perplexed about some things when it comes to you and her."

I took a seat across from him. "What is it you don't get?"

"Why you were so damn afraid of Nathan three years ago? Why'd you let him run you out of town?"

I'd never told Dad about what truly happened the day Mr. and Mrs. Spade were killed. My parents knew I was with them and that I'd escaped injury, but that was the extent of it. Christmas Eve might not have been the opportune time to confess everything to my father, but he'd opened the door for this conversation. My pulse sped up.

Over the next several minutes, I told him everything, from the wailing cries of Farrah's mother to the way I charged at the assailant. For the first time, I cried over it, something I'd always managed to stop myself from doing. I guess everyone has their breaking point.

Understandably, my father sat there in shock.

"Son, I'm so sorry. I can't believe I never knew you were suffering with this. Why didn't you think you could tell me?"

"I guess I just never wanted you or Mom to carry the guilt that I did. It wouldn't have helped or changed anything if you'd known."

"We would've gladly carried some of the burden and could have helped you see the situation more clearly. I would've done everything in my power to convince you that doing what you feel is right is always the best decision, even if the outcome doesn't turn out in your favor. Their deaths weren't your fault, Jace. You were a kid. You went with your gut, and your actions were well-intentioned. I'm so sorry you had to go through it, but now I certainly understand better why you stayed away all these years."

"I'm not running away anymore, Dad. Losing Mom helped me realize I don't have forever to deal with my demons. So I'm here facing them head-on. I just wish I wasn't hopelessly in love with someone I still feel guilty about hurting."

"Farrah doesn't blame you. Nathan doesn't blame you for anything anymore. Sounds like the hardest thing is going to be learning not to blame yourself. Self-forgiveness is the hardest kind. But if you can manage that, son, you can manage anything."

"I'm trying..." I hesitated.

"And I'm happy you're seeking help," he added.

"I am too. Talking to my therapist helped me remember something. I haven't told Farrah or Nathan, though."

"What is it?"

"Mr. Spade wouldn't give up the money that day. I have no idea why. Elizabeth was begging him to. So was I. But he wouldn't turn it over. It was like he didn't think the guy would actually do anything. I knew better, which was why I tried to get the gun. I wonder now if the whole thing could've been avoided if he'd just given the guy the damn money."

"Absolutely." My father blew out some air. "That's unbelievable."

"But I don't think I could ever mention it to them."

He nodded. "You don't want them to think badly of their father."

"Yeah. What's the point? Who knows what he was thinking, and it will only make them feel worse. I don't want that."

"I agree. And I'm proud of you. Now that I know the whole story, I realize how much you've kept from us over the years. Please don't hesitate to talk to me if you ever need to. I know I'm not perfect, but you're my greatest accomplishment. Your mother would've felt terrible about you holding this in for so long. I'm sure she's looking down on you right now, though, feeling just as proud of you as I am."

"Thank you, Dad."

After my father went to his room, I was surprised to find I'd missed a text from Farrah about a half hour ago.

Farrah: Any chance you could come back here tonight?

Say what?

My heart came alive.

Hell yes.

I typed as fast as humanly possible.

Jace: I'm sorry I missed your text. I was in the middle of a long conversation with Dad. I finally told him everything...about what happened a decade ago.

Farrah: Oh my God. Wow. Why tonight?

Jace: The old man wouldn't go to damn sleep. Then he started prying about you and me. Before I knew it, I was bawling and talking about the past.

Farrah: I'm sorry you cried...but it's good to let it out. I'm glad you did.

Jace: So, back to your original question.

Farrah: Never mind. It was impulsive. I know it's late.

Jace: Um, the answer is "fuck yes." It's never too late to see you. I can be there in twenty minutes. Is Nathan sleeping?

Farrah: Yes.

Jace: That's a good place for him.

Farrah: LOL. Not that I care what he thinks anymore, but text me when you get here and I'll let you in. I'd prefer he stay sleeping.

Jace: Be there soon.

My father was finally snoring, so I left him a note explaining where I'd gone in case he got up and didn't find me. I could only imagine the wiseass comments he'd make tomorrow. He'd be happy for me, though; that I knew.

The ride back to Farrah's seemed to take forever.

When I finally parked in front of their house, I texted.

Jace: Here.

Feeling like I was walking on air, I made my way to the door and waited.

A couple of minutes later, she opened and placed her index finger over her mouth.

My heart pounded as Farrah led the way.

Once inside her room, I noticed she was fidgeting. Taking her hand, I prompted her to sit down next to me on the bed.

"What's up, beautiful? I would've thought this was a booty call, but you look *way* too nervous for that."

"I *am* nervous..."

"Don't be nervous. Talk to me."

"When you left, it was torture because all I wanted was to be near you tonight. It scares me a little."

"Don't be afraid to tell me what you want, Farrah. Because it's most definitely the same thing I want."

"I didn't call you over here to talk. But I feel weird saying it...asking for it."

My dick rose to attention.

"Let me try to decipher what you want to convey, then—so you don't have to say a thing. May I?"

"Yes." She smiled. "I'd like that."

"Okay, so...here's what's happening." I took a deep breath. "You want me. But you don't want to give me the wrong idea...because understandably, I haven't earned your trust back yet. You're still not sure letting me in is the right thing. But when you're around me, your body remembers. It remembers that it belongs to me. You want me inside of you, even if your mind is telling you otherwise. You can feel how much I want you, too. And that only makes it worse. Am I right?"

Farrah licked her lips and nodded. "Yes."

"And you called me here tonight because you want me to fuck you like I used to, without drawing any conclusions about what it all means. You want pure, unbridled, raw fucking with no words. You just want to get lost in me without worrying for once."

She closed her eyes and breathed, "Yes."

"I can do that, Farrah. I can *so* do that for as long as you need me to. I just want to make you feel good. Screw putting a label on it. We never have to label it if you don't want to."

Her chest heaved. "We have to be quiet. Not that I'm hiding from Nathan, but I'd prefer he not wake up and find you here."

"I mean, as of late, we're known more for our screaming." I winked. "But I can do quiet if you can?"

She stood no chance of answering that question because before she could say anything, my mouth was on hers. The warmth of her breath and her familiar taste were my own personal heaven.

I spoke over her lips. "Forget about all the reasons this is a bad idea. Just be with me. Relax your body and let me do the work."

She fell back onto the bed, and I hovered over her, spreading her knees apart.

"Oh my God," she muttered as I lowered my mouth and buried my face in her pussy.

She winced in pleasure, pulling on my hair. "Yes," she breathed. "You're mouth feels so good. I'd forgotten how amazing it is."

"You don't know anything yet," I said as I flicked my tongue along her clit.

Moving back, I circled my thumb through her arousal before slipping my fingers inside of her. She let out a sound that bordered on too loud. I groaned before taking her delicious mound into my mouth again, savoring every bit of her flavor.

"I missed this so much," I whispered over her tender flesh.

She threaded her fingers through my hair and pulled to guide my movements.

I stuck my tongue deeper inside of her, pushing in and out while she moved under me.

"Tell me what you want, baby."

Farrah bucked her hips. "I want you inside of me."

Kissing my way to her mouth, I was dying to feel her wet pussy wrapped around my cock.

We kissed frantically as I unzipped my pants and kicked them off. I nudged her legs apart before sinking into her, marveling at how tight she was.

"Damn, I forgot how good this felt, too," she panted.

I'd told myself I was going to go slow, make love to her, but apparently that was impossible. Slow and easy didn't last very long. I couldn't take it anymore, speeding up my thrusts. I tried to regulate my breathing to keep from coming, needing to prolong this. That was no easy feat because it had been so damn long, and she was so wet. I fucked her harder as she dug her nails into my ass, the friction of her tight pussy nearly undoing me with every thrust.

Earlier, I'd thought maybe she wasn't ready for this, but the way she gripped my body, urging me to go faster, harder, deeper, took away any doubts.

Shutting my eyes, I silently thanked God for allowing me the opportunity to be inside the woman I loved again. I'd never take this for granted, would never hurt her again. The only hard part was going to be convincing her of that.

At one point, she let out a loud gasp, prompting me to cover her mouth so she wouldn't wake Nathan. Her muscles spasmed around me, and I let go, too, emptying my cum inside of her.

We lay together in sated bliss as I softly kissed her face.

"I lied," I whispered.

"About what?"

"About this not meaning anything. It means everything to me, Farrah. And so do you. I love you so fucking much, and I never stopped." She was quiet as I continued. "When you first told me you loved me three years ago, you told me not to say it in return. You didn't want me to feel obligated. I loved you so much then, and I love you even more today. But you don't owe me those three words or any validation right now. The only thing I want is for you to let me show you every day through my actions how much I love you. Let me make up for the time we lost."

She didn't say anything in response, but her eyes filled with tears. And that was good enough for me.

• • •

She woke to find me watching her. I'd been up early and unable to go back to sleep.

"What are you looking at?" she teased.

"Just thinking about how lucky I am to be here with you on Christmas morning. It's the best gift I could've asked for."

Her delicate fingers traced the stubble on my jaw. "Do you need to get back to your dad?"

"I'm in no rush. Pretty sure he'll be thrilled once he wakes up and realizes where I went. I left him a note." I kissed her forehead. "Do you want me to leave before Nathan wakes up?"

She wrapped her hand around my waist and pulled me close. "No. I want you here."

"Good. Because I'm not ready to leave you." I kissed her firmly on the lips. "Let me handle any awkwardness with Nathan this morning. Okay? I don't want you to stress."

"I will gladly let you handle it." She laughed.

We lay together for another half hour until we forced ourselves up and got dressed. I could hear Nathan puttering around in the kitchen.

"You ready?" I held out my hand. "Here we go..."

"Yup." She threaded her fingers through mine and sighed.

Nathan was at the counter pouring a cup of coffee when we emerged together from Farrah's room.

His eyes widened. "Oh...okay then." He chuckled.

"Good morning," I said.

His eyes went from Farrah's to mine. "Morning..."

Farrah stayed quiet as she poured herself some java. She fumbled with the mugs, definitely nervous, even if the fear wasn't anything like it used to be.

Nathan pulled a chair out and sat down. "I, uh, didn't realize you came back here last night." He took a sip of his coffee.

I nodded. "I did. Your sister wanted me here." I pulled up a seat across from him, looked him dead in the eyes, and got straight to the point. "I love her very much. I never stopped." I paused to look over at Farrah, who'd ceased what she was doing to listen. "And I'm not leaving this time, Nathan. In fact, I don't ever want to spend another night away from her. Given that I live with my father at the moment, that means you're gonna see a lot of my ass around here until I get my own place. I'd ask you if you were okay with that, but honestly, it won't matter. I'm not making the same mistake twice. I don't give a shit what you or anyone thinks anymore. I only care about her. If you have any questions, you can let me know."

Nathan nodded several times. "I do have one question."

I tightened my jaw. "Okay..."

He snickered. "What are you making me for breakfast?"

Chapter 25

Jace

Six months after Christmas, I'd kept my promise—I'd spent every single night with Farrah. That was the one constant, despite the many other things that changed.

I'd fully transitioned into my role as head of Muldoon Construction, with my father taking a backseat in the company. If I'd encouraged him to sell, he probably would've listened to me, but deep down, I wanted this. Continuing my dad's legacy was something I'd always be proud of, and running the family business helped ground me here—not that I needed a reason to stay in Palm Creek. Farrah would always be that. But now that I knew I was here to stay, it was time to build roots. That meant having a place where Farrah and I could have true privacy, a place all our own. I'd made a decision I hoped she wouldn't be upset about. As we drove down the street where Farrah grew up, I was about to find out.

"Why are we in my old neighborhood?"

"Brings back memories, doesn't it?"

A minute later, I parked my truck at a house diagonally across from the home Farrah and Nathan had grown up in.

Farrah scrunched her nose. "Why are we visiting Old Man Dickie?"

Dick Lombardi—"Old Man Dickie"—didn't live here anymore, but apparently Farrah didn't know that. Dickie was a curmudgeon who used to yell at Nathan and me for various things when we were younger. Whether we were speeding by too fast on our skateboards or egging his house, we'd given Dickie plenty of reason not to like us. He was mean even when unprovoked, but we definitely deserved some of his wrath.

"This isn't Dickie's house anymore," I announced.

"He passed away?"

"Yeah."

"Oh no. That's sad. As mean as he was, I feel bad for his kids."

"I actually know his son, Major. He's a client."

"Does he live here now? Are we visiting him?"

I unlocked the car doors. "Let's take a look inside."

Farrah followed me out of the truck, and I used my key to enter.

Dickie's house had been completely redone. The old carpets had been ripped up to reveal gorgeous hardwood underneath. The kitchen had been gutted, and new cabinets installed over white Corian countertops. Basically, Dickie's house was just the shell, and everything on the inside was brand spanking new.

Farrah wandered the place in amazement. "This looks nothing like I would've imagined."

"After he passed away, Major redid everything before putting this place on the market."

"Oh my God. I love it."

"Good. Because...it's mine." I smiled. "Well, hopefully ours someday."

Her mouth hung open. "You bought this place? How could you afford it? The houses in this neighborhood are not cheap."

"I saved a lot over the past five years, and Muldoon is doing really well right now. So I gave myself a raise."

Farrah ran her hand along the beige sectional in the living room. "I can't believe this is all yours." She walked over to the window. "I can see my old house from here."

"I know. That's part of why I picked this place. Even though we've been trying to forget certain things, there's much more I'd rather remember in this neighborhood." Standing behind her at the window, I wrapped my arms around her waist and rested my chin on her head. "A long time ago, you told me one of your greatest wishes was to get back the peace you had before your parents died. I want to create that idyllic life with you again, one day at a time."

She turned around to face me. "Am I supposed to be moving in with you?"

I chuckled. "Well, I hadn't gotten that far. I didn't want to throw this on you and put you in a position where you felt you had to say yes. Of course, I want you here with me, but it doesn't have to be today. For now, this can be our sanctuary, a place where we can finally be alone without anyone breathing down our necks. One of these days, when you're comfortable, I figure...maybe you just won't leave."

Farrah moved her head back and forth. "I can't believe it."

Feeling like a giddy kid, I took her hand. "Come on. I haven't even shown you the best part."

The one thing Dickie never had was a pool. I wasn't going to buy a house without one, so over the past couple of months, I'd had one installed.

Farrah's mouth dropped when she got a load of the inground, screened-in pool.

"This looks just like the one Nathan and I had..."

"I know. That's why I designed it like this. The pool is completely new. It's the one thing that didn't come with the house."

Beaming, Farrah walked around the perimeter. She suddenly lifted her dress over her head and jumped in, causing a deluge of water to splash me. *What the hell?* I tore off my shirt and yanked off my pants before jumping in after her. We spent the next several minutes playing in the water like we used to. This was going to be my new happy place.

When we finally emerged from the pool, Farrah squeezed the water from her hair. "I can definitely get used to this."

I ran inside to grab a couple of towels.

After I returned, I handed her one. "Maybe if Nathan is good, we'll invite him over for a barbecue. Dad, too. The beauty is, we get to choose who comes here and when—no one intruding on our space anymore."

Farrah wrapped the towel around her waist. "It's honestly the first time in my life I've ever had privacy."

"We can fuck as loud as we want. Do anything we want. Make Dickie roll around in his grave."

"That dirty old man will probably enjoy watching us." She giggled.

"The ghost of Dickie..."

She sighed and looked out at the pool. "This is going to seem like an odd comment after all of this talk about our new fuck den, but I feel like my parents are with us right now. And your mom, too. They're blessing this house."

I hoped that was true, but still wondered if I'd have Farrah's parents' approval. But it didn't matter. Despite my lingering self-doubt, I no longer let guilt rule my life.

Farrah's mentioning our parents reminded me there was another thing she hadn't seen yet.

"Get dressed. I haven't shown you the bedrooms."

On the way inside, I stopped in the hallway to show her a photo I'd had framed on the wall.

It was the one picture I knew of that had Farrah, Nathan, and both of our parents all together. It was taken the day Nathan and I graduated high school.

"Wow," she whispered as she traced her finger along the frame. "That was, like, the saddest day of my life, because I knew you were leaving for college soon."

"Hanging this up wasn't easy for me. It's part of my therapy. The more I stop to look at it, the more I just see the happiness of that day, rather than the sadness of two years later."

"I've never seen that photo before." Farrah continued staring at it. "I love it. Thank you for framing it."

Wrapping my arm around her, I squeezed her side. "Let me show you the bedrooms..."

"Is there an ulterior motive to that?"

Kissing the top of her head, I said, "Only if you want there to be."

I showed her the master first, which had an attached bathroom. The other two rooms were smaller. I'd made one into a guest suite, and the other into something I hoped she'd love.

Her eyes widened when she got a look inside the final room.

Two yoga mats lay in the middle of the floor. I'd strategically placed plants and candles around the space, along with some wall mirrors and hanging bohemian decorations.

"This is your private oasis, yoga room—anything you want it to be."

She covered her mouth. "This is amazing. How did you put all this together?"

"Literally ripped a page out of a magazine on how to design a yoga space and copied it to a tee."

"I'm gonna use the shit out of this room!" She reached up and planted a long kiss on my lips. "Seriously, this is the most thoughtful thing anyone has ever done for me."

I lifted her into the air. "Maybe we can try that spine yoga again together—the kind you had me do that one time. What was it called?"

"Kundalini." She laughed.

"No. I don't think that was it. I think it was... *cunnilingus*, wasn't it?"

She covered her face. "I was so mortified that day."

"I loved it. And I loved you in your hot yoga pants, too—a little too much. Wasn't supposed to be feeling that way then. That was why I had to escape to the bathroom, if you know what I mean."

She cackled. "No way! I remember that. I thought you actually had to go."

"Nope. Couldn't contain my excitement." I pulled her close. "Anyway...I prefer *cunnilingus* yoga."

"You built a special place to go down on me, didn't you?" She winked.

"I can't think of a better use for this room than pleasuring my beautiful, vibrating vagina."

Farrah buried her face in my chest. "I can't believe you remembered that."

"How could I forget?"

Farrah looked up at me. "It doesn't vibrate anymore, by the way."

"Give me five minutes to change that."

She lowered her hand, cupped my package, and laughed over my lips. "Things are definitely looking up."

Epilogue

Farrah

Jace and I were headed home after dinner out one night when he surprised me by pulling into the parking lot of The Iguana.

Well, this is a blast from the past. "What are we doing here?"

He put the truck in park. "You haven't come here in years, right?"

"Yeah. It's been forever."

"Well, I called and checked, and tonight is Pour Your Heart Out. Can't believe they still do it. Thought maybe we should check it out."

Smiling, I took off my seatbelt and followed him out of the truck.

It was spring of my junior year in college. This week had been stressful, working on law-school applications. I couldn't wait to kick back and have a couple of drinks in my old haunt.

A wave of nostalgia hit me the moment we entered The Iguana. Even the smell was familiar—alcohol mixed with a blend of various perfumes and sweat.

We found a table, and Jace headed to the bar to get a mojito for me and a beer for him.

When he returned, we sat facing the stage. As the confessions started, it brought back all my feelings from the time I'd put my fears aside and gotten up on the stage myself. Tonight's confessions were chock-full of emotion—from a girl who hadn't told her family she was pregnant yet to a man who admitted to stealing his roommate's panties. As much as I loved listening, some of them served as a reminder of how lucky I was to be in a stable and healthy relationship.

About six months after Jace had first showed me his new house, I moved in with him. We'd been living together for over a year now. At first, I'd been hesitant to leave Nathan, but it turned out to be the best decision, not only for me but for him. Living alone really pushed my brother to put himself out there and start dating again. Who knew what Nathan needed all along was to live apart from me?

I saw Jace nod to a man in the corner.

"Who's that?"

"No one."

Jace had been bouncing his legs up and down and fidgeting a lot tonight. He seemed tense.

He suddenly stood.

"Where are you going?"

"I'm the last one up." He winked.

What?

What is he doing?

Once on stage, Jace adjusted the microphone to his height. A couple of women heckled.

Seriously?

He tapped the mic a few times. "Hi, I'm Jace."

"Hi, Jace," the audience said all together.

I covered my mouth.

"I'm here on this stage confessing tonight...because I had the audacity to seduce my best friend's little sister."

A mix of claps, cheers, and whistles rang out. My face felt hot.

"Sounds like a simple affair, right?" He looked at me. "But the story is far from simple."

I got chills as I continued to watch him.

"Farrah was six years younger than her brother, Nathan, and me. When everyone is young, that's a huge age difference. But she was one of those kids with an old soul. You'd look into her eyes and see compassion and understanding well beyond her years. I knew about her little preteen crush on me. I thought it was...cute." He chuckled. "When I went away to college, she was still a kid. That was the end of it."

He paused as the audience waited with bated breath.

"Then let's just say something really painful happened, and it kept me away from home for several years. During that time, Farrah lost her parents, and I was just...lost. By the time I came home to Palm Creek again seven years later, that sweet little girl had grown up. At twenty-one, Farrah was more beautiful than ever. I ended up moving in with her and her brother to help them pay rent." He paused. "I bet you can see where this is going?"

I looked around as the audience laughed.

"Sexual attraction is a bitch, isn't it? It has a way of grabbing you by the balls and not letting go until you give in. Resisting the pull toward someone you're not only attracted to, but who makes you feel good on the inside, someone you can relate to...well, it ain't easy. And I failed miserably. I gave in to the temptation and went behind my friend's back. It was the hottest sex of my life, by the way, and worth every second of the risk we took."

My face felt flush as the crowd reacted with great enthusiasm.

"At first, she and I told ourselves we wouldn't get attached. How well do you think that went?"

Everyone cracked up.

"Yep. That's about right," he continued. "We couldn't stop seeing each other because we were addicted." He exhaled into the mic. "I'm gonna make a very long and complicated story short. Nathan caught us and freaked out. Shit went down. And I somehow convinced myself she would be better off without me. So I left town and didn't see her for another three years."

When some of the people gasped, I realized how crazy our story sounded. But I also realized we'd been through *so* much together.

Jace's eyes met mine. "Not a day went by that I wasn't thinking about her. You can run someone out of town, but you can't tell them who to love. I threw myself into a meaningless relationship with someone else to help me forget. When I was forced to come home at the end of that three years, so much had changed. Farrah could barely look at me. I couldn't blame her. She'd lost the spark I remembered. I knew I was the one who'd taken it from her. Nathan had forgiven me by this time, which was unexpected. I never thought the person who had hurt me the most would be the one who'd teach me about forgiveness. But the hardest person to forgive is always yourself. It took me a while. Once you can do that, so much becomes possible."

Jace paused. "So what's the moral of all this? It's that sometimes sordid stories...become love stories. You can have everything working against you, and in the end, it still works out because it was meant to be. Love is not a choice. Don't let anyone tell you you're not supposed to love someone. Sometimes, the negative voice you have to ignore is your own."

A few people clapped, and I thought that was it until he said one more thing.

"I've actually never gotten up in front of an audience in my life. This bar was always one of Farrah's favorite places. She hasn't been back here in years, but she's sitting right out there in the audience watching me tonight." He pointed as all eyes seemed to turn in my direction at once. "She's probably going to kill me, because she had no idea I was going to do this. Thank you for listening and God bless..."

Jace received a huge round of applause. As he walked back toward the table, I smiled wide.

I rubbed his shoulder. "You did great. Thank you for that. I'll never forget it."

He leaned in and kissed my lips. "I figured you'd be surprised."

"You were amazing."

As we stayed and finished the last of our drinks, Jace kept checking his phone. I'd assumed his nerves from earlier had to do with the fact that he'd planned to go up and speak, but why was he still anxious?

He looked down at his watch. "We'd better get going."

I downed the last of my mojito before we got up and headed toward the door.

The last thing I expected to see was Nathan walking into the bar just as we were leaving.

"Shit," my brother said.

What the hell is going on?

Jace kept shaking his head as if to tell Nathan to stop talking. Nathan was practically panting.

"What are you doing here?" I asked. "And why do you seem so out of breath?"

"No reason...uh...Jace told me to meet you guys here."

I looked between them. "You both are acting very strange."

"Fuck," Jace muttered.

"I'm sorry, Jace," Nathan said. "I tried."

My eyes narrowed. "Tried what?"

"Excuse us for a second," Jace said as he took Nathan aside.

They walked several feet ahead of me so I couldn't make out what they were saying. Then my brother left without even saying goodbye.

"What's going on?" I asked when Jace returned. "Where's Nathan?"

"He had to go."

"Why?"

He placed his hand on the small of my back and guided me toward the door. "I'll explain to you in a minute. Let's take a drive."

Still confused, I followed Jace out to the truck. As we drove off, I just stared at him. "You need to tell me what's going on!"

"Please don't worry. It's nothing bad. I'll explain to you when we get home. I promise it will all make sense."

When we got back to the house, Jace led me out to the pool area. It was a beautiful, cool night.

"Relax here. I'll be right back."

Confused as hell, I waited on one of the loungers as I looked up at the starry sky.

A minute later, he brought out a plate. As he got closer, I realized it was chocolate-covered strawberries, my favorite treat.

"What is all this?"

"This is Plan B." He set the plate down at the edge of my lounger. "Take one."

I lifted one of the strawberries and bit into it. Speaking with my mouth full, I said, "This is so nice, but—"

"But you're confused as hell. I get it." Jace sighed. "Farrah, this night was supposed to be perfect. I called the manager of the bar a while back and arranged to make sure I could be the last to go up there. I was...supposed to ask you to marry me on that stage tonight, in front of all those people."

"Oh...Oh my God. What?"

"Yeah."

"You changed your mind?"

"No." He laughed. "I didn't have the damn ring!"

"It's lost?"

"I have to back up a little."

I took his hand. "Okay..."

"Before my mother died, she told my dad that if anything ever happened to her, to make sure he kept her wedding ring so I could have it for the woman I eventually married. The only problem is—and this is going to sound shallow as fuck—my mom's ring is pretty small. I wanted to get something bigger for you without hurting my dad's feelings. I went to ask Nathan for his advice on how I should handle it, and something freaky happened. He left the room and came back with a diamond ring that was exactly the same size as my mother's. It was *your* mom's ring."

My eyes widened. "Really? I knew Nathan had it, but I thought it was for him."

"He wanted *me* to have it for you. I thought... what am I gonna do with two rings? I'm a one-woman man." He winked. "But then...I had an idea. I'd take both stones and put them on each side of another one. I went to that local jeweler—Fred Seales. He helped me design the perfect ring for you. He told me it would be ready this week, so I planned this whole thing around that. The problem is, when I went to pick it up earlier, the damn jewelry store had closed early."

Unable to contain my laughter, I said, "Oh no."

"I nearly canceled my plans at The Iguana, but then Nathan somehow had the bright idea to track down the owner's home phone number. It turned out his wife went into labor, so he closed the store before I had a chance to pick up the ring."

"Oh my God."

"I was with you by this time, but he agreed to leave the hospital really quick to meet Nathan and open the store so I could still propose to you tonight on stage. The entire time I was up there, I was praying Nathan would burst through those doors with the ring just in the nick of time."

"So that's why Nathan showed up when he did? He had the ring, but he was too late?"

"He *still* didn't have the ring!" Jace laughed. "The guy had to turn back around because his wife started to push. It was either get me my ring or miss the birth. Nathan didn't want me to have nothing to give you tonight. So he went to Walmart and bought a temporary zirconia ring, thinking he could make it on time. But of course, he was too late."

"Poor Nathan." I covered my face. "I'm sorry I made you tell me. I ruined everything."

"Don't feel bad. I don't think I could've held it in another second. The stress nearly killed me."

We were interrupted by loud banging.

Jace ran to answer the door, and I followed.

When he opened, Nathan stood there with his mouth ajar, looking like he was afraid to say anything.

Jace put him out of his misery. "It's okay. She knows."

Nathan's shoulders fell. "I'm sorry, sis. We fucked this up."

I shook my head. "What are you apologizing for? Don't you realize how ridiculously lucky I feel tonight? Not only that my boyfriend tried so hard to make tonight special, but that my brother cared enough to run around like a chicken with his head cut off?" I started crying. "I love you both so much."

"The jeweler called from the hospital and told me to meet him there." Nathan handed the ring box to Jace. "Here you go, man. Congratulations."

A shiver ran down my spine.

"Don't congratulate me yet. She didn't say yes."

Nathan patted Jace on the shoulder. "Before you do it, I have to tell you both something amazing." He paused. "Guess what they named the baby?"

"What?" Jace asked.

He looked like he might cry. "Elizabeth."

I whispered, "Mom's name."

"Yup."

Jace wrapped his arm around my waist. "I prayed for their approval and asked for a sign. Maybe that's it."

Nathan looked between us and asked, "Should I go now?"

"Nah." Jace waved his hand. "You might as well stay. Fitting that your ass will be breathing down my neck when I do it, just like always."

Nathan stepped back a bit and smiled. When I looked over again, Jace was already down on one knee.

"Farrah, this didn't turn out anything like it was supposed to, but honestly, has anything we've ever experienced together gone according to plan? That's how we do it. I love you so much. You're gonna be the best damn lawyer there ever was. And I can't wait to be by your side every step of the way. I'll be there for you no matter where the road takes us next. I love you more than life itself. Will you be my wife?" He opened the black ring box.

Tears filled my eyes as I looked down at the gorgeous sparkler. A large center stone was adorned on each side by the two diamonds that had belonged to our mothers, who'd be symbolically protecting our union forever.

"I love you so much," I managed to say through my tears.

"Is that a yes?" He smiled.

"Yes!" I laughed. "Of course!"

Nathan fist-pumped. "Yes!"

Jace turned to him. "That's a yes from you, too?"

I wiped the tears from my eyes. "I think this proposal worked out exactly the way it was meant to."

"You know what?" Jace smiled. "I agree."

Nathan clapped his hands together. "Can we celebrate?"

"I happen to have some sparkling cider in the fridge leftover from Thanksgiving," I said.

"Pop it open, then!"

Jace kissed me on the cheek. "I'll get it."

I couldn't stop looking down at my ring. Jace returned with three champagne flutes and the bottle. After popping the cork, he poured us each a glass.

Nathan was first to toast. "To my brother from another mother and my sister. May you have a long and happy marriage. And to the lucky woman I've yet to meet who will someday become the proud recipient of a fifty-dollar zirconia solitaire. Salud!"

We broke out into laughter.

This night...gosh, it was perfect.

Pulling my *fiancé* close, I lifted my glass and made a toast of my own. "To family...the one you're born into and the one you make."

Other Books by Penelope Ward

The Anti-Boyfriend
RoomHate
The Day He Came Back
Just One Year
When August Ends
Love Online
Gentleman Nine
Drunk Dial
Mack Daddy
Stepbrother Deares
Neighbor Dearest
Jaded and Tyed (A novelette)
Sins of Sevin
Jake Undone (Jake #1)
Jake Understood (Jake #2)
My Skylar
Gemini
Park Avenue Player (co-written with Vi Keeland)
Stuck-Up Suit (co-written with Vi Keeland)
Cocky Bastard (co-written with Vi Keeland)
British Bedmate (co-written with Vi Keeland)
Playboy Pilot (co-written with Vi Keeland)
Mister Moneybags (co-written with Vi Keeland)
Rebel Heir (co-written with Vi Keeland)
Rebel Heart (co-written with Vi Keeland)
Hate Notes (co-written with Vi Keeland)
Dirty Letters (co-written with Vi Keeland)
My Favorite Souvenir (co-written with Vi Keeland)
Happily Letter After (co-written with Vi Keeland)

Acknowledgements

This book was written in 2020 during a really challenging year for all of us. In these unprecedented times, I'm so happy to be able to help provide an escape for you. I consider myself the luckiest gal in the world to have readers all over the world who continue to support and promote my books. Your enthusiasm and hunger for my stories is what motivates me every day. And to all of the book bloggers who work tirelessly to support me, please know how much I appreciate you.

To Vi – Forever my partner in crime. Hopefully you don't get tired of me singing your praises. Each year our friendship becomes more invaluable to me. I couldn't do any of this without you. The best part of this career has been our collaborations and getting to work with my friend each and every day.

To Julie – My late-night watch dog. Thank you for your friendship and for always inspiring me with your amazing writing and attitude.

To Luna –Thank you being there day in and day out and especially this year for being such an inspiration. The best is yet to come.

To Erika –Thank you for always brightening my days with your daily check-ins and virtual smiles. It will always be an E thing!

To Cheri – An amazing friend and supporter. Thanks for always looking out. Can't wait 'til the day we can all get together again.

To my Facebook reader group, Penelope's Peeps – I adore you all. You are my home and favorite place to be.

To my agent extraordinaire, Kimberly Brower – Thank you for everything you do and for getting my books out into the world.

To my editor Jessica Royer Ocken – It's always a pleasure working with you. I look forward to many more experiences to come.

To Elaine of Allusion Book Formatting and Publishing – Thank you for being the best proofreader, formatter, and friend a girl could ask for.

To Julia Griffis of The Romance Bibliophile – Your eagle eye is amazing. Thank you for being so easy to work with.

To my assistant Brooke – Thank you for hard work in handling all of the things Vi and I can't seem to ever get to. We appreciate you so much!

To Kylie and Jo at Give Me Books – You guys are amazing! Thank you for your tireless promotional work. I would be lost without you.

To Letitia of RBA Designs – My awesome cover designer. Thank you for always working with me until the finished product exactly perfect.

To my husband – Thank you for always taking on so much more than you should have to so that I am able to write. I love you so much.

To the best parents in the world – I'm so lucky to have you! Thank you for everything you have ever done for me and for always being there.

Last but not least, to my daughter and son – Mommy loves you. You are my motivation and inspiration!

About the Author

Penelope Ward is a *New York Times, USA Today* and *#1 Wall Street Journal* bestselling author.

She grew up in Boston with five older brothers and spent most of her twenties as a television news anchor. Penelope resides in Rhode Island with her husband, son and beautiful daughter with autism.

With over two million books sold, she is a 21-time *New York Times* bestseller and the author of over twenty novels.

Penelope's books have been translated into over a dozen languages and can be found in bookstores around the world.

Subscribe to Penelope's newsletter here (http://bit.ly/1X725rj)

CPSIA information can be obtained
at www.ICGtesting.com
Printed in the USA
LVHW091418220221
679624LV00032B/171

9 781951 045463